GW01451385

THE CASABLANCA CASE

Simon Swift

A Wild Wolf Publication

Published by Wild Wolf Publishing in 2012

Copyright © 2012 Simon Swift

All rights reserved. No part of this book may be reproduced, stored in a retrieval system or transmitted in any form or by any means without the prior written permission of the publishers, except by a reviewer who may quote brief passages in a review to be printed by a newspaper, magazine or journal.

First print

All Characters appearing in this work are fictitious. Any resemblance to real persons, living or dead, is purely coincidental.

ISBN: 978-1-907954-21-4

www.wildwolfpublishing.com

Praise for Simon's debut novel, Black Shadows

"Black Shadows is a great, hardboiled detective story from back in the day."
Debbi Mack, New York Times bestselling author of Identity Crisis.

"Black Shadows is Raymond Chandler or James Ellroy reinvented for the 21st century. There's a real authenticity about the period; the setting – New York in the 1940s – the characters – all coming together in a detective story that really hits the heights.
From the dramatic opening onwards, the reader is hooked. It's a proven formula: a wisecracking detective, exotic female characters and shady gangsters, but here everything works so well."
Jake Barton, bestselling crime author of Burn Baby Burn

"Black Shadows is a tightly written piece of noir fiction, inviting obvious comparisons to Raymond Chandler and Dashiell Hammett."
HarperCollins

"Bodies pile up fast in Swift's rollicking debut. Reads like a psychedelic ode to history and the cliché ...and maybe that's the point."
Andy Straka, bestselling author of Witness Above

"Just when you might think: they don't write 'em like they used to ... an author comes along with a true passion for classic rat-a-tat-tat, shoot 'em full o' holes, gumshoe crime fiction."
John Walker, Suspense Magazine.

"A cracking homage to old school detective pulp fiction."
Paul D. Brazill

To Sarah, of course.

To Harvey, always.

And to Ruby, forever.

I would like to say thank you to cover designer, Sessha Batto.

I would also like to thank all the people that have helped me guide Errol Black through the pages of another hardboiled romp.

My last, but most important, thanks go to my amazing family – to Sarah, to Harvey and to Ruby. Thanks for making me smile and laugh each and every day. You keep me grounded, you keep me busy, you keep me happy! Thanks.

Prologue

As the teenager ejaculated, he became aware of two unfamiliar sounds. One was the very pleasing sound of his girlfriend gurgling with pleasure, her mouth full. He looked down and smiled to see her eyes widen momentarily and then swallow heavily. She looked up at him, flashing her teeth and beaming a beautiful smile.

The second noise sounded like the gentle tapping of a drum.

Moments before, as the jeep had ploughed through the sand dunes and come to a halt five hundred yards away, he had slid his fingers under her clothing, reaching for her breasts, caressing them tenderly through the bra. Not taking his mouth from hers for a moment, he reached for her belt, undoing it violently and slackening her jeans. She followed suit, both unaware they were not alone on the idyllic beach.

The driver of the jeep, a tall heavyset man with ashen hair, killed the engine and stepped out onto the sand. His two passengers followed suit, covering the vehicle with a sandy tarpaulin. All three of the men were dressed in desert camouflage and carried silencer fitted .45's in shoulder holsters.

The tricky part had been unclipping the bra, but soon enough his fingers passed over her naked breasts, fondling them each one in turn, pressing and pulling the erect nipples. Opening his hand so as to encompass every part he squeezed softly before lifting the clothing right up and putting his mouth where his hand had been. He spent time kissing her nipples, slowly revolving his tongue around them and then nibbling gently.

The men edged up on the shoreline towards the small gathering of sleeping bags, which lay silently between the jeep and the young lovers. Their movements were covered by the noise of the sea. As they danced across the sand it all looked peaceful and calm. One of the men – a small, black man – crossed himself and pulled his weapon.

She had pushed him onto his back, their mouths parting, and pulled at his jeans, carefully releasing one leg at a time. Her hand then moved upwards and closed around him. She kept her fingers there stroking faster to increase his excitement then slowing into a pleasurable rhythm. Suddenly, she released him and moved down slowly, kissing first his chest, his belly-button, and then lower until he filled her mouth. His head slammed back against the sand as her tongue went to work; licking every inch of his erection from top to bottom, side to side. She held it with one hand and sucked the tip, at first softly, but harder and harder making him cry out in pleasure. He just lay back gyrating in rhythm, letting the pleasure flood over him as he fucked her mouth beautifully.

Two of the figures in the sleeping bags sat up, hearing the climatic cry of the teenagers. One said something in Spanish and they both laughed. As one cupped his hands around a cigarette the other flared a lighter but suddenly his head slumped forward.

She still held him in her hand as the men reloaded their silenced pistols twenty yards away.

Now he took over sliding his hand down to her stomach, pushing her jeans right down and tossing them on the sandy beach. Her muscles quivered and tightened at his touch, and he steadily reached lower. His hand travelled down between her thighs.

Again he heard the tap tapping...

She moaned as his middle finger entered, exploring her moist, warm inside. He moved his hand in a soft, languid motion, gradually increasing the speed of his strokes, pushing a second finger in. He felt elated, he had finally got there.

The thudding of the three silenced guns, firing over and over again spoilt the perfection of their lovemaking. The muzzle flare lit up the whole beach as the sleeping bags were torn apart by round after round.

A minute after starting, the shooting stopped and quiet now descended on the beach.

"Are they all dead?" asked the black man.

"Oh yes," said driver, as he kicked the bloodied remains of the six sleepers.

"Make sure," said the tall man, who lit up a cigarette as the other two loaded fresh clips and shot the corpses point blank in the face.

They waited.

8

Not daring to let go, she clung on to his penis but as she slowly resurfaced to kiss his smiling face, it was no longer smiling. There was a dark, bloody hole in the centre of his forehead and he slumped backwards, carrying her with him.

The sun first appeared just after five. The trawler emerged not long after that.

"Two hundred yards," said the driver, quietly.

The others nodded.

The trawler got nearer and the hum of the engine got louder. At fifty yards the black man walked over to the bloody sleeping bags and waved his arms at the boat.

There were two men on the deck of the boat. They both died waving back at the shore. The force of the bullets sent them crashing backwards into the railings, where their bloody bodies lay still.

Twenty minutes later the jeep was heading away from the coast, bouncing off the sand dunes a little easier in the daylight. Trussed up in the back, lay the girl.

The small trawler exploded several miles from the coast...

Chapter one: Going Back

Going back was never easy.

The road ahead stretched out for miles, clinging tightly to the coastline. It continued over the undulating Blue Hills, cutting through the valley of Heaven Springs. The sky was pure blue, mixing on the horizon with the shimmering waters of the Atlantic Ocean. Small, scraggly islands littered the coast, some as small as tennis courts and as green as emeralds. Others rose majestically from the ocean, with sheer cliff faces and flat tops, covered with swaying palms and pretty, colourful flowers.

Sitting in a beat-up rental Ford, I was getting the same feelings as when I fell off the wagon. Anticipation flooded my veins, so much so, I was shaking as I passed the 'Welcome to Casablanca' sign. I could taste it and at first it tasted good.

A seaplane flew overhead, making a colorful mosaic of the sea below. In the distance the white buildings of the Moorish West Island reflected the sunlight, their gardens running out to the white, palm-lined beach. The sand was so white you just wanted to run barefoot until you reached the crystal-clear water, which looked turquoise from above, due to the coral reef, but was clear enough to see the multi-coloured fish if you swam with your eyes open.

I turned off the engine and wound back the roof, letting the hot sun burn the back of my neck. It was sure warm, summer was just around the corner, and the waterfront cafes would be doing a roaring trade. I watched the plane as it rose high above the South Isle and dropped down in the distance towards Samui Cove Bay.

A lot of years had passed; a lot of life elapsed. It is often said that you should never go back, but sometimes there is no alternative. This was one of those times.

I started the car and descended the spectacular mountain drive down to the outskirts of town. It felt like going on a date with your childhood sweetheart when you had not seen each other for twenty years; or waking from a coma and walking back home alone with only vague memories of what your life really was. Would you recognise your friends, or even your wife? Would you be disappointed or contented?

I found myself on George Street, a big, wide, palm-lined boulevard with grassy sidewalks and glass-fronted bars. There used to be a park right in the centre of this busy, shopping street. Not exactly Central Park, but still a little oasis. Now I found a housing development of exclusive, high-rise flats. Hell, they were new and shiny and clean but different, that's all.

I drove on, finding more and more changes. There was nothing wrong with most of them, a lot of construction work was going on but it looked classy and brought a feel of affluence to the town. Despite this, I still couldn't help feeling that for every million-dollar apartment block, or five-star hotel, or whites-only casino, a little piece of character had been chipped away, a small shred of history tossed into the fire.

I swatted a sand fly on my neck and wiped away the bloody mess with my handkerchief. The weather had not changed; still hot and clammy. It was warm enough to bring out the pretty girls in their bikinis under the watchful gaze of their natural predators; the hot under the collar guys. It was warm enough to soak a shirt right through before lunchtime. Warm enough to make that first beer of the day taste like liquid moonlight.

I crossed the spectacular West Bridge and headed north towards the Downtown. In spite of the changes, and they were numerous, I could still feel the old Casablanca magic. Its mood fluctuated from block to block; from elaborate Georgian architecture to Byzantine tavernas. Every now and then I passed an ugly tower block, or I spotted a piece of filthy, New York-inspired graffiti, or I caught a whiff of urine on the street, but then it was all extinguished by a piece of outstanding beauty.

I was nearly at the Yellow Brick Road, where the cobbles were made from gold and led into the heart of Casablanca. Here there were no ivy-wrapped oaks, ten-foot tall sunflowers, tidy, manicured parks with gleaming fountains and squealing gulls. It was here that the fantasy ended and the harsh reality of modern urbanism began. The Golden Triangle was a three pronged mile of City life, where businesses thrived, commerce ruled and beach-life took a backseat. Incidentally, two thirds of violent crime was also committed within the Golden Triangle, but I suppose that's not surprising as more than three quarters of the money was housed here.

Chapter Two: The Yellow Brick Road

It had clouded over when I pulled in by the sidewalk and got out of the car. The Yellow Brick Road spread out ahead of me and for some reason I was apprehensive to ride on into town.

I looked around me and found a familiar old building. Rico's tobacconist had survived for decades. It was nothing fancy, just a thousand types of baccy, over one hundred and fifty different designs of pipe, and as many different zippo lighters, all housed in a glass cabinet as big as the Oval Office. I stayed with the cigarettes, but then there was a whole shelf of those too.

I picked up a packet of Lucky Strikes and waited for the big, black face to appear from around the corner. When a small Chinese face appeared I asked what had happened to Rico. This seemed to unnerve the man and he simply held out his hand and repeated the price of the cigarettes. I held out a note and he snatched it away before disappearing again round the back. I stood for a moment in the old store and lit up a Lucky. When the man returned with a couple of younger men at his side I tapped my hat and turned on my heels.

I opened the car and got in. Would it just be a new hairstyle, or had my baby gone about a whole transformation? She certainly seemed about as pleased to see me as I was her. Maybe it hadn't been a good idea after all. They had cops in this town so, why on earth would they need a washed up ex Private Eye sniffing around? I was sure nobody here would appreciate me pissing in the wind. Sitting back in the car with the window down, I considered turning around and just driving right out again. Putting the sunroof up and going for a real long ride; but it wasn't gonna happen and I knew it.

I arrived at the Casablanca morgue a little after eleven. There was a red Chevette parked by the side of the building with the side-lights still on. In the passenger seat sat a heavily built Caucasian man with a ruddy complexion. He was wearing a suit that looked thirty years old, white shirt, and blue and green striped tie that hung hopelessly to his left. He had a dirty, tan trench coat over the suit with pockets spilling food. He was smoking one of those thin cigarillos that look like droopy pencils, in between bites of a hefty sandwich. He saw me approach and wound down the window.

"Black?" he asked with his mouth still full. "I thought you might take my advice and keep the hell away."

After finishing off the sandwich, he pulled out a small hip flask, took a large slug down in one and sighed deeply. He then tossed the still flaming pencil onto the gravel car park and heaved his bulky frame from the car.

"I told you, you'll get no help from my boys. They're very particular who they work with."

"You should turn off those lights, you're battery will be drained right down. Next time you try and start the car all you'll hear is a whining noise that grates right on your nerves."

The man reached through the open window of the car and switched off the lights. He then locked the door and started walking towards the entrance of the morgue. I followed, staying half a pace behind him.

"How long you planning on hanging around here?" he asked with no emotion in his tone.

"As long as I have to. When the job is done I suppose I'll leave. How's it going, can you can tell me that?"

When we reached the reception desk the man nodded at the security guard and headed down a long corridor.

"We've rounded up the regular suspects, although I don't mind telling you, nobody's gonna waste much time on this one."

"They never did."

The man stopped and looked at me square in the face. He had an ageing, craggy face. A face that looked like it has seen it all before and had had enough. His eyes were slightly crossed but he held his gaze admirably. "You're from round here? How long since you last been here?" he asked, softening a little.

"Too many years than I care to remember."

"It's changed, ha?" he said with a laugh and started marching down the corridor again.

"That's what I intend to find out."

Arthur Peru was my link in Casablanca. He ran a bunch of unorthodox homicide investigators on a very tight budget. A kind of independent force somewhere between the regular police and an agency, with himself as the omnipotent head. He answered only to the Commissioner, who rarely interfered. He arrived in Casablanca not long after I had departed. He had a great reputation as a man who got results, achieving straight A's when failures were the norm, and he managed it without breaking the bank. All his officers were hand-picked from as far afield as Seattle and Daytona and they usually fit the bill as loners with flair. Peru was a team man, in contrast to his protégés; his aim was to tame them, bond them and shape them into a cohesive unit that was steadily cracking the crime-ridden streets of Casablanca. At least according to the county newspapers. I had heard a lot about him. His record was immaculate, he kept his nose spotlessly clean and his men were fiercely loyal. Although I didn't expect much in the way of help from him, his co-operation would be invaluable. He had friends in all the right places, but according to heresy was lily-white and not afraid to rattle a few cages to get what he wanted.

Today he had something I wanted.

He showed me through to the ice room, put the key in the correct drawer and left the room. For a moment I stood frozen to the spot. There was no noise in places like this, just a constant deafening silence. Everything was impeccably clean and gleaming white. The place smelled of a mixture of detergent and formaldehyde.

I took out a Lucky and lit it up before stepping towards the drawer. A couple of deep inhalations and I heaved the drawer open. It was a lot heavier than I expected and I clumsily dropped ash right onto the white sheet below. As I brushed it off with the back of my hand, I could feel the shape of a head below the sheet and it was cold, icily cold. My hand lingered until I finished the cigarette and then I pulled back the sheet.

It wasn't the first time had seen a dead body, far from it in fact, it wasn't even the first time I had seen the dead body of a friend. But still it took me aback. The body was bloated and the skin leathery. His eyes were wide open as was the mouth and there was none of his usual cockiness. In his nakedness he looked vulnerable. Usually the epitome of confidence, with the body and looks to match, now he looked a little sad. A slightly overweight, untanned body with a tiny penis and two ugly bullet holes in the chest. I looked into his eyes a moment longer and then covered the body with the sheet. As I was pushing the drawer back in, Peru walked through the door.

"Doesn't look too great, does he? Fancy a beer?"

I tossed him the bunch of keys and walked out through the open door.

"I don't know how you drink that shit straight," said Peru, as he handed me a large bourbon and took a seat. "Makes me fuckin' breathe fire. Can't imagine what it does to your fuckin' liver."

"Cheers," I said and emptied the glass.

Peru looked at me in horror and sipped his Budweiser. "You can buy your fuckin' own next time. Either that or drink something sensible. Something that lasts longer than a quick poke."

He took out a cigarillo and offered me the pack. I refused and went to the bar, returning with a bottle. Peru didn't bat an eyelid. He knew the score.

"So what's your story, Black? What are you really doing here?"

I watched him smoke his cigarillo. I would have to be careful around Arthur Peru; he was a shrewd customer. On the surface he acted with disinterest and put on the superficial friendly face, but underneath he was worried. Why's a big-shot fed coming back to Casablanca, on his own, for the murder of a nobody? Sooner or later he would find out the truth and if he was as good as I suspected he was it wouldn't be long.

"Like I told you on the phone, the stiff in your morgue was on our books. That's all. I'm no more than an errand boy."

"So I've done you a favour. He won't be bothering you anymore. Now you can cross him off your list and concentrate on other affairs of national importance."

"I don't want this one swept under the carpet. I want to know who killed him and why."

"Well that's very noble of you, and if you ever wanna run for the civil liberties commission you've got my vote."

He blew out a thin line of yellow smoke.

"What else is there? I've met those whiter than white jew-boy federal agents before. They swear on their mother's life that they only want justice, to uphold, life, property and the American way before going home and slapping the wife. You don't look like one of those, Black, so what is it?"

I said nothing.

He coughed a chesty cough and spat into the ashtray. Looking at me all the time, almost as if he studied me long and hard enough he would find out the inner thoughts. A minute or so passed of silence. He just looked at me and I returned the gaze, before he broke the deadlock with a sentence of incomprehensible Italian.

"How well do you know Casablanca, Black, can you still jive?"

I smiled.

"I hope so," I said vaguely. "I'll always find my way around."

I gazed through the grimy window and sighed, "This town used to be…"

"Beautiful, right?" Peru finished the sentence as I stumbled over the old scars.

He laughed a sardonic laugh. "Maybe you're gonna be disappointed. Fields of long grass and sweet smelling flowers are in short supply since the dime flashed its shiny side. If you do stick around you'll realise it's not all bad."

"Another drink?" I asked.

Peru swore again and looked at his watch. "Gotta go. You got a place to stay? I can recommend a good sofa."

"Thanks all the same, but I think I'm gonna look up an old friend."

Peru studied me again like he had done in the morgue. "Is that wise?" he asked. "Like I said, things around here have changed. Maybe your old friend has moved on. Maybe he doesn't live here anymore."

"Maybe," I said, and poured another drink. "When can I get my hands on the case notes?"

Peru sighed. The suit he was wearing was two sizes too small and it shook with his body when he sighed. He rubbed his thick curly, grey hair with a small, stubby hand and then straightened his tie. "Why don't you come round the office tomorrow? Don't expect no fuckin' red carpet treatment though because you'll be lucky if you get as much as a hello. You know where it is?"

"I'll find it."

"Yeah, I'm sure you will. Oh, and one thing before you go, Black." He grabbed me roughly by the shirt collar. "My department don't sweep things under no carpets. You got that? We prefer linoleum! And we don't even own a fuckin' broom!"

Chapter Three: On The Waterfront

Driving through the main avenue of downtown Casablanca was like taking a walk in the past. On the surface little had changed. Sure, the odd shop had changed names, the news banners had a different date on, but it really could have been all those years ago. Except somehow it just didn't feel the same. It was like one of those dreams you have when you come back from holiday. For nights after you return home vivid stories invade your slumber and you almost believe you're back there. But there's a fogginess around the edges making it all a little bit unreal. I pulled up by the docks and got out. I'd always found pleasure from a walk down by the docks.

The Casablanca docks were a murky affair. Home of a thousand vessels, their sails rattling hauntingly in the wind. Once it was a place for majestic liners, queens of the ocean that cut through the choppy waters and disappeared to far away lands. Romantics and boat lovers were drawn to the docks in droves. It was a place to come and spend the day watching the forces of nature harnessed by humble crafts. There used to be a selection of eateries and bars overlooking the whole sprawling den of activity and you could safely bring the kids. But with the war came the bootlegging. The things that people wanted became scarce on the open market leaving a gap to be filled by cynical opportunists, usually with a .45 tucked into their belt. So the docks gradually changed becoming an import point for anything illegal; first it was bananas and boot polish, nylons and lipstick, but now it was more likely moonshine and narcotics.

Of course, there was a Union presence, although it was probably the team leaders running the rackets. What began simply as market forces quickly became corruption and vice, breeding on people's worries and expectations.

No matter what, there was still something a little special down by the docks.

There was a fresh food market in a large piazza by the main fishing quarters. Men and women of different shapes and sizes waving their arms about and shouting like lunatics, whilst crates of freshly caught seafood were hauled in. Truckloads of ice drove down the gangway of the long fishermans pier loading up the dozens of awaiting boats. It was quieter than I remembered and the fishing side of things had been pushed further and further away into the corner.

There was an argument going on as I strolled along the waterfront. It was between a dockyard worker and a market vendor, who was precariously balancing a basket of fresh fruit. The docks man was waving his arms about aggressively and kept taking a step closer to the other man, who in turn, stepped back. A couple of steps further and he was gonna end up in the water. They stopped and looked in my direction as I walked by. I touched the brim of my hat and kept on walking.

I could feel the heat in the back of my head as they fell silent and stared until I was out of earshot. Just as they recommenced, a black car pulled up by the side of the pair and out got a well-dressed smoke in a beige suit. I stopped and turned around. He said something and they both shook their heads. I got brief eye contact with the black man before he got back in the car and it drove off.

I think I detected a glimmer of recognition, but it was hard to be sure from such a distance. Jarvis McSwarve hadn't been around long before I upped and left, although we had met and I knew he'd remember. Jarvis wasn't the type of guy to forget a face. He was becoming a big man years ago, and by the look of his car and attire a few moments ago, had continued to ascend. He owned and ran a bar on the west side of town. A kind of refuge from the mad world we all lived in. It had unique status amongst Casablanca's establishments in that it was loved by good and bad alike. The cops thought of it as their home insofar as the chief of police had a reserved table in the restaurant. And the criminals also frequented the place. There was an unwritten truce of toleration. The cops would not interfere with the bad guys; they would let them keep their pieces and even accept drinks on their tab. In return, there would never be any trouble there, no deals done and the place remained clean. All of which was to Jarvis's immense benefit. He gladly took the sugar from both harvests and kept a shine with both sides of the rusty coin.

The two men had stopped arguing now and disappeared from view. I took out a Lucky and breathed in a lung full of salty air before lighting it. Maybe the old girl had cleaned up her act. There was certainly no evidence to the contrary as yet. Rico's absence I could live with. But I didn't get carried away. There was worse to come.

Chapter Four: Sarah

One thing about going back to a former lover is the sex is usually mind blowing. The rose coloured spectacles resting on the bridge of your heart blind the old ugliness, which crept in and suddenly she looks like the most beautiful girl in the world again. Shorn of all your inhibitions and with no real burning desire to impress, the performance improves accordingly. You can remember all those little things that work wonders between the sheets without suffering the niggling irritations. Worries of sleeping in the wet patch pale into insignificance and the lack of the basic but essential everyday problems – like putting out the garbage or fixing the kitchen cupboard – don't get in the way of a bloody good bout of physical gratification. But soon enough the reality creeps back in. You realise you can't fuck forever and forget about living. The world will stop for a day or two. Maybe a week if you try hard enough, but soon it slips into first and starts the perpetual wheel again and rolls right over those glasses, crushing them into the ground.

At first, Casablanca had all the old appeal. I could sense the change from day one but didn't really want to admit it. A bit of cosmetic surgery simply gave it a newer edge. Like it had made a real effort to impress and was not going to lose out on looks alone. It was the moments after the love affair had been re-consummated that I feared. When, all of a sudden it becomes awkward, and problems which simply didn't matter before, creep in and form a barrier to any practicality.

One barrier that I wasn't quite ready for showed its face all too soon. Catching me quite unprepared, she presented herself like a twenty- foot barricade, blocking any path back to a smooth reunion. I stood frozen to the spot in the middle of the street and just watched. Cars started to swerve around me and honk their horns angrily but I didn't move. Standing there with a glazed look on my dull features, I prayed she wouldn't turn around and see me. I wasn't ready for that just yet.

She didn't. She just glided down the sidewalk and then, when the door opened for her from the inside she gracefully got in. She was wearing a short, pale blue suit with high heels and bare legs. Her hair was a mass of curls and was stuck on the top of her head in a great, silky pile. There was a glimpse of thigh as she bent over to squeeze onto the back seat. Soft, smooth, milky thigh that suddenly looked so very tempting. And then it was gone.

No matter how many years it would have been, I don't think I would have been ready for the first sighting. Old wounds are easily re-opened, however long ago they healed. I didn't know whether it was five years or twenty but when I scratched the scar on my shoulder it still hurt like yesterday. It bled and bled until I was covered in crimson and there was nobody gonna come and save me. As the car sped off with her delectable body concealed within, it was least of all gonna be her.

I noted the car – a red Dodge – and the number, but the windows were slightly tinted and it was impossible to see who else was in there. Maybe it didn't matter. There was no reason why it should, but after coming all this way I wasn't gonna get by without so much as a hello. That much I was sure. The rest just followed.

Sarah had been the one that I left behind all those years ago. I remember the day we met like it was yesterday. There was now so much water under the bridge but that first meet and the subsequent virginal days, when romances are in their incubation stage, stick like the proverbial glue. Untarnished and complete; a little love short story all of their own.

Back in the Thirties I was heavily into the personal security racket. There was heaps of work on those lines and it was extremely lucrative. The obvious drawback being the almost ever-present shadow of the mob. People tended to disappear in the gangster ridden days of thirties America and if a bodyguard got in the way than so be it. The old unwritten law of mobsters only killing one another was still in its incomplete stage and needed some ironing out.

Casablanca had never had a reputation as a mob town. Whilst the Eastern Syndicate and the Capone Mob carved up most of the country between them, Casablanca was a rare safe haven. Maybe it was down to the influence of Senator Ishmail

Ouzanti, the incorruptibility of the law enforcers, or the simple lack of a golden goose, it managed to ride the rocky years of the Volstead Act and emerge relatively clean. There would always be crime, but it mostly lacked any real organisation and was certainly not under the control of the big boys. But even without this mafia control there was always a presence.

Sarah Hill was not supposed to be involved with the Outfit. Not at any personal level, she was simply the secretary of a bent attorney who was getting the lean from the big boys. If he was under threat then so were all his family and friends, and particularly his employees. He was defending a pickpocket, who had crossed the local gang in New Orleans. Old Marcus had taken rather a shine to young Sarah, which I would soon understand to be quite a natural reaction and came to me spitting blood.

I had dealt with Marcus Trainer before in all manner of roles but never had I seen him in such a state. He came bumbling into my office unannounced, stinking of alcohol and totally shaken. His tie was all loose at the collar, his suit rumpled and he looked like he'd forgotten to shave for days.

Oh and he was waving around a wad of twenties as big as a telephone directory.

He swore blind that he'd narrowly missed the big train only hours before. He already had his security tied up through the state. Twenty-four hour gorillas with sub machine guns and rocket launchers concealed down their pants. But now he was worried about Sarah. As far as his wife was concerned, they could have her gift wrapped, but his darling Sarah, she was worth preserving.

"Casablanca's supposed to be free of all this wop shit. That's why I moved here from New York," he complained.

I sympathised.

"I want you, Errol. That's all there is too it. I don't want one of your bloody assistants or some mad ex army fuckup, I want you personally. What's your rate these days?"

"Fifty a day," I said, tongue firmly in cheek, but he didn't even notice. "But what do you expect for your hard earned?"

Before I had finished my sentence he had already peeled off five greasy notes and slammed them on the table. I raised my eyebrows and loosened my morals. "I just want her safe. This whole thing's gonna blow over in a few weeks, just stay by her side and make her feel safe."

I took the money and put it in my inside pocket. "Marcus, you've got a deal."

We shook hands, and on his way out, Marcus stopped and turned around. "Errol, I'm relying on you on this one, don't let me down. And don't get any ideas of your own, you little bastard."

I smiled and waved him out, but as I closed the door I paused. All the usual good humour had drained from his voice in that last sentence. He meant what he said.

Her hair was a mass of golden curls. She had pale skin with a gentle brown trail of freckles over a pert nose. She had a delicate mouth with inconspicuous lipstick and big blue eyes. Her eyebrows, although rather thick and unplucked, were unfashionably beautiful and she had the sweetest smile. She looked about sixteen, and in fact was only a few years older, but had the body of an erotic dream.

She was sitting at a small desk, busily typing away, when I strolled in for the first time. She looked up immediately and smiled. "You're the private eye."

I perched on the edge of the desk and smiled. "Errol Black. You must be Sarah, pleased to meet you."

She held out a hand and I graciously accepted it. I planted a clumsy kiss before holding on a moment too long. She smiled nervously and took her arm back.

"Would you like a drink, Mr Black?" she asked, her voice like silky velvet.

"Bourbon, no ice," I replied, and watched her glide over to the drinks cabinet.

She was wearing tight, black trousers and a figure hugging white blouse. Her rounded buttocks were squeezed tightly into the trousers and stood up firm and inviting. As she poured the drinks I caught a hint of a bra through her whiter than white blouse. I accepted my drink and took a large gulp, momentarily lost in the sheer sensuality she exuded.

I finished my drink and put the glass down on the table. She continued to smile sweetly. "Okay sweetheart, you know just why I'm here and this is the way we're gonna play it."

She nodded somehow making a look of mild concern seem erotic.

"I'm gonna be tagging along with you for the next week or so..."

"That would be just fine," she interrupted. "I don't have a boyfriend at the present so there won't be a problem there."

"Okay. I'll put a man in the office with you here at all times. I will personally escort you to and from here and we'll be taking most meals together."

"Marcus is really pushing the boat out," she said, and gently nodded her head.

"If ever it gets too much for you just let me know and we'll sort something out. Where do your parents live?"

"I've just got a flat of my own on the Eastern side of town."

"That's no good. I'll get you a room at The Dockside. That's where I'm staying temporarily."

She was nibbling away at her nails. I don't know if it was a nervous thing or if she was bored. Either way I was content to leave her be. She stopped all of a sudden and giggled. "I'm sorry I'm being rude. Would you like another drink, Errol?"

"That would be swell sweetheart, just swell."

On the way to the drinks cabinet the telephone rang and Sarah picked it up. I was on guard and immediately reached for the extension. Instead of the nasty, gruff voice spitting threats and obscenities, I was surprised to hear an extremely well spoken, polite young man. He was in the middle of a long and gushing monologue and Sarah was sat back, playing with her hair, all glassy eyed. She was smiling sweetly and lapping up all the glowing compliments.

For some unknown reason I felt the first pang of jealousy. I wouldn't admit it to myself at the time, but it is now unmistaken. There I was sitting with a girl that I'd met for the first time and the fact she was talking to another man was getting to me. It was a wholly irrational feeling and one that I didn't like one little bit, but there it was large as life and there was nothing that I could do about it.

I got my own drink and threw it back recklessly. Sarah put the handset down just as I was filling my glass for the third time. She walked right up to me and played with my tie. Her breasts were brushing against my open jacket and I could feel her hot breath on my neck.

She smiled and said, "If you're staying at The Dockside maybe you have a couch I could use?"

"Maybe I do."

"Well then I will move in with you. That would be safer all round wouldn't it?"

"That would be ideal if you're sure you can trust me."

She giggled and her eyes lit up like the brightest stars. "Of course I can, Mister Black. The question really is, are you sure you can trust me?"

Trust her was something that I certainly should never have even considered. Unfortunately, she was one of those girls that just didn't offer you a choice. Whether I wanted to or not I simply acted, usually in a foolish manner, without thinking about the consequences. Everything passed by like a dream and before I knew it, we were spending a great deal of time together. I seemed to forget just how fate had led our paths to cross and what the real point of my presence in her colourful life hinged on.

For days we were constantly in each other's company. At first, I at least put on a pretence of professionalism, sticking to the procedure of an op in the office and myself on transportation duties. But this soon phased out and the job became a personal pleasure. I went to bed at night looking forward to the morning when I could see her sweet face again. I drank and smoked a great deal less and I even began to sing in the bath.

In the meantime, Sarah appeared to take it all in her stride. The fact that her life may be in danger was easily glossed over, and it all seemed like an exciting adventure to her. She always got up early and cooked breakfast and insisted on listening to tales of daring and intrigue from my life as a private investigator. Most were made up on the spot and although I think she realised this it didn't seem to put her off, or temper her enthusiasm. Maybe it was her own unique way of putting away the reality and hiding behind the cloak of a fictional danger. Whichever, I was made aware early on just how tough a cookie this little lady was. She was not one to run and hide behind the sofa and was not for scaring without a fight.

Although at first, our relationship stayed firmly associates, or I suppose mild friends, she always displayed an open warmth toward me and I found it simple to return this gesture tenfold. There was hardly ever any unease between us and we found we could talk about anything and everything. Sometimes we would both sit quietly for twenty minutes or so and there remained a calm atmosphere. When the silence was broken we would then talk non stop for hours.

It's amazing just how much we had in common bearing in mind the stark differences of our background, although I am sure that a lot of the similarities were invented in my hopeful mind. The restaurants we dined in were to our mutual pleasure, as were our musical or cinematic tastes. Never when we were together did she mention any past or present boyfriend but insisted on hearing all about my own love life, which I toned down accordingly. Marcus also dropped conveniently into the background as he became more and more concerned about his own health, which didn't seem to affect Sarah one way or the other.

It was the second week of the assignment that we began sleeping together and this just topped off the perfect job. I accepted Marcus's fifty a day, handed in the expenses promptly and slept with his girl.

Those days now seem a lifetime ago, but remain in my mind as if yesterday. As that red Dodge sped off I knew it wouldn't be the last that I would see of Sarah. Sometimes I wish it was, but others I admit to myself that I am glad it wasn't. I couldn't go back to Casablanca and not meet up again with my old love, it would be like an alcoholic jumping off the wagon only to drink low alcohol beer.

After standing still in the middle of the road and nearly getting myself knocked over a number of times, I eventually found my walking boots again and headed off to The Dockside Hotel. This was one place that I knew would still be here when I arrived. I had checked as much over the telephone.

The Dockside Hotel was an icon of the town. Frisco had the bridge and New York the statue, whilst Casablanca had an inn offering rooms for hire. More like Raffles to Singapore than the Flamenco to Vegas, The Dockside usually got pretty good press and was frequented by clientele hoping for sanctuary and sophistication rather than an all over rub down and six lucky sevens.

Towering twenty storeys over the gentle waters that divided the Downtown from the mountainous West Side; built from colonial white stone and covered in clinging ivy, as green as the lushest meadow, it was nearly one hundred years old, but beautifully maintained. Never falling prey to the onrush of commercialism and big city modernism, it resisted the casino and only rarely took gigs, jazz being an erstwhile companion.

The Dockside remained a favourite amongst the town's bohemians, a little like Greenwich Village in the big apple or Venice Beach in LA. Many a struggling writer would drain a bottle in the Short Bar, searching for inspiration, hoping that elusive idea could be plucked from the smoky atmosphere and several painters gave their own unique interpretation of its homely comfort. Because of its ability to draw in the artists it became a good place for detectives to visit when in need of a break. If nothing practical came up there would never be a shortage of supposition or speculation in the thriving conversation.

I crossed the modest front gardens, my bag over my shoulder and entered under the familiar wooden sign. After giving my name, my bag was politely taken from me and forwarded to my room. I followed, pleased to be in one of the higher, premium suites. From there I could look out from the steel balcony over the bay; gazing far into the mountains searching for that lost clue. More likely I would become helplessly reminiscent after a couple of stiff ones and let the old romance of it all fill my veins. I would have to steel myself. Old memories were dangerous enemies of which I could afford few encounters.

Opting not to use the elevator, I strolled through the lobby into the central courtyard of the hotel. The steep balconied sides appeared to lean forward over the open gardens of sweet smelling flowers and intricate wood carvings. A nice touch having an indoor park as your centrepiece of a city hotel, but The Dockside always aspired to be a little different, even insofar as the rainbow parakeets shipped from Magnetic Island, Australia to annoy and amuse relaxing patrons.

Along the sides of the courtyard ran several shops ranging from traditional hotel accessories; the barber, the boutique, the jeweller, to a whole selection of tailors. Casablanca was well established as the suit capital of the county, with the Downtown alone boasting over a hundred different outlets. Along The Dockside centrepiece you could be offered every colour, size, shape or design of suit known to man. And incredibly none of the shop front salesmen were actually selling, every one without fail was offering you a chance to, "Just look."

I couldn't help but think of Sarah and how stunningly beautiful she still looked after all these years. She emerged from my past like a spectre, casting a painfully beautiful shadow across my life. How much I missed caressing her smooth naked body and our marathon love making sessions. I felt anxious to meet her again, to look into those clear blue eyes and smell the sweet aroma of her perfume. To see her soft, pink nipples pop out of her dress and hear her innocent giggle echo in the night. I would have to bide my time and pick the right moment; if there was such a thing.

Word travelled fast round here and I was sure that the grapevine would already be in overtime. One thing was for sure and I mustn't lose sight of it. Certain people in this town would not be at all pleased to see me and the wolves would be out. I would have to be extremely careful and use my courtesy time with Peru's boys wisely.

Dusk was settling in when I got in the car and set off for Heaven Springs. Heaven Springs is a small village of maybe a few hundred people at the foot of the Blue Hills in the Broadlands. A couple of miles north of Samui Bay, it is in the remotest, some would say nicest, part of town, and about fifteen minutes walk from downtown. Cattle ranches are scattered around, alongside pretty little cottages and the barest village amenities.

I arrived just after seven. The fog was rolling in, thick and heavy, suffocating the ground and obscuring what used to be a wonderful view. The old streetlights struggled to pierce the haze shining a pale, indistinct glow of orange.

I parked up my heap and got out. The fog pressed tightly against my face; to a newcomer it may be a little disconcerting, but it made me feel at home. Heaven Springs seemed always to have a thick blanket of fog, even when it was 100 degrees in the City and the sun was shining. The elements were nobody's fool. You can change the surface of a town, but you can never change its heart. That rang true as I stood in the fog, inhaling the clean, fresh air.

I walked up the sidewalk on Main street until I reached Heaven Springs General Store. I opened the door and there was no bell. I had got used to the chime of the bell every time the door opened and was taken aback. It's funny what little things stick in your mind. Fragments of useless information that find a little crevice in your brain and lodge themselves in so they are never forgotten, no matter what else the passing of years erode.

Apart from the bell, I was pleased to see the General Store had not changed. Not one little bit. I suppose it was a typical country store; the kind that is forever stuck in a bygone age. A long wooden floor that creaks as you walk, tightly packed shelves of jars of preserves and pickles of all different kinds. On the counter was a huge collection of cheeses, all displayed in their original wheels. It was beautiful.

I walked along an aisle, momentarily lost in the sheer nostalgia of it all. Revelling in the feast of oddities that only village delis provide, from the odour of old wood and fresh bread to the wonderful sight of an array of cold and spiced meats.

A young blonde haired girl of no more than twenty stood behind the counter. She smiled sweetly, showing off a perfect set of sparkling white teeth and asked if I needed assistance. I told her I was looking for Winston Bishop, who I believed was the proprietor. To my relief he still was. She showed me through to the back room.

Winston Bishop was standing with his back to us. He was a small, stocky man. His skin was as black as coal and his hair as silver as a fox. As he turned, I saw he was wearing a large, white apron covered in flour. In his large paws was a huge tray of freshly baked bread rolls, straight from the oven. The aroma was delicious and it took all of my restraint not to break off a wedge of crust from one of the well-risen loaves.

Winston put the tray down on the large wooden table in the centre of the room.

"Hello Winston," I said.

He looked at me blankly for a few seconds, but said nothing. Then recognition suddenly hit him and his round bearded face formed a wide grin. "Errol Black. If it isn't young Rolly?"

"Not so much of the young anymore, Winston."

"Jeez Rolly, it's been a long time. What's it been, five years?"

He came towards me and shook my hand firmly. Still had the grip of an ox. He must have been seventy if he was a day, but still looked exactly the same as the last time we met. He was right it had been a long time. It had been eight years.

"You're looking good Rolly, you lost a little weight?"

I shrugged, "Maybe a pound or two. You're looking pretty good yourself."

Winston let out a big laugh and flexed his muscles mockingly. "Keeping young boy, keeping young. Do you want a drink?"

"Sure, why not, and a piece of that bread wouldn't go amiss."

"No problem buddy. Gimme a minute to tell Tammy she's on her own for a while. Come on take a seat."

I took off my hat and perched myself down on one of the four old, wooden chairs. Winston ambled out of the room. I found myself in a spacious kitchen that looked like an archaic farmer's utility room. The floor was polished wood and the walls were predominantly old stone. The table stood in the centre of the room and there were pine units all around the perimeter. A huge stove pumped out hot air and nice smells and there was a spice rack as big as a bookshelf. One door led back to the store and another to a yard at the back.

Winston returned with a couple of beers and put them down on the table. In the other hand he held a platter filled with a selection of cheeses and cold meats that made my mouth water. I could barely wait to tuck in as he handed me a loaf of warm bread.

"Still like your food Rolly?" he said, and sat down to join me. So did he! He ate his way through almost a whole loaf. We ate and drank for five minutes barely saying a word. We then talked casually for a good half hour. It was nice. Damn nice.

There was a short silence and then Winston said, "Is this a social call Rolly? I mean, have you just come here to eat my bread?" He said it in a pleasant enough voice, but I could detect an air of inevitability.

I sipped my beer and sighed. "I was hoping you might be able to help me with something."

Winston nodded, his smile fading. "The police have been. I thought that you were out of that game."

"I keep trying Winston. I really do." Now it was my turn to sound distant. "But there's always something to bring me back."

"There always will be son. I should know that. But it's the living that matter, the dead are beyond us."

"Tell me about Hermeez, Winston. Was he in some trouble? Was he involved in something?" I sighed. "Or was he just unlucky. Another statistic on the violent crimes register?"

"I don't know the answers, Rolly. Hermeez came to Casablanca to retire. To do some fishing, soak up the sunny weather and to take it easy. We went down river together a few times. We got away from it all and had some fun. But what happened was a terrible, terrible thing. Unfortunately these things do have a habit of happening."

I got a sudden feeling of foreboding. I shouldn't have come here, not like this, and now I regretted it. Raking over the coals was not what the old man needed and I shouldn't have been doing it to him. I should be poking fun at his apron and making him laugh. Being the friend that I used to relish being, not digging up the life of the one he had so recently lost.

"I got your card," he said, referring to the condolences card I had sent a couple of summers previous. "I understand you couldn't have come. Whitney would have appreciated you thinking of her. She talked a lot about you."

"Did Hermeez talk about me?" I asked.

"Yeah. Now and again. Hermeez knew the score. He knew it would have to be big to bring you back here."

I didn't know he was here, I wanted to say, but the words didn't come out. I honestly didn't know. It might not have made a difference even if I had known.

"How long are you gonna stay in Casablanca, Rolly?" asked the old man, his eyes suddenly brightening up a little.

I patted his shoulder.

"A while. I'm not rushing off anywhere. Maybe *we* can go fishing, what do you say?"

"Ah, maybe. Casablanca's changed since you were last here boy. Have you seen much of the town?"

"A little, and I'm not sure I like what I see."

"It's different, ha? Don't worry. You stick around, it'll all come back. Ideals have changed, surface has changed. Deep down it's the same people."

"It's better out here," I said.

Winston smiled, "It always was."

At that moment Tammy appeared with another couple of beers. "I thought you two could do with a refill," she said, handing over the bottles. "If you need anything else just shout."

Again, a flash of those sparkling white teeth and she left.

"She's a wonderful girl is Tammy," said Winston.

I agreed.

34

"She moved in after Whitney died. Practically runs the store now, although I wouldn't tell her that."

"Are you…" I let the question hang and Winston let out a huge guffaw.

Shaking his head vigorously he said, "No.No.No."

It felt good to see the old man smile again. I could see that Tammy would certainly ease the pain, even if it was just as a hired help.

We talked for another twenty minutes. Nursing the beer, but resisting another one. Winston talked a lot about the past; about Whitney and about his native Antigua. I was happy just to listen and let all the nice memories wash over me. That was a good thing with Winston, he never dwelt on the unpleasant. Talking of all the good times was an effective way of erasing the bad ones.

I only briefly mentioned Hermeez again, but there was nothing Winston could add. As far as he was concerned, Hermeez was simply a man enjoying his retirement in a quaint old town. Sure, he liked a bet on the horses and the dogs, sure, he liked a drink and the ladies, but then that wasn't telling me anything that I didn't already know.

Just before I left I asked him about Jarvis McSwarve.

"He's still around," I said. "I always thought that Casablanca would get too small for Jarvis."

He paused before smiling. If there was a reaction I couldn't read it.

"As far as I know, Jarvis McSwarve is doing very well for himself. Hermeez mentioned him briefly, admiring his business prowess. That's all. I don't think they were friends, if that's what you want to know."

I smiled.

"You know Jarvis is married now," he said, but before I could ask any more Tammy came bursting in.

"I'm so sorry," she said, looking at me with her angelic eyes. "Winston it's that bloody Mrs Williams again. She wants to talk to you."

"It's okay," I said to Winston and stood up, "I've gotta go anyway."

Before I could shake his hand he held me tight in a bear-hug, pummelling my back with his heavy paws. I managed to break free in time to take Tammy's hand in my own and plant a delicate kiss. "Very nice meeting you Tammy," I said. "Winston, I'll be in touch."

Instead of going straight back to The Dockside, I drove South on the Canal Highway towards the Samui Bay. The bay is only a couple of miles long and less than a mile in width. Along the bay there are a collection of oyster farms, tiny seafood restaurants and nature reserves. The weather here is always less wild and windy as it is sheltered by a ridge covered in pines that run along the beach.

I parked up the car and took a walk down to the water. This is what I had wanted to find when I decided to come back. Lovely clean, fresh air and views to die for. It was incredible that only fifteen minutes from the nudie bars and freak shows of the downtown you could find this.

Behind me the tree covered hills blurred into the sky. The narrow beach ran down to the gently lapping water. Soft, silky sand with not a trace of litter or debris.

I stood there for twenty minutes in silence, just looking out at the water; at nothing at all. Letting the feeling of nature approach me, and the tension flood out. I wouldn't get many moments like this and I knew it. For Hermeez there would be no more. They were precious, like the pearl bearing oyster. To be cherished as best I could.

Eventually I turned up my collar and returned to the car.

Chapter Five: The Wild West

I awoke about eight and took a cool shower to wash away all the cobwebs of an unsettled night. I had slept fitfully and still felt tired. The old feeling was creeping back steadily. I felt excited at the prospect of my first full day back in Casablanca.

I laboured through a full breakfast in a Downtown diner and wondered just what my baby would have in store for me today. The short walk to the Arthur Peru's HQ opened my eyes to how things really had changed.

Very little of beauty remained in Downtown Casablanca. The Yellow Brick Road proved a false dawn. It seemed that was the only road in the Golden Triangle that had kept its soul. As soon as you drove a block either side the change was stark.

I felt shocked and betrayed. How I had loved this town, but Peru was right. It was now up for sale, and there were many buyers. I brushed past several raincoats similar to my own, only I wasn't sneaking into 'erotic' nudie shows. The topless bars were overshadowed by the bottomless ones. Wall to wall neon signs, flashing grotesquely made it all look like Las Vegas gone mad.

The building Peru had made his team's home was inconspicuous enough, in that it fit nicely into the graphitised decor and made no attempt to advertise just what lay inside. The cracks in the sidewalk were covered in weeds giving off the impression of being vacant. To the passer by it was just another anonymous run down tenement with cracked glass windows and rotting damp walls. Inside, however, was different. Although it was no hotbed of detective activity, it was a world away from the main station house. Telephones were ringing, typewriters were being slowly pummelled to death, the two fingered way, and voices were raised so that they challenged the noise pollution limits. And in the middle of it all stood Arthur Peru with a short wooden cane in one hand and a cigarillo in the other.

He was running the edge of the cane along a chalkboard, which was a mass of illegible scribblings, as his audience watched captivated. The audience being a small bunch of men who could easily have passed for extras in *High Noon*. At first, I thought that the villains had all escaped their cells and taken over the building, but then I realised that these were the good guys.

Everything fell silent as I walked into the room and all eyes settled on me. Peru smiled as enthusiastically as he was ever going to manage and shook my hand before introducing me to his own gang of crime busters.

"Boys, this is our guest, Mister Errol Black. Treat him as you would treat any visitor."

I smiled a friendly smile. "I look forward to working with you guys," I said, regretting it as soon as the words left my lips. These fellas would only look forward to the day I walked out of the door. For good.

Peru introduced the six present gunslingers, one by one.

First John Wimpon, tall, thin Caucasian with thick, black hair. Timmy Matthews had given me the background on all these guys, in as far as was possible. They all played on being shadowy loners but certain characteristics stuck out like The Empire State Building. John Wimpon was said to be a workaholic. Cold, methodical, arrogant with irregular behaviour, sometimes described as having psychopathic tendencies. Peru simply introduced him as his organiser.

Noah Thomas was the intellectual of the crew, with a string of letters after his name. He was a former fed, although the rest of the crew appeared to have forgiven him this minor indiscretion. He was blonde, chunky, smartly dressed and clean shaven.

Unlike Lloyd Stone, who had a constant three day growth. Lloyd was down as a maverick; nasty, cruel, cynical and a real womaniser. He was also a good looking son of a bitch.

Dan Vincent and Ahmed, a naturalised Kenyan, were the specialists of the crew. Vincent was said to be a genius with ballistics and weaponry. As a former military special he could identify any shell in the world, which weapon had fired it and usually a whole heap more of vital information. Ahmed was a face man. He was reputed to have more faces in his head than any police filing cabinet in the world.

Nobody else offered a hand and not a word was said.

The one that really did stand out was Jackson Travers. He seemed genuinely attentive as Peru introduced me, but still offered little warmth. He smirked to himself wickedly and creased up his wrinkled features awkwardly. He had a thin, droopy moustache that hung over at each side of his mouth and he wore a cloth cap straight out of thirties LA. I eyed him inquisitively but he refused to hold my gaze for longer than a second, preferring to take out a small tin from his inside pocket and roll up a miserly cigarette.

Jackson Travers had acquired the affectionate nickname of The Weasel. It wasn't difficult to understand why this was as he cowered away in the corner of the room, his whole creepy demeanour was oily and weasel like. Arthur Peru became a fan the minute they met, recruiting him to his motley crew of desperados.

He was said to be an expert on gambling and the rackets. Rumour was that as a young man in Chicago, Jackson Travers mixed with Edward J O'Hare the former bootlegger and dog track owner that turned Judas on Al Capone. It was not clear whether they were friends, lovers or simply employer/employee, but I guess that was where the old romance with the dogs began.

When O'Hare was gunned down on November 16 1939, Travers was no longer in The Windy City. He was in prison for assault and carrying an unlicensed weapon, where he would be recruited by Peru. Like most of Peru's warriors, Jackson Travers had unorthodox history and had spent the early part of his life on the wrong side of the law. It was up to me to discover if they were still there.

We all stood there in absolute silence for a good few minutes. I surveyed the rest of the bunch carefully and it didn't take me long to come to the conclusion that I was gonna be surplus to requirements. Not one of them offered as much as a smile, let alone a welcoming gesture. They would be difficult to win over and I would have to play it by ear if I was to get anywhere. Travers meanwhile kept on chuntering to himself and smirking.

When the briefing was over Peru nodded in my general direction and wandered off into an office at the far end of the room. I followed, walking around his crew who all stood their ground admirably. The office was very basic; a cluttered desk, a wall full of pinned up newspaper clippings or wanted dead or alive pictures and an ashtray that hadn't been emptied for a month.

"Sit down, Black! Take the weight off your feet."

I did as he asked and lit up a Lucky. It was strangely silent in the adjoining room. All the cops were pretending to be doing something but were taking a keen interest in this room.

"Some of my boys are not happy about you being here, Black."

"Is that a fact?" I remarked looking at Peru over the desk. He remained on his feet and spoke without looking at me.

"Like I told you yesterday, they don't appreciate any outside help on this one. They think it's kind of strange on such a small-time case. After all a fatal shooting is no longer headline news here in Casablanca."

I smoked my cigarette and listened.

"They're all loners you see which admittedly gets pretty tiresome at times, but they get the job done. They don't like help from anyone outside their own little circle and get all uptight when it's pushed on them."

"Especially from a fed, right?"

"Right."

I looked through the glass. Most of Peru's men were sitting around a small table all close up together. It looked like they were planning the defence of a small bar in the Wild West. Some of them looked my way and when I smiled they scowled and turned away. Travers was the only one alone. He was sat at another table with his feet up and his head buried in the Racing Times. He sneaked a look over the top of the paper and smiled a greasy smile back at me.

"Bearing all of this in mind they seem extra cautious over this one. I explained who you claim to be and the most admirable recommendation and glowing reference you come with, but something just won't leave them alone. They don't like it, Black, not one bit."

I shrugged.

"Now why do you think that is?"

I shrugged again. "Nobody wants their toes treading on. I'm sure there's nothing more to it."

Peru sighed. "The federation usually do more than tread on toes. I'm a little wary, being as I am in a position of certain responsibility, you understand?"

I nodded, giving an appreciative look.

"Now you're here, I suppose you're here to stay. For the time being at least," he added, looking briefly through the window.

I expected the lean. I would have got the lean whatever the reason for my being there. Hell, I would have given a federal agent the lean myself if I was in their shoes. Intrusion of territory is a major player on the hacking off register. I could appreciate that. But then I kept telling myself that this was a homicide investigation for Christ's sake. Nobody had yet given a satisfactory reason for the gun going off and the fact remained that it had done and as a result, a man was dead. The man in question was on the agency books so why the hell shouldn't a representative pay them a visit? It made perfect procedural sense. Only problem, these guys didn't follow procedure.

I decided to play stubborn, maybe that way they would leave me well alone. That would suit me just fine.

"If you want me to tell you how long it's gonna take, I'm afraid I can't do that. I'm just gonna do my job."

"Do your job. Do your fuckin' job!" Peru swore in Italian. "No fuckin' freak comes to Casablanca simply to do his job. Listen, Black, I know this town, I live and breathe the sickly air that makes it unique. Don't tell me you've been here before, okay, because it don't mean shit."

"I'm finding that out."

Peru almost smiled. "That's good," he nodded. "That's good, you're learning. Maybe you'll learn that you're not needed here, not on this one and not on any other one."

"Okay Peru. Is that the lecture or are you gonna go right into details about local jurisdiction and how you don't want yours stamped all over? Because if you are don't bother."

I geared myself up for a little speech of my own.

41

"You know the rules, Peru, just as well as I do. Like you say I come with a glittering reference. Now I don't expect a pat on the back for that, but I do expect, no demand, a little respect.

"All I ask is for some slack, co-operation may be too much to ask for your..." I looked through the glass at the creatures staring in, "...your colleagues. Now I'm going to cover everything there is to cover on this case, I'm gonna do all the donkey work I usually get someone else to do for me."

Peru smiled at that one.

"And I intend to do that without causing any ripples, or putting anyone's nose out of joint." I smiled. "Unless they deserve it. And when I find what I am looking for, I will, of course, hand over any criminal evidence to your department to follow procedure and take whatever action is necessary. Anything pertaining to federal business I will advise you first before informing my superiors. I owe you that courtesy."

Peru shook his head wearily. "It was a house shooting, Black, a fuckin' house shooting, that is all. You have no business here at all and you damn well know it!"

"But I am here," I cut in. "And until the crime is solved..."

"...the crime is solved?" Now he laughed.

"Until I finish my business, I stay. Now how do you want to play this? Who is attached to this investigation, or is it already filed away under unsolved?"

"We have too much work to give every one constant twenty-four hour attention. Anything you need to know is in the file. If you can't find it in the file you ask me or Jackson Travers."

"What about the local naughties. You mentioned the 'usual suspects'. I need to know who they are and what they do."

"You don't need to know shit, Black. However, you want to dress this thing up we both know it was a house robbery that somehow ended up with the owner getting shot dead. Who did it? -that's your only puzzle and more importantly that is your only jurisdiction on this soil. You would do well in remembering that."

"I've heard a lot about your team, Peru," I said. "You have a lot of admirers. A lot of good results that are all down to you. I don't want to cause no friction. I'm not here to upset the applecart or to muscle in on your little party, because it seems to me that you got everything under control…"

"But you must be allowed to 'do your job'!" The sentence sounded like a filthy habit.

"Yeah, that's about the size of it."

He said nothing. His gaze was at his wild boys through the window.

"I don't expect them to open their legs to me, don't worry. I can handle a little cold shoulder. But that's not really what's eating you is it? You don't think I'm playing straight with you, and neither do your boys." I stubbed out my cigarette. "I know you've already checked me out and I don't doubt a few of your protégés have had a poke around as well. What did you find?"

Peru slammed his cane down hard on the desk, knocking piles of papers and reports to the floor. The noise rang out loud and everything in the whole police room fell deadly silent. I stopped mid sentence and looked into his eyes. Gone was any trace of friendliness and his jowls were more puffed and red than usual.

"Don't patronise me, Black!" His voice contained the most emotion in the whole time I had known him. "Without me you are nothing in this town. You would do well in remembering that, whoever the fuck you are."

"I'm on the level, okay. I'm not on a Mafia hunt or an organised crime chase. I'm simply here to dot the i's and cross the t's."

He put the cane down and composed himself before returning to the usual monotone, "There are no unaccounted for gangsters in this town. Wentz was a small time boy and his murder should be of no consequence to anyone. It was a burglary gone wrong. Nothing more. We have them in Casablanca every day. Why should one more make a difference? Now you have asked for the case notes and as a guest of the Casablanca PD I will be happy in handing them over to you, but please…" he held out his open palms, "…insult me no more and tell me what the hell you are really doing here."

I finished my cigarette.

"On the record I've told you, but just to prove to you that I'm playing straight I'll tell you a little more."

For the first time since I had met him Peru gave a true smile. It didn't suit him. "Hang on," he said. "He was a friend of yours, right?"

I said nothing but then I didn't have to. Peru knew he was right and for the time being this would put his mind at ease.

"You wanna tell me the story?"

"Nope."

He sighed. "Don't fuck me, Black. I don't want no vigilante on my turf. You play ball and I play ball. Just don't fuck me, okay."

I smiled.

"That wasn't so fuckin' hard now was it? If playing straight means making my blood pressure go up with silly games of cat and mouse, I'll take you crooked. Okay, so now we start again."

He searched through the big, heavy filing cabinet in the corner of the room and pulled out a brimming file.

"You got this for a week, no more," he said and handed it over. "And you're lucky. You've also won yourself the services of Jackson Travers, the finest of all my detectives. On twenty-four hour call, if that's what you want. The others don't even want to see your face so you've been warned. They'll leave you alone as long as they don't have to clean up after you."

"I'll work alone," I said a little too bluntly.

Peru stopped and looked at me hardly. "You wanna play the lone wolf, ha? Well if you've really done your homework on me then you should know that I don't allow it. If that's what you want then I'll be having the file back." He held out a chubby paw.

I shrugged again and Peru smiled. "He may not look up to much but he's invaluable in this town. Tonight he's gonna take you to the dogs."

I preferred the nags but what the hell. The Greyhound Track was as good a place as any to start investigating this little number. Hermeez Wentz had been a keen gambler all his life and for the most of it a good one. Countless times he had come away from a meet with a small fortune whilst I had to beg for my taxi fare. The fact that he had a half of a betting slip in his dressing gown pocket when he was found dead made it all the more interesting.

Travers was due to pick me up at The Dockside at eight. I spent the remainder of the afternoon scouring through the case notes. Peru was right; there was nothing of particular interest. Hermeez Wentz, a former PI and resident of Casablanca for five years found shot dead in his own bathroom by a nosy neighbour.

It said in the file that Hermeez was a well-respected member of Casablanca's elite. He lived in an apartment in the Cocoa Heights area of town on the border of the Downtown district and an extremely good residential area of the Trimbles. He had no long-term romantic interests since the death of his first wife six years before he moved to Casablanca. Similarly he had no regular employment, although he made a good sideline income by contributing an interesting column to the local rag about a PI's view on the world. A real cliched Phil Marlowe outlook on real life events, which Hermeez was qualified for by his own private eye experience. I read a couple of the columns and laughed out loud. It was quite good.

Apart from that, there was very little. Apparently he had few close friends and no family to speak of. There was no timetable to the killing. I would have liked to see his movements for the twenty-four hour period before he died. I made a mental note to ask Peru about this the next time we met, although I didn't hold out much hope. If he wasn't under surveillance it would take some detective work, something the Wild Bunch did not want to offer to this particular case.

His banking details were added almost as an after thought. Looking through them I realised why. When he arrived his account was quite healthy and over the years there was a gradual decline. There was nothing special here, that's what you would expect from a man enjoying his retirement. When he died, however, his bank account was overdrawn to the tune of $10000. One possible item of interest was a large withdrawal the week before he was shot. It was certainly worth following up.

He was said to be a keen gambler. He liked the horses and loved the dogs, and wasn't averse to an after hours game of cards. There were unconfirmed sightings of him outside a top quality massage club on the West Island, although when it was pursued the management denied any knowledge of it. The police put it down to simple gossip columnists cashing in and left it at that.

Chapter Six – Death of a friend

A friend was dead. I'm not sure that you can say 'former friend' because if they're no longer a friend then the word even by association seems false, uncomfortable.

Hermeez Wentz had been my longest friend. We had not only grown up together, forming that enigmatic bond that boyhood pals create and adults cannot even hope to understand, but carried it on further into manhood. I had consumed my first beer alongside him, made love to my first woman with him doing a similar act in the next room, a paper-thin wall away, and I had even killed my first human being shoulder to shoulder with my dead friend.

Hermeez was an incredibly handsome man. A shade over six foot with a fit, lean body and piercing dark, broody eyes. His hair was kept short and brushed back. His nose was small, well sculptured, sitting nicely in the middle of a charming, charismatic face. He was always clean shaven and well attired, priding himself on an appearance of sophisticated bravura. He was quite often told he looked like a gangster and I had to admit that if he didn't keep away from the fedoras, that he did. His German ancestry was well hidden behind a silky, accent-less voice.

When we left Casablanca we were quickly separated. I joined my old buddy after a short gap of 3 months. He had moved back to New York to head up The Shadow Man Detective Agency in the absence of our mentor, Terry Shadow. Hacked off with being paid to act as nursemaid to ageing mobsters or bent officials, dodging the bullets and taking the heat, he loved it in the Big Apple. Despite my problems there was a promise of a job whenever, or if ever, I wanted.

So, when I walked into Joe's Diner on 5th Avenue, my arm still in a sling we were reunited after our first separation.

Hermeez nursed me through all the hurt and all the anger. Listening patiently at all those odd and unsociable hours, when after days of silence and indifference, it all came flooding out in a tidal wave of wrath and venom. Calming the fires of my anger, keeping a cool head when I lost my rag in a bar or restaurant, flailing my arms, or worse, at any punk that looked my way. He would drink with me, sleep alongside me and if the situation could not be avoided, he would fight with me.

You often wonder when you read all those hard-boiled novels of lone-wolf heroes prowling the mean streets of Los Angeles or San Francisco, shoving their guns in people's stomachs and pulling the trigger, being beaten

senseless by a gang of Outfit yobs, or seduced by the resident femme fatale,
you wonder just what made them like they are. Did Phillip Marlowe ring his
ma and pa at weekends, or go round for Thanksgiving dinner? Did Mike
Hammer have to wait by the telephone whilst Velda went to the clinic for a
pregnancy test, or did he always carry rubbers, or did he really not give a
fuck? They never tell you the other half. All you get is half a life, hell it's the
only half worth reading about that's for sure, but you still wonder.

I suppose I read the secret half of Errol Black in those first few weeks
back in New York. I read it, understood a whole lot more and burnt the
fuckin' evidence. You could say that my turning point in life had arrived. I
became a most wonderful cynic and a terrible rogue. Turned my back on
reality and crept onto the pages of Hammett's typescript. Hermeez knew it
was a facade, a shell that I had carefully constructed around me, that one day
he would help me smash to pieces. I'm sure he had it all planned one day in
the near future; a cathartic return to heal all the old wounds and tie up all
the loose ends. Unfortunately, I don't think he planned to persuade me to
return quite like this.

A month after my return to New York we left The Shadow Man
Detective Agency in the hands of Dyke Spanner and took a trip to the Far
East. We marvelled at the wonderful waterways of Bangkok, took in the
history and culture of Malacca and drank Singapore Slings in the Long Bar
with Sir Stamford Raffles. On the way back home we stopped for a short
break in majestic Venice.

I found the address to the apartment listed at the bottom
of the file and took a look. Everything had been returned to the
scene after examination and the whole place was due to be
demolished.

Hermeez had never been a tidy man. Dishes were never
washed up and cleared away immediately after eating, and clothes
were frequently strewn around the place. Folding was not a
favourite habit. Whoever killed him was not fussy either.

The bed was torn to bits, with foam stuffing all over the
place. Nasty looking springs protruded from the mess. A chest of
drawers was knocked on its side with the four drawers emptied
of their contents onto the floor. The carpet had been lifted and
hastily put back down, and the walls had all got marks from a
small heavy implement.

It was a beautiful job, all right, a real thorough search, and there were things missing as well. A neighbour claimed there used to be paintings on the wall and certain ornaments. They were found to be missing from the wreckage.

I walked through the junk on the floor, broken glass crunching under foot. Old newspapers and torn pages from books, some candles and a few clothes. One of his old coats was in pieces with a packet of cigarettes still in the top pocket. On the surface of it all was the white film of dust, used by the forensics to sweep it all for evidence. From what the file would have us believe there wasn't any.

The window was open and a gentle breeze blew in. I closed the window and trudged back through the junk. Kicking a small metal object into the door, I stopped and picked it up. A small zippo lighter, engraved with a "HW". I put it in my pocket and left the apartment.

If anything it looked a bit too messy to be a simple burglary, but then so many of today's criminals were either high on drugs or complete lunatics that this might not mean anything. It no longer scored you any points with the chief to point out minor irregularities which cast doubt on an otherwise cast iron case, as they were often proved to be of no consequence later thus wasting a lot of time and money.

I flicked to the photographs at the back of the file. The close ups of the body were pretty gruesome affairs. Wearing nothing but a white towelling dressing gown, which was awash with crimson, the colours magnified this. There were two point blank gunshots to the chest an inch apart. Again, it crossed my mind that a burglary would be unlikely to be so violent and frenzied but I put it out of my mind.

I sat back and fixed myself a drink when it caught my eye. The only other item he was wearing was a watch tightly strapped around his hairy wrist. The watch itself was old and of little value, but it looked good. I remembered when Hermeez picked it up twenty years ago. It was at a Malayan bazaar and cost a mere four ringets. It probably took a factory full of twelve year old labourers a month to make which fed their families for a year, but was not even worth the wrist space of the would be robber. My thoughts were interrupted by the telephone...

Chapter Seven – Jackson Travers

I picked up the handset, "Yes."

"Mister Black?" came the bland voice down the telephone.

"Who's calling please?" I asked authoritatively.

"Leave Casablanca, there's nothing for you here." The voice was icily cold; every word spoken without a trace of emotion.

I paused a moment and lit a cigarette.

"Who's calling?" I asked again and instead of the chilling voice I expected, I could hear muffed laughing.

The caller composed himself and said, "Get your wallet and be down in the lobby in five. There are things happening at the Racecourse."

I sighed, packed up the case notes safely in the deposit box and went down to meet Jackson Travers.

The drive to the Racecourse took twenty minutes and there was little conversation between us. Jackson Travers looked every bit as odd close up as he did from afar. He still wore a chequered cloth cap on his head, with no trace of hair underneath, with jeans and a long camel coat. He had been waiting in the hotel lobby, sitting inconspicuously with his legs crossed and his head ducked behind a racing newspaper. I spotted him immediately and when I tapped him on the shoulder from behind he carefully folded his paper and slipped it in his coat pocket without saying a word.

"So you like to work alone?" he said, his thin, slimy lips barely moving.

"Ahem. No offence intended."

"And none taken." He took out his little tin of tobacco and began the painstaking process of rolling a cigarette as we walked to the car. "I hope I didn't startle you," he said with a smirk on his face, as we reached the car park and he opened the door.

"Well I was all packed and ready to go," I said and lit up a Lucky.

Jackson looked at the cigarette glowing between my lips with distaste and said, "A pair of real jokers that's us."

"I'm starting to think that this whole department's a joke."

Travers stopped and looked right at me over the roof of the car. He looked as if he was evaluating further physics. "Why do you say that, sweetheart?" he eventually muttered.

"Well nobody seems to be taking this case seriously. If every unlawful death is treated the same way, no wonder Casablanca's gone to the dogs."

He smirked at the unintentional irony and got in the car. "Casablanca's okay," he said and fired up the car.

"You reckon? I took a walk down the Yellow Brick Road today."

Jackson ignored that, instead choosing to sing along to an old Irish tune on the radio. I sat back and enjoyed the view of a town gone bad.

Conversation then dried up a bit as Jackson seemed more interested in playing with the radio dial and making more poor attempts at smokes. Twenty minutes later we pulled in outside the main entrance of the Casablanca Greyhound Centre.

The Casablanca Greyhound Centre was a major player of the small local economy. It was under used and under funded in the old days, but had since been restored and was now a highly impressive sight. A large cantilever stand with comfortable seats for a few thousand people hung over the carpet like oval. Around the manicured field was the track of finely combed sand, the traps to the far left and the mechanism for the electric hare. Half way up the stand, between the two tiers you could watch the action from behind glass in the luxury drinking and gambling club.

Travers strode into the Gentleman's Suite: a huge room full of all kinds of people; ladies as well as gents. The race meet might not be due to start for a couple of hours yet, but the party was in full swing. The suite had a certain grandiosity to it, with a long bar which filled the far wall; a wall which was adorned with portraits of greyhounds of all colours and size, mounted in elaborate, gold frames. Leather loungers were filled with rich-looking folks eating olives with cocktail sticks and caviar from silver platters. The suite had a dark, polished hardwood floor

52

with a huge oriental carpet in the centre and several smaller rugs around the edge. There was a grand concert piano in the corner expertly played by a dapper smoke in a white suit, who was the spitting image of Dooley Wilson.

Waitresses were marching back and forth carrying buckets of champagne and whole smoked salmon amongst other things, and wearing very little, but wearing it well.

Travers snatched a flute of champagne from a passing tray and held it up in the air. "Cheers," he said and creased his face up into that awful smile that looked so like a grimace, before throwing it down in one.

"What do you think, Errol, do you like how the other side live?"

"I like my eggs bigger and from hens and I like my grapes sweeter and growing on a vine, but it's okay if you like this kind of thing."

"Not really my cup of tea either, but as I am sure you have gathered, a most useful venue for gathering intelligence." And he looked at me in what I guessed was supposed to be an enigmatic expression, but only succeeded in looking like a man sucking a lemon. A very ugly man at that.

"Faces are all around us. Faces that are pulling the strings, tweaking the nipples and tickling the toes of our little kingdom."

"Is any of this relevant?" I asked.

"Relevancy is not always transparent. I don't think that your friend, Wentz, will be worrying to much about relevancy, do you?"

A small, plump man with thick black hair and a heavy beard appeared by my side and shook Travers' hand. He was wearing a blue, navy suit with a red and yellow tie. He had a huge, fat cigar smouldering between his thick, purple lips and a chunky, gold bracelet that jangled as he pumped Travers' rather limp hand.

"Jackson, it is good to see you here again, supporting the Centre. Join me for a drink, will you, after the racing." His voice was surprisingly high and his eyes were constantly on the move, as if searching for his next victim.

"Jim, of course. May I introduce you to Errol Black, a guest of Mr Peru." And he giggled to himself childishly.

I shook hands with Jim and we were left to introduce ourselves as Travers looked away disinterestedly, got out his tin and started rolling up a cigarette. He was Jim Jacobs, the president of the Casablanca Bank. He proudly extolled the virtues of the Bank's investment policy and enviable record in the world of high finance. He tried to act nonchalant but his ears pricked up when I told him I was a detective on a special assignment. I was going to leave it at that but the Weasel blurted out about Hermeez Wentz and then quickly moved on.

"Jim's a very important face," he said, and walked away.

I searched for a Lucky in my coat pocket and as soon as it was between my lips there was a spark and it was lit. The culprit smiled sweetly and curtseyed and I winked in return. Travers took another flute of champagne before marching right through the room and through a solid, wooden door.

The next room housed the bookmakers that were presumably the exclusive reserve of the Gentleman's Suite. The room was no less ornate despite some of the archaic stands that were being set up. It was quite comical watching champagne swilling, chain-smoking turfies cranking their chalkboards up on heavy, expensive Persian carpets. Everything here was quiet, with just one or two early starters setting up their stalls. Wiping their chalkboards clean and drawing fresh lines in their books. Nobody seemed bothered that we had sauntered right through the complex. Few even gave us as much as a passing glance, the ones that did looked briefly before turning abruptly away.

We reached the end of the room and passed through a heavy door. Now in a corridor, Jackson Travers stopped abruptly and turned around. "You like the tour?" he asked and then gulped down his drink.

"You're such an informative host, Jackson," I quipped.

"Now the fun will begin. Tell me are you a dog lover?"

He didn't wait for an answer, letting out a choky laugh and turning quickly on his heels. At the end of the corridor there was a right angle turn which led to a flight of steps. At the bottom of the staircase was another set of double doors which led out into a marquee. Two gorillas stood outside, the bulges in their jackets not hidden. Instead of blocking our path, turning us around and marching us right back where we came from they smiled and opened the door. It was cute to see and Travers was enjoying it immensely. On the way through he handed over the empty champagne flute and pushed a dollar bill in the doormen's top pockets.

Chapter Eight – Scamper

"Isn't she beautiful," said Travers as we found ourselves in a palatial dog pen.

The tent was huge with dog kennels to the immediate right. The most of it was a sanded track, which was used for training. A rope separated us from the track, which ran the length of the marquee. Tables and chairs set out neatly in rows.

The beast in question was a silver greyhound with white flashes across her ears. She certainly was a magnificent creature, parading around the carpeted pen with an arrogant air. Thick muscles powered her painfully thin legs, hidden behind a soft main of silky hair. Her almond eyes were almost human, showing off an intelligently mind behind the wet nose and sharp bark.

"Mr. Black, meet Scamper; the finest looking greyhound in the whole of Casablanca."

Travers stumbled towards the rope which cordoned off the dog kennels from where we stood. "Come here girl." He held out his hand and a long pink tongue shot out of the dog's mouth and licked it.

The lady was now satisfied and trotted back to her kennel, leaving Jackson Travers watching in admiration. Every movement was slick and graceful. Each step was smoothly taken and she was equally as graceful in full flight.

Jackson Travers stood back up and smiled in my direction. I had no inclination to return the gesture.

"How much do you know about dogs, Black?" he asked.

I was tempted to fire back the obvious cheap jibe, but for some reason held off. I sensed that for the first time that day Travers was serious. I told him the truth, which wasn't much.

"Greyhounds are different from other dogs. They're not only sleek, well-muscled and fast, but extremely bright and high-natured. Everybody thinks dogs are blind as bats, but Greyhound Racing has its origins in coursing where the hounds used their eyes not their ears. In ancient Greece they were well respected species, proficient in all forms of hunting, whether it be stags, foxes or badgers, but of course their main quarry has always been the hare."

"Even the mechanical variety?"

Travers looked at me in disgust. "The name has been so aptly coined over the years from great hound. A corruption long since forgiven and easily overtaken."

He smiled cryptically and moved on.

I had played it right. Jackson Travers would have made a hell of a poker player and now showed another side to his nature. For the next ten minutes he talked non stop about racing, with a passion. For a non-believer he made me shiver. He sounded like an Irishman describing a pint of Guinness.

At the far side of the training track stood a short, stocky, man. A flat cap covered most of his head and a pair of binoculars the remainder. He was following a jet black greyhound saunter around the sand, swapping between his wristwatch and the glasses.

"That there is Scamper's trainer, Johnny Dragapetto. Mean son of a bitch, trains most of the good dogs round here."

Travers waved and Dragapetto put down the glasses and stomped over. He was scowling openly, despite the little man's silly smile. "He's pissed because he lost a race on Saturday. Usually sweeps the board."

When he arrived the scowl had dropped a little and his face mellowed. "Jackson, always good to see you," he lied looking straight through me.

"Johnny, this is Errol Black," he nodded. "He's a good guy, so I'm told."

Johnny grunted and again looked at his watch before scribbling the time down on his clipboard.

"Got any form for me, Johnny?"

Dragapetto looked at the Racing paper under Travers arm and shrugged, "What's wrong with your guide?" he snorted. Before shouting across the yard for the next one.

"How's Scamper shaping up?" he persisted. "Can she take the State record?"

"She could take the world record could this one, but one step at a time." He looked at me. "But she needs to be allowed to train."

I lit up a Lucky and stared hard at Dragapetto.

"Jackson, I don't mean to be rude, but is this business or pleasure? You know how busy I am."

"Just wanted to show Scamper to my new friend, Mr Black. That's all Johnny, don't you get grouchy it's bad for the blood pressure you know."

Steam came out of the trainer's ears. "You know Mr McSwarve don't like people coming into the enclosure." He kept looking at me. "Especially people he don't know."

"It's okay Mr Dragapetty, me and Jarvis are old friends," I said with a shit-eating grin on my face.

"Dragapett-o, the name is Dragapett-o."

"Whatever, pass on my regards when you see him."

He sneered, "Jackson, I'm sorry I'm busy." He put his pencil back behind his ear and trudged off. "Lots to do. Don't go bothering Scamper, please. That dog's worth more than you'd believe."

It was foggy outside and the sun was submerging behind the huge oak trees that circled the splendid racetrack. I felt a tap on the shoulder and took the steaming cup of coffee Travers offered me. He dunked a chocolate coated bagel in his coffee.

"Horse Racing, the sport of kings. Never could abide the bloody aristocracy. The dogs, now that is something else."

It was amazing what a transformation Travers went about around the track. It was as if he was swept up in the romance and intrigue of another world. Far away from the filth and degradation of what Casablanca had become, he had now crashed out of his creepy little shell and spoke with enthusiasm and fluency.

"The oldest breed of domesticated animal released back into the wild and allowed to follow its natural instincts. Beasts of grace and elegance, of long powerful legs and the softest, smoothest mane of silk.

"No whips. No riders. Just freedom, a hair's breadth away. Poetry, Errol my friend, pure poetry."

I sucked in the cool, fresh air. Let a little poetry cleanse the soul.

I lit up a cigarette and surveyed the impressive centre. There had been none of this back in the old days. The only dogs in Casablanca were ferocious guard dogs or slavering frothing at the mouth strays, left to wander the beautiful town as an urban vermin. In a way Travers was right, these beasts were freer than ever before, even if it was only for the time until Smith's mechanical hare circled the oval and the bets were placed. But incarceration was better than destitution. I knew that all too well.

A car pulled up in the distance and it looked familiar. I was taken aback to see Jarvis McSwarve get out accompanied with Sarah. She was conservatively dressed in long, black trousers and a polo neck sweater. For a brief moment our eyes met, but she wouldn't hold the contact and looked away sharply.

Anger burned deep inside.

"Ah, you've spotted the royalty have arrived. Shall I tell you a story?"

I looked at Travers. He had chocolate smeared all around his mouth and was in the process of rolling a cigarette.

"I'm all ears," I said and walked on.

"Once upon a time there was a town," he said, expertly tipping a little tobacco into a white sheaf. "A beautiful town, with pretty ladies in bright, white dresses and shiny satin shoes, of leafy suburbs with big houses and double garages. Where the gentlemen took their girls dancing on an evening and it was safe for little kiddies to play out in the neighbourhood unsupervised."

"Sounds nice."

"Sounds familiar you mean. But then it changed, not overnight but gradually. The world got smaller and nasty villains and scoundrels ran out of playgrounds. So they moved into our idyllic town. With them came everything bad that you can imagine, all those nasty demons from the drunken nightmares that we've all had.

"Prostitution, drugs, theft, murder. They all arrived at once, and the town changed irreversibly. No longer could you go down to the cinema house because all they played was filth, pornographic filth that has no place in a family environment. You couldn't even go to the park for a picnic with your sweetheart because you might step on a spent syringe, or get mugged by a gang of delinquent tearaways. No longer could you go for a drink in one of the many watering holes without the good chance of getting caught up in a bar brawl or a spot of criminal warfare."

"I thought Casablanca was okay."

Travers sighed and looked over my shoulder.

"It is," he said. "But it's not always been this way. I admit it has lost its innocence, popped it's cherry so to speak, but like the rebellious teenager that was once a sugar pie, lily white sweetie, it took a distinct turn for the worse. You think it's bad now, then you should have been here ten years ago."

I remembered Casablanca as exactly what Travers had described; a beautiful town, but that wasn't the only reality. There had been crime in the old days, just not so damn much of it, and certainly no Syndicated set up. But sure, there had been crime, even some Outfit presence to a degree. However, Casablanca had always been beautiful.

"So what are you telling me Travers? Are you saying that all of this transformation is down to Arthur Peru?"

"Yeah, I guess I am. When Arthur Peru arrived in Casablanca it was bad, you could say it was make or break time. There was a real chance that this once great town was gonna become another gangland right-off. The homicide and vice squads were working around the clock and most were probably getting the greasy thumb treatment, meanwhile the disease was spreading. The feds had enough on their plate, what with Nitti in Chicago and the big boys out East, they didn't have the time or the inclination to come out here. If they couldn't save Cuba, what would Casablanca matter?"

"What about Senator Ouzanti, nobody ever described him as small fry and got away with it?"

"It was Uncle Ishmail that detailed Peru. Brought him in personally and gave him a free hand. No official brief to speak of, just a final aim."

"Which was to clean up Casablanca and kick the mob out?"

"Your guess is as good as mine but I would think that you're not far out with that. We're not the Untouchables by any means, but each and every one of us is straight down the line and dedicated to do whatever Arthur Peru asks of us."

I smiled. "Okay Travers, I'll leave off the Peru jibes, but I'm still not convinced of his omnipotence just yet."

"This friend of yours, Wentz," he said, changing the subject promptly. "How long is it since you last spoke to him?"

I shrugged. "A long time."

He licked one length of the would-be cigarette and sealed it perfectly before lighting up. "You knew he was a gambler, right?"

"The betting slip."

"One of many, my friend, one of many."

We strolled around the long, crisp grass surrounding the track.

"Who did he owe?" I asked, not expecting an easy answer.

Jackson chuckled to himself. "There were a few," was all he said before the loudspeaker crackled into life, announcing the race meet would begin in an hour's time.

"He didn't always lose though. Won as much as twenty thousand in one night. On the roll of dice, so the story goes."

"But he was in debt, right?"

"Oh yeah, he never stayed black for long. He owed a couple of big ones to his bank manager for one."

"Jim Jacobs."

He nodded. "A very important face."

"Any names on the undesirable list?"

"Not that we know of."

Jackson stopped and blew out a thin stream of yellow smoke. It smelled faintly of marijuana. "Jarvis McSwarve was into him pretty heavily."

I tried not to react, but Travers' expression told me I had failed miserably. Jarvis McSwarve. It was exactly the name I had been hoping for.

And there was Sarah.

I had seen them and they were together. That much was unmistakable. They were together and not just as race companions. Already I found myself hating him; it was searing deep inside, scorching through any sense of logic or common sense I possessed. He had to have killed Hermeez, maybe not

61

personally but it was his decision. He was in some way responsible.

"My my my, do you not like that. Don't worry yourself too much, there were others."

We took our seats in the stand as the race meeting commenced. There was something beautiful about watching those hounds sprinting around the small, sandy oval. At times I found myself shouting with the best of them; urging them on to find that elusive extra yard which would enable them to catch the hare. Five thousand punters all seemed to think they were in with a chance.

When it came to Scamper's race I even upped my stake to a cool ten bucks. Travers droned on, "Easiest money you'll ever earn…I hope you'll be buying the next round…" he went on and on, but it all washed over me.

I got the feeling that Sarah was the hare and I was the prized greyhound. Bounding after her, stretching out my long legs in a desperate race against time. Ten yards from the end I almost caught her. A mere hairs breadth away and then…

"I'll be damned."

Jackson Travers stood up, mouth open, face aghast. He stayed frozen for several seconds before blinking his eyes in disbelief. There was a general hum of displeasure and surprise amongst the substantial crowd. I tore my slip in half and looked around the stunned arena. Scamper was being shepherded to the finishers' enclosure as the winner was doing a lap of honour.

It proved a dampener to the remainder of the evening.

We stopped for a drink in the Carlton Bar. Travers had champagne, I had bourbon. I tried to pump him on some names that had cropped up. He described McSwarve and Sarah as the King and Queen of the racecourse and told me he was the Chairman of the Racing Commission before apparently clamming up and changing the subject.

He talked sketchily about some of Hermeez's debtors, but it turned out they were mainly small fry and he had checked them out anyway. He handed me a slip of paper with the results on it. There was little of interest.

I asked him about Dragapetto, the miserable trainer, but he brushed this off with more vigour than before.

"He's the best damn trainer in the State. He was bound to lose a race eventually," he said referring to Scamper. "Nobody ever went through a whole career unbeaten. Maybe I should have stayed away."

"He sure is a handsome mutt," I said.

He screwed up his weasel face at the sound of the word mutt like I'd poked him in the eye.

"I'll take you back," he said.

"What, no drinks in the Gentleman's Suite?"

He shook his head. "Not tonight. I'll take you home."

And he did. I felt like a naughty teenager, who'd taken his girl's signals too far and put his hand up her skirt only to be scolded and told to slow his goddammned self down.

I don't know if Travers felt embarrassed or genuinely disappointed, but from the moment his golden girl trailed in second the spark was lost.

He dropped me back at The Dockside, driving the whole way without uttering one word. When we arrived I got out and he drove off without even as much as a goodbye. I held out a hand waving at an empty space and went inside.

Chapter Nine – The note

I saw the note immediately.

An aching belly full of baked potatoes and porterhouse steak, and a good bottle of claret with the stains down my shirt to prove it, made me tired. The elevator ride up had been spent half asleep, dreaming of my creaking double bed and crusty pillow. My senses were dulled, nerves frayed and body exhausted. I wanted to sleep.

I was slow to react, my guard down, but for once I could escape a sloppy moment. No sooner did I have my gun in hand and my ears pricked when I saw the handwriting. Neatly scrawled in gold ink was my name 'Errol'.

I could feel the old warmth soaking my muscles and alerting my loins and it felt good. The tiredness was fought off, the fatigue washed out. All of a sudden I felt young again, I felt excited and anxious. The angels were dancing up and down all over my porterhouse.

At first I bled, now I could fly.

We were back at the country ranch overlooking the beautiful coastline stretching out for miles in either direction. The air was crisp and the stars were twinkling in a clear sky.

Lavender was scenting the cool air; drifting up in wafts of yellow smoke from the lantern by the log fire. The lights were dimmed and the majestic flames reflected in the glass of the patio doors.

I picked up the note and the fragrance hit me; the musky smell of her body, hot breath on the back of my neck. The reflection of the wobbling flames was replaced by the profile of a slender beauty. We danced tightly together, smooching slowly to the music drifting in and out of our lives.

The country ranch was now a blur. Fuzzy around the edges, but the thought of it made me feel warm inside. It used to be our special place. A sanctuary away from the world of flying bullets and jealous lawyers. Over the years I had had mixed success in pushing it out of my mind but it always crept back. From time to time I willingly let it.

I sat down and poured a drink. The note was short and to the point. I read it five times but it still said the same thing. She wanted to meet me on Tuesday night at nine. That was two days from now. There was only one place.

It could be a trap. The thought struck me immediately, but I dismissed it. Even if it was the chance was worth taking. This was one rendezvous for which I would not be taking the cavalry for back up.

I tucked myself up in bed and drifted into a deep, comfortable sleep. Hazy dreams invaded my slumber; of breathtaking chases and wild gunfights, but there was a constant warmth, which protected me through it all.

I was awoken by the telephone.

Arthur Peru said hello as if I had just killed his cat. He was calling from the station-house and sounded done in. I told him so and he told me to go to hell. At that point I thought he was gonna hang up the phone, but he didn't. Instead, he arranged to meet me in an all night diner on the Camel Canal.

The Camel Canal was a plain and simple affair. It had yellow walls and tall creeping cheese plants. The tables and chairs were bare and wooden and practical. The staff were polite and efficient.

Peru was waiting with a half-empty pot of coffee for company. When he saw me open the door, he signalled for another pot. I took a chair and smiled a toothy grin.

"What's wrong, you guys don't like to sleep in this town anymore?"

"Busy night. I'm on my way home. You could always head off yourself if the hours are not to your liking."

I smiled and stayed right where I was at.

"You're gonna stay, ha?" he set his coffee cup down and refilled it. "Maybe this will change your mind."

The waiter brought the fresh pot and I poured a cup.

"The coroner's report." He handed over a single piece of paper.

The report was nothing special. Two point blank gunshots to the chest an inch apart. The first had missed everything vital and exited cleanly. The second went straight through the heart and killed him right where he fell. They were fired from a .33 calibre weapon, one of several thousand on the streets of America.

There was evidence of a minor scuffle prior to the shooting, torn clothing and bruised knuckles, indicating they had been used to hit something hard, although this was inconclusive. His body showed traces of alcohol, but nothing out of the ordinary.

The rest was usual stuff.

"Nothing to disprove the original verdict," said Peru and took the report back.

I nodded.

"He was probably sat at home enjoying a quiet drink. Burglar stumbles in and interrupts the peace. Scuffle ensues and the burglar shoots him. Twice. All smooth and simple."

"Too simple."

"Sure. They usually are, but then that *is* how it usually happens."

There was a short silence between us. I was wondering if the night at the races was simply a perk for the unwanted. Butter him up, tempt him with a few stories of piling debts and then shut the case. Finish it before it begins and send the outsider packing.

"I'll tell you what, Black. I'm gonna cut you a little slack because I'm feeling compassionate. You get to keep Travers and for a limited time you get to keep the case open. But it's a two man job, I can spare nobody else. Keep it short and keep it tidy. When you decide you're happy with the verdict come and let me know and I'll wave you goodbye at the airport."

"Have you done a timetable?" I asked.

"A timetable?"

"You know the kind of thing. The last twenty-four hours of a dead man; what he did, who he came in contact with, what his state of mind was. Helps build a profile…"

"Yeah, I know what it does. Talk to Travers. He was working on one. Maybe he's finished. They take a while you know, especially on John Does. It shouldn't make any difference,

Wentz was an unlucky SOB, that's all there is to it. You'll come round."

On the way out I mentioned the debtors Jackson Travers had given me earlier. Peru shrugged and told me to check them out, only he had already done it. Not a thing on any of them. For a burglary he had been quite thorough. I told him so.

All except one, that is.

One was off limits.

It was Jarvis McSwarve.

Chapter Ten – The Penitence

The Penitence was overlooking the coast on the west side of the West Island. It was a ticket only joint unless you had a gold badge in your wallet, or a ten thousand dollar slate. The queues were already running right down the street when I arrived. I jostled my way to the front and had a quiet word in the ear of the doorman. His smile betrayed him but he waved me through nonetheless.

De-frocked of my hat and coat I entered the bar, walking right into the golden age of black and white cinema. Rows and rows of tables were full of chattering people, dressed in evening wear of all design. The tables were stacked high with drinks, cocktails, chasers, bottles of beer from all around the globe. Food was being carried around by beautiful waitresses; all dressed the same, but with different faces; Caucasian white, African brown, Oriental off-white and deep brown of Bangladesh or Sri Lanka.

I managed to squeeze onto a bar stool on the corner of the forty foot wooden bar, which was so full of flowers and bowls of nibbles there was no room for my elbows. I cracked a peanut from its shell and ordered a beer. It arrived quickly, ice cold and still in its bottle.

There must have been a piano somewhere, although it was too busy to see just where, as I could see the notes gently floating around the air, not too loud so as to drown out the sound of social conversation, but just enough to provide background music.

I sipped my beer slowly and studied the menu on the wall above the top shelf of spirits.

"You can eat anything in blue in the bar, but anything in black must be taken in the restaurant," said a young, black lady called Cherry. She had a label on her maroon blouse above her breast. "Unless you got a table booked I'm afraid the restaurant is fully taken for the next four hours, Sir."

"Then I guess I'll eat right here, Cherry," I said and she smiled a sweet smile, her brown cheeks almost blushing pink under my gaze.

She took a notepad and a pencil from the pocket in her black waistcoat and said, "May I take your order then, Sir?"

I ordered a plate of nachos with melted cheese and watched Cherry disappear down the bar, swinging her hips.

There was not an empty table in sight. I guessed there were at least a couple hundred people in the main bar and most looked like they were enjoying themselves. The ladies looked classy, real ladies with powder puffs in their purses and a thousand dollar a month clothing allowance from their fellows. The guys were harder to categorize. Most wore black dinner suits with bow ties, no clip ons here, a few were still in uniform, be it police or military. One, who looked like Captain Renault leaned over the bar and ordered another couple of bottles of champagne. He took the tray and didn't pay a dime.

My nachos arrived with another beer and I signed the bill. They were delicious and vanished in quick time.

As I got to my feet to wander I was accosted by a large, black gentleman in a white tuxedo. He had a well-pruned goatee beard and shoulders the width of a six lane overpass. Grabbing my free hand he pumped it until my shoulder almost came loose.

"Haven't seen you here before, Sir, pleased to meet you. I am the show manager, Hunter McSwarve." He smiled a big smile, showing a perfect set of white teeth, interspersed with a little gold.

"Errol Black, pleased to meet you Hunter. I have been here once before but it's been a long time."

His eyes narrowed and then he smiled again, "Everyone is welcome at The Penitence Mister Black. My staff are all very well trained to attend to your every desire. Vacation is it?"

"Yeah, vacation. Thought I would check out the famous club that everyone raves about." I looked around. "I can now see why."

"That is good, Mister Black. You are so kind. I stress again my wish that you enjoy yourself this fine evening. You have a ticket for the show I presume?"

I shook my head. "No, I'm just here to have a couple of beers and soak up the atmosphere. I didn't even know that there was a show tonight."

"Oh, but I insist. Tonight we have an extremely good act, you must join me at my table as a guest of the management."

There was no point in resisting and anyway I was curious so I agreed. There was also a chance that I might find out something about his brother, the owner of The Penitence.

Hunter McSwarve was the youngest of the three brothers, Jarvis and Irwin being older, in that order. I was a little surprised, at first, to be approached but then as I discovered more about the nature of the club it added up. These guys would know every single patron of their establishment. There might be hundreds of members but they would make it their business to know them. As we left the bar I wondered if there was something going on, if I had slipped in some way and was being led into a trap. But as we made our way through to the arena, Hunter must have stopped twenty times to pump the arm of someone else, just as he had done with me, only they already had tickets for the show.

"You said that you have been here before, Mister Black. I do not recall seeing you at The Penitence, so I take it that you mean Casablanca?"

"That's right, I used to live here. A long time ago now, things have changed a lot."

"Everything changes, Mister Black. Casablanca has both the good and the bad of the world within its humble boundaries. I like to think that The Penitence is one of the good."

"Oh, I'm sure it is. I've seen nothing to the contrary so far."

"That is very good. I expect all my guests to enjoy their stay here. Whatever goes on in their home lives or the pressures of their work they can forget about it all once they have stepped into The Penitence. Flush out the bad vibes and be refreshed." He looked at his watch, a chunky, solid gold affair and frowned. "Oh, you must accept my sincere apologies, Mister Black, so rude of me."

"Not at all, I look at mine all the time."

He smiled. "If you would now take a seat I must introduce the show."

There was an aroma of perfumed oils and burning candles. The room was a circle with a slightly raised, carpeted stage and a metal pole in the centre. Around the stage there were circular tables, most of which were full of people, both men and women.

McSwarve did a quick circuit of the room, shaking hands with yet more men and holding the hands of the ladies gently as he brushed his lips over them. He then went to the centre of the stage where he was joined by a tall black girl in a long, straight dress. A simple introduction and McSwarve left the stage to Jemma Vowle, who began to sing in a low, throaty voice that captured the mood immediately.

At my table sat two couples, both in their fifties. Neither said a word to me, they were all staring straight ahead at the stage, transfixed. There were two empty seats. I took a drink from a waitress as McSwarve was escorting a portly, white gentleman, who had a beautiful, young blonde far from her fifties, on his arm. She tried to walk elegantly in her foot high heels, stumbling twice before clinging onto her partner for dear life.

The portly gentleman – who I would later discover was far from gentle – wore a well-tailored black suit with a red bow tie; he also had thick, steel-rimmed spectacles, hiding dark, alert eyes. His nose was red, going on purple and he had a thick cigar glowing from between his narrow lips.

McSwarve led them towards me and they took the empty seats. He introduced them as Jeremy Darchville, Oriental rug importer, and Virginia, his lovely wife. I shook his hand and kissed Virginia on the offered cheek.

"He's a damn good man is Hunter McSwarve," said Darcheville, as McSwarve went on another circuit. "They're all good fellas, but Hunter is a hell of a guy."

"Friendly sort of chap," I agreed.

"Can't do enough for you. Don't recall seeing you before Errol, do you know Hunter well?"

I lit up a Lucky and sucked the smoke deep into my lungs.

"Nope. Just met him tonight," I said. "Picked me up at the bar and offered me a place at his table."

"That's Hunter all over. He's always picking up waifs and strays. He won't sit here though. Much too busy."

That was Virginia, her lilting accent hailing from somewhere Deep South. Decked out in a clinging white suit with gloves and jewellery, rubies and diamonds. Her large breasts faced skywards and barely moved as she clumsily jigged to the music.

Jeremy leaned over conspiratorially. "Those two over there," he nodded at the farthest away couple, who both looked remarkably alike; they both wore bland, grey suits with grey ties and white shirts, only the broad had forgotten to shave tonight, "Never say a bloody word. They just sit there mesmerized."

He blew out a thick stream of cigar smoke and said, "Clergy."

The following pause presumably finishing the point.

"What is it you do then, Errol? You don't mind me calling you Errol do you? You see in my business you gotta talk on a personal level. None of this Mister or Missus nonsense, it just won't do."

"A formal address keeps you at arms length, and an arms length away is too distant for the selling game." She almost said it without moving her lips and then turned away, fanning herself with a beer mat.

"I'm a detective," I said. "Well I used to be. I'm currently retired."

"Tried that once Errol, retiring." He shook his head. "Didn't work for me. I need the cutting edge, the harsh dog eat dog world of business. It's what keeps me young, aint it sweetheart?"

Virginia smiled a bright, red smile and wrinkled her nose.

"Take today for instance. Looked like it was going to be a total, bloody write off. Three twenty foot containers due in from the Orient."

I had expected Virginia to produce a map from her cleavage and point it out with her lipstick.

"For weeks the bloody dockyard workers have been causing trouble. One day they're in the next day they're bloody out. It's like the fuckin' hokey cokey.

"Anyway I was anxious. Sixty thousand square feet of carpets and I've got orders for at least half of them. My only problem is to get the bloody things cleared and unloaded and then Ginny can hit the high street, you know what I'm saying?"

I smiled, clapping politely as Jemma Vowle wrapped up her routine with a barnstorming rendition of Mac the Knife.

"Gets to eight o clock, my men are wanting to unload the first shipment and low and fuckin' behold out pops the shop steward and blows the whistle. Everybody out in five minutes if you want to keep your kneecaps intact."

"What's the problem?"

"The problem? Who fuckin' knows what the problem is. Not enough money, too long hours, not long enough tea breaks, too rough shit roll? The problem is basically whatever fuckin' Berry decides on the day."

"Berry?"

"Pat Berry, Casablanca Union supremo and all round dipshit. He's over there with that black piece." He nodded to the far side of the room where a tall, white man with a thin, grey beard and round spectacles sat talking to Jemma Vowle who was leaning over the table and laughing; her beautiful figure trembled as she laughed.

"Takes his orders from way above." He gestured into the heavens with the stub of his smouldering cigar. "Who knows what rules they live by and who wants to know? But today he just pulled 'em for no reason, all the boys said the same. Likes his own fuckin' power that guy and quite often he strikes for the sake of striking. The dockers don't like it, I should know, I talk to them. I fuckin' feed most of them, but when Nero speaks they obey. No choice in this game."

Drinks were being replenished by one man and two women, not in Penitence uniforms. Their bodies were oiled and glistening in the dingy light of the candles. The women were both young and beautiful with large, exposed breasts. The man was also bare chested and looked like Johnny Weisimuller.

Virginia grabbed Jeremy's arm and breathed heavily. Her cheeks flushed and eyes followed the trio, as did most of the spectators in expectation of the erotic show to follow. Conversation died down, although Jermey continued in a whisper.

"Took me two hours to even get a meet with the guy. Gorillas and spooks all over the place, patrolling the fuckin' docks like it was the Federal Reserve Building or something…"

Gentle music filled the room, softly but slowly building a rhythm. It sounded Irish; bells and drums dominating, the tempo slowly increasing. A long, continuous, repetitive beat.

The trio were highlighted in a spotlight, looking sensuous and beautiful as the music created a unique atmosphere. I looked around. The whole room were focused, transfixed on the three beautiful bodies.

"I pulled a few strings, scratched a few backs, cracked a few heads, you know the score. I just had to do whatever the fuck I could to get a meet with Berry. To try and find out what the hell was going on."

"Did he see you?" I asked, not really listening. I was becoming enticed by the show, but Darcheville carried on regardless…

"Oh yeah, he saw me… eventually. I laid into him all guns blazing. I told him the way it was and the way it was gonna be in the future. Fuck we can't go on with a cowboy like that running the show. Folks just wanna do an honest days work."

"Honey," squealed Virginia. "Watch the show! Talk after." and she gripped his arm tighter.

They slowly circled the stage; the women back to back, always keeping one hand on the centre pole; the man prowling round the outer of the stage like a predator waiting to pounce. Occasionally they brushed past each other, but the movements were subtle. It was like a game of cat and mouse, neither party wanting to commit until ready.

Virginia gulped her drink. Some missed her mouth and dribbled down her chin without her noticing. Jeremy gave me a look as if to say, "Okay, let's humour the ladies."

The tempo of the music picked up and the three bodies all shed their clothes in one lucid movement. A gasp rang out from the audience as the man stood tall, his arousal there for all to see. One of the women began stroking his sides as they swayed together in tune. The other sank to her knees, her oily fingertips caressing him across his thighs, his buttocks and round to his

74

testicles. His head faced skywards, eyes tightly closed as he languidly descended to the carpeted floor.

I sighed inwardly and smiled to myself. In this room were the powerbrokers of a most wonderful town, the makers and shakers of a town of culture, beauty and history. Maybe it really had changed, that's what everybody kept telling me. Maybe they were right. What at first seemed only superficial changes now looked deeper. Here I was in the premier nightspot of Casablanca, and the golden-ticketed entertainment turned out to be nothing more than a live sex show. Hell, a damn good live sex show, but nevertheless, that is what it was.

The music became quicker and quicker and the actions of the threesome increased accordingly. The actions now more frenzied than calculated, the sensuality of the stroking and kneading giving over to a more carnal desire and base need. The two women urged their partner on, one hovering over his groin, lowering herself onto him until he was inside her and then bouncing up and down. The other doing a similar action over his open mouth, his tongue probing and penetrating.

The drums were now deafening, building up a crescendo of noise as the three moved in concert towards climax. Getting faster and faster until the wall of noise was almost unbearable

And then it was all over. The performers were gone and the audience were breathing again, some flushed, breathless and giddy. Others were stunned into silence. Most began talking, although not really knowing what they were saying, coherent sentences being a struggle.

Jeremy Darcheville gave a whoop of approval and then clicked his fingers for more drinks. As the lights came up I noticed the grey couple had disappeared.

Jeremy caught my eye. "Fuckin' prigs," he said with venom. "Don't understand art some people. They probably preferred the fuckin' trigger. Anyway, Errol, where was I?"

"Pat Berry," I said tiresomely, awaiting an opportunity to leave.

McSwarve was circulating, taking the praise from his punters, smiling and nodding as if he was exhibiting a piece of fine art. Most of the audience appeared to be pleased with the show, either unaware that they had been cajoled into watching and paying top dollar for an X-rated show of pornography, or too polite to point out the fact to the management.

I took another drink and flared up a Lucky.

"Have one of these Errol, trust me they're good."

I looked at the box of huge cigars, took one out and had a sniff. It smelled of cow dung, not tobacco and came from Paraguay not Cuba, so I politely put it back."

"Did you get the containers cleared?" I asked, watching McSwarve shake hands firmly with Pat Berry across the room. It was a friendly shake, there was a sense of familiarity and respect between the two.

"Oh eventually, sure I did. I usually get what I want in the end, Errol, don't I Ginny?"

Virginia flushed red and giggled.

"Took a good deal of negotiating and horse trading though. I nearly ended up slotting that arrogant piece of shit, but in the end we came to an agreement. I gotta, you see, I'm a businessman, it's what runs through my blood. I thrive on it."

McSwarve was now one table away. I would thank him again and turn in for the night.

"Sold me some bullshit story about the dockside labourers not getting a fair deal. Too many private importers using their own crews and paying top dollar for the privilege. I told him that it was tough shit, if you want a good job doing you get reliable men and you pay them good. There's nothing against the law about bringing in your own team.

"He didn't like that one little bit, said the Union boys were gonna press for a fee regardless of who did the work. I told him today was a one off, next time he can whistle. Hell I already pay a healthy fuckin' levy that goes fuck knows where. They even broke one of the seals the clumsy fuckin' dumbos. I tell you one day... Ah, what a wonderful show."

Hunter McSwarve stood beaming a big smile. Jeremy Darcheville shook his hand and patted his back. Virginia blushed redder as her small jewellery encrusted hand was plucked and kissed tenderly by the friendly host.

"Thank you very much for your hospitality, Mr McSwarve, it was most kind."

"Not at all, Mr Black, I'm pleased you enjoyed yourself, but now you are leaving?"

"Yes I am. It has been a pleasure."

I shook hands with Darcheville and kissed the lovely Virginia. "Maybe next time I will meet your brother Jarvis, it's been a while."

The smile faltered slightly and his eyes narrowed again, just like the first time we met.

"I hope so, Mr Black. I didn't realise you were old acquaintances, you should have said. Jarvis is away for a couple of days but when he returns I am sure he would love to meet you. Let me have your number I will give you a call."

I scribbled it on a beer mat, turned around and left The Penitence.

Chapter Eleven – Breakfast

The morning arrived before I was ready for it. Today was gonna be a long day. I took a cold shower to shake out all the fatigue. The heating wasn't too fiery so I followed it with a hot shower. Looking at myself in the mirror, I didn't like what I saw. Shaving would have been easier with a set of garden shears, but I eventually spruced up and made myself look respectable. A new tweed suit finished the transformation and I was ready for a new day.

The breakfast room of The Dockside hotel was a huge, airy room filled with plants and flowers. The bland decor of cream was contrasted by the beautiful, colourful vegetation. There were staff everywhere, which was good if you were in a hurry, but to the relaxed, no rush diner who wanted a slow, peaceful breakfast it was hell. I couldn't take a sip from my coffee without some little Chinese man in a burgundy penguin suit filling it back up again, so when I absent mindedly reached for the cup it overflowed onto my fingers. Of course then a whole bunch of them emerged, napkins at the ready, dabbing and wiping.

"You mind if I join you?" said a voice.

I looked up into the crystal blue eyes of Noah Thomas, who was smiling, probably in amusement at the over fastidious waiters.

"Not at all," I said. "Take a seat. Another coffee over here," I said to the penguin.

"Sorry about the rather cold welcome yesterday. It's just…"

"Don't worry about it," I said. "I didn't expect anything else."

Thomas was a tall, plumpish man. He wore a well cut, navy blue suit with a handkerchief sticking out of his breast pocket. His voice was soft and accentless. His blond hair was swept back and held together with a block of grease.

"I got a similar reaction when I first arrived," he said. "Took them a while to figure out I was handpicked the same as they all were. Peru does his own choosing, simple as that. My history had no bearing on me being selected, it was Mister Peru's decision, same as it always is. With you though, it's different."

"Not really. If I was gonna become one of the team then you would be right, but that's not why I'm here. I'm on secondment, that's the difference, and I don't ask for much, just to be left alone will do."

"But if everybody really did leave you alone you couldn't hope to get to the bottom of this."

"Don't bank on it sonny. I've done it before."

The coffee arrived with a plate brimming with steak and eggs. I tucked into it hungrily.

"The guys are nervous of change, hostile even, that is all I'm saying. Maybe they won't all come round, but maybe some of them will."

I looked up from my breakfast into the clear eyes of Noah Thomas. "It makes no difference to me whether they come around or not, you understand that?"

There was a long silence.

"Look, do you really want to help me, is that what you are saying?"

"Maybe I don't want to be awkward for the sake of it. Maybe that's it. I've been in your shoes, being sent all over the place on turkey runs without any backup. Going into hostile territory without so much as a drinking partner on the long, fruitless nights. Maybe I can't really help you, even if I want to. From what we've turned up so far you're probably searching up a blind alley, you probably know that already. But I don't want to hinder you, okay."

I smiled. "Okay. If you really want to cut me some slack you can start by telling me your opinion of the unaccounted death of the subject."

Thomas sipped his coffee and then dabbed his mouth with a napkin.

"My opinion aint all that important, but for what it's worth I think the preliminary reports are probably right. Everything points to a house robbery that went badly wrong. The papers say we expect an arrest soon and I have to say officially really I hope that they're right."

"Now tell me your real opinion."

"Well, like I said all the evidence points to a house robbery, but what we got to be asking is, how a mere burglarizer could shoot and kill a man like Hermeez Wentz without too much of a struggle? What was he trying to burglarize? And if there is such a dangerous man on the loose, why does everybody seem to be playing it right down and acting as if nothing happened?"

"The papers reported it."

"Hardly. It got three lines on page seven of The Post and has not been mentioned since."

"What do you mean, 'A man like Hermeez Wentz?'"

Thomas finished his coffee. "I looked into his background. He was quite an impressive character: a former United States serviceman, fought in the war in some of the most brutal battles, highly decorated on his return to the US, holder of a Private Investigator's badge even when he died. He was well regarded by all his traceable clients, which I have to admit don't number too many. One puzzling thing about him was nobody seemed to know why he left New York and came to live in Casablanca."

"He retired. He used to live here back in the Thirties and decided to return. There's no mystery in that."

"The other thing that's been puzzling me is just exactly why you are here, Mr Black."

"Are you now gonna give a little biography of me?"

"I know that you served alongside Wentz in the war, and that you too have been a Private Dick in your time. What I don't quite understand is why you are here. The Bureau doesn't send operatives out on burglary hunts, no matter who the victim was. Never used to in my day anyway. No, there's something more to it."

I finished my breakfast and pushed the plate away. It immediately disappeared.

"Why don't you take a guess?"

I laughed. Thomas laughed with me.

"I've got a few ideas on the matter. It could be to check up on Mr Peru's outfit, although that's not really necessary. I think that we are doing very well."

He licked the tip of his finger and smoothed back his eyebrows.

"It could be to keep a closer, more centrally trained eye on Mr Earl. Maybe Edgar wants to close Senator Ishmail's little party?"

I held out my arms, opened my palms and shrugged. Thomas smiled and shook his head. "Again, I think not, but what else could it be. Maybe you're not from the Bureau at all."

Noah Thomas looked hard at my face, his smile now gone, replaced by a kind of scowl. He was searching me, stripping me down of all outer layers and taking a look on the inside. I hoped I was stained right through to the core like a stick of Brighton Rock, so as he could not find the truth. We looked at each other for what seemed like a couple of days.

I relaxed the smile and poured another cup of coffee. "Keep searching boy. There's nothing to find, but hell keep on searching anyhow."

"Come on, Mr Black what is the deal? I checked you out with all my old buddies. They never heard of you. Either you are here on a covert assignment, in which case Arthur Peru needs to know what and why, or you're here as an imposter on some kind of vigilante mission. Which is it?"

"I told you, I'm here to catch the murderer of Hermeez Wentz, that is all. And when I do, I will hand him over to the appropriate authorities. Now if you want to help me I welcome you, if not that also is fine by me. Good day."

Chapter Twelve – The Neighbour

Janice Crouter was easy to find. She was a tall, thin lady with very defined bones. Her face was terribly creased, the excess skin hanging loose on her rigid profile. She wore a long, flowing dress which looked like it was made from an old pair of curtains. It hung off her spindly body like it would a coat-hanger. Her hair was grey and pulled back in a knot, exposing her wrinkled forehead. She was listed as being seventy-eight, but looked as if she might be one hundred and fifty.

In spite of her advanced years she had very piercing, alert eyes which held my glance firmly as I introduced myself.

"I've already had a visit from the police," she said, as I flashed my badge.

Her voice was strong, yet warm.

"Yes I know, Mrs Crouter, but would you mind going through a few more details?"

"Not at all, come through," she ushered me through the door. "And call me Janice, please."

I followed her into the apartment across the avenue from Hermeez's. The file Peru kept named her as a nosy neighbour. She was the only one that could point out to the police just what had been taken in the burglary. I started on this point.

"There were two lovely pictures stolen," she said. "One was from the wall above his desk. Lovely picture. It was an oil painting of a burning ship on a fiery ocean. Very moody with a heavy, cloudy sky. The other was from the bathroom. I think that it was a Tintaretto, although not an original. I don't know why Herm kept it in the bathroom, as it was his favourite. It was of the tower in Venice. A really lovely scene."

She poured two cups of tea and shoved a plate full of biscuits towards me. I politely took a biscuit.

"Don't stand on ceremony, Mister Black. There's plenty more of those, you don't have to take mouse nibbles."

I smiled and sipped the tea.

"Was there anything else that was missing, Janice, anything at all that you can think of?"

"I couldn't say for sure. I'm sorry, Mr Black, but it was such a mess. The police assured me that there was no sign of the paintings, so maybe they were the only items taken."

"But why would anyone burglarize a couple of fake paintings? They may have been pretty, but they were copies nonetheless?"

She shrugged. "Makes me wonder if it wasn't a simple burglary after all."

Peru's file also said that Janice Crouter was a notorious gossip. Although she lived alone and was in full control of her faculties, she had a bit of a reputation as a storyteller. Her evidence was therefore of negligible value to the police.

"Why do you say that, Janice, is it just the paintings, or some other reason?"

She shrugged her bony shoulders. "Just seems that something's not quite right. I know we live in an awful world, Mister Black, you hear it everyday. But why would anyone do this to Herm? He was such a nice young man. Never had a bad word to say about anybody. It makes me wonder if it wasn't some drug-crazed youth with a scrambled brain. It says in The Post that they'd do anything to keep their filthy habit going, even kill I'm sure."

I nodded. "Hermeez was a good friend to you, wasn't he?"

"Oh sure he was. He wasn't like the others. Even my son treats me like some mad old crone. He speaks two octaves higher to me and mimes as if I'm deaf and stupid. Herm was twice the man he is. Treated me like a person, a real person.

"He would often join me for a glass or two of wine and a game of chess. Always lost, mind you, but he never tired of playing. He gave up some of his time because he wanted to, not just a moment here or half an hour there when the guilt got too much for him. No, Mr. Black, Herm genuinely cared.

"He even helped me out with those two tearaways next door, when they played up."

My ears pricked up. "How do you mean played up?"

Janice poured another cup of tea.

"Well, they were playing their music at all hours of the night. Kept the whole neighbourhood awake they did. I told

Hermeez that my sleep was suffering, so he went round and had a word."

"Did that stop them?"

"Not at first. It got worse to begin with. Some nights my whole living room trembled. My little pussy cat fell off the mantelpiece and smashed. I've had that cat for thirty-five years."

"So Hermeez went round again?"

"Yes he did," said Janice Crouter. "Now I don't condone violence Mr Black, I never have done and I never will do. Hermeez knew that. In fact I let him know in no uncertain terms." She smiled. "But it did do the trick. I suppose he won't go to hell for giving them a bloody nose, will he? Especially when it made an old woman very happy."

I shook my head. "I don't think he will, Janice." I made a note to question the two tearaways. It was a long shot, but who could tell what a public reprimand could do to a pair of wild youngsters.

We talked for a further twenty minutes. I mainly listened, fascinated by the strong bond of friendship between my buddy and this dear, independently willed, old lady. It was clear she absolutely doted on him; she often popped in, cooked him meals, cleaned the flat for him and basically mothered him. She had an opinion on most things, whether it be politics, art, or the neighbour's gardens.

She told me there were few other people in Hermeez's life that she knew about. And she knew most things. He was the member of a Club, although she couldn't remember the name, and he often stopped at a diner around the corner. He spent a lot of time either fishing or writing his private eye column for the local newspaper.

As I stood up to leave I asked her again about any female company.

"There was one girl," she said, as if she had just remembered. "Although I only met her the once and Hermeez never talked about her, so I don't really think she was a girlfriend. Pity, she was very attractive with long, silky, flame-red hair. She was taller than he was, six foot, maybe six foot-two, with long, straight legs."

84

"Can you remember her name?" I asked.

"Never knew it to forget," she said. "She did have a very distinctive mole, although it didn't spoil her beauty in the slightest. It enhanced it if anything." She frowned. "I didn't approve of her clothes, though, she was dressed head to foot in black leather. Pretty young thing she should be wearing dresses, not ugly menswear."

I thanked Janice again and promised to return. The affection she felt for Hermeez was clear to see and at times the tears welled up in her grey eyes, although her ancient face held firm and any sympathy I offered was stoutly rejected.

Two young men caught sight of me as I left Janice Crouter's house. They were walking up the sidewalk, carrying a crate of beer and huge drum of popcorn. Instead of heading for my car, I turned around and punched the popcorn from their hands. Before they could react I had my gun out and in the face of the leader of the two.

He dropped the beer, bottles smashing all over the road.

"You upset a friend of mine!" I growled.

The boys were shaking and any bravado they had considered showing had already evaporated.

"We already said sorry to the German guy," pleaded one.

I lowered the gun.

"When was this?" I asked.

He took a deep breath and thought. "Few days ago. He came round and…" he rubbed his side, "…convinced us of our insensitivity. We haven't had the music on since."

"Good."

"In fact, we came round to apologise again, but he sent us packing."

"Seemed in a hurry," the other one chipped on.

"Yeah, he said it was cool."

"A hurry?"

"Yeah, he had a car waiting."

"A car?"

"Yeah a car."

"What car? Come on, what car?"

85

The boys shrugged and looked at each other. One held out his hands as if to say he couldn't really remember.

"A red car. Maybe a Dodge. I can't be sure."

"Okay boys, you better find a broom," I said and walked back to my car, crunching the broken glass with my shoes.

Chapter Thirteen – The Casablanca Post

The Casablanca Post was one of three local rags, the only one of which came in a broadsheet format and therefore the one with the most prestige. It was founded by a local businessman, Ivor Cramer, who reputedly made his fortune illegally selling booze during the Prohibition. Knowing just where his bread was buttered, The Post became a vocal supporter of the Volstead Act, right up until its abolition 5th December 1933. It survived the change in the law by establishing itself as a quality newspaper that challenged and harassed all forms of authority. Few Casablanca households went without a copy of The Post, and few political, entertainment or Establishment figures survived its cutting editorials. This all changed five years ago when Cramer suddenly died of a heart attack, whilst enjoying his favourite meal of lamb chops, roast potatoes and stewed cabbage in a public restaurant. The newspaper was taken over by a consortium, thought to be headed by Senator Ishmail Ouzanti, although publicly by the McSwarve Group, and quickly changed its outlook on Casablanca politics. Ever since Cramer's untimely death The Post became middle of the road, uncontroversial and stoutly defensive of the Establishment it had previously sought to embarrass. All of this was achieved once again without any threat to its huge circulation. It became both a sounding board to future policy implementations and a back-slapper of apparent achievements.

With the change of owner came a change of location. No longer based from a poky, backstreet office in the Downtown area, the new consortium managed to attain planning permission for a shiny, new, two-story building on the West Isle, looking over the magnificent views of the East Bay.

It was whilst admiring the beautiful views that I was tapped on the shoulder and offered a real handshake.

The hand belonged to David First, the puppet editor of The Casablanca Post. First was a tall, thin man, smartly dressed in grey, double-breasted suit. He had grey hair, greased back and a pale, greyish complexion. The only colour he allowed on his attire was a blue handkerchief perfectly folded in his left breast pocket.

I shook First's hand and smiled. "Pleased to meet you, Mister First, thanks for seeing me."

"Don't mention it, Black; we'll do anything here at The Post to find Wentz's slayer, anything at all. Why don't you follow me I'll show you to his desk."

I followed the editor-in-chief into the building, through the spacious lobby, up a flight of stairs and down a long corridor. I counted seven framed photographs along the way featuring Senator Ouzanti. First looked at every one and smiled in admiration.

Hermeez's desk was old, heavy and built from solid wood. It was in the far corner of an open-plan office that was partitioned by filing cabinets and eight-foot bookshelves. There were eight or nine desks in the room in all, but none had as good a view out over the bay as the empty one. Empty that was except for an old Triumph typewriter and a telephone. There was a box by the side of his chair which was stuffed full of files and cuttings.

"I'm afraid we had to collect all his belongings together, Mr Black. Not that there was much, you understand. Nothing of any monetary value."

He waved at the box. "It's all in there, you're free to look through it. In fact you may as well take it with you if you like. We didn't really know what to do with it. The police don't want it."

"Thank you," I said. "I think I will take a look. I'll be fine on my own now."

First nodded and smiled. "I'll get Muriel to bring you over a coffee. If you need any assistance just call."

I nodded and watched him march down to the far end of the office and sit down with a group of people.

I emptied the box on the desk and spread the contents out across its leather surface. First was right, there was little here. Most of it was cuttings from Hermeez's own column, dating back two years. It was a weekly piece. I skimmed through them all, finding myself recognising some of the stories and even myself in them. Of course the names, places and vital statistics had all been changed, but it was all there; a little piece of our past all laid out in black and white. There was a lot of Phil Marlowe as well, only the tales were more believable.

The usual reference books were there; dictionary, thesaurus, book of dates and book of quotations. I checked for markings in all of them but there was nothing.

At the bottom, was a single, framed photograph and a large, flat diary.

Muriel arrived with the coffee as I turned over the photograph and looked into the eyes of a beautiful young lady.

"Isn't she pretty?" asked Muriel, planting the coffee on the top of the diary.

The lady in the picture was a girl from long ago, now dead. Someone that Hermeez never truly got over, although he insisted to me a thousand times that he had.

"She certainly is," I agreed. "Was there… anyone else in his life, did you know?"

Muriel frowned.

"It's okay," I said softly. "I'm furthering police enquiries. Check with Mr First before you say anything if you like."

That seemed to reassure her. She was a large, friendly looking woman in her mid forties. She cupped her own coffee and sighed. "There was somebody," she started. "Although it was over before…well a few weeks ago. She was a lovely lady. Alison I think she was called. She never did like him keeping that photograph, like she was a rival or something. Silly really, it was obvious to all of us in the office how much they were good for each other."

"How long did they see each other?"

"Oh, only a month or so. Hermeez never spoke much about his private life. Always kept himself very much to himself. I think she works at a leisure club out in the Trimbles."

"You don't know why they split up?"

"I'm sorry, he never did tell me the reason. Probably something to do with his fierce privacy. He hardly ever took her back to his flat you know. We…me and the girls, overheard her one lunchtime. She was quite upset, accused him of seeing other women and...oh I suppose I shouldn't say anything really, but he threw away a lovely woman there."

I smiled and drank my coffee.

"I better get back to work. Sorry I can't be much help."

"You've been plenty, Muriel. Just one thing, did Alison have red hair?"

Her face creased up. "Oh no, Alison has dark hair. Long, dark brown. Red wouldn't suit her at all."

The diary was largely a business calendar. It contained reminders of deadlines, sale fluctuations of The Post on column day, meetings with various people and so on. There were no personal contacts at the back, no record of private rendezvous, no telephone numbers and very little clues. I checked out all the names of the people in the diary with David First and then with a clerk at the station. They were mainly journalists and regular Post contacts and nearly all of them were clean. The two names that had a record with the Casablanca P.D were Benjamin Jacobs, pimp and all round thug, and Clyde Gabriel, a local businessman who was suspected of illegal gaming and prostitution rackets.

The only other thing of note was a collection of numbers at the back of the diary. No words and no reference to work off, just a jumbled collection of numbers. I showed it to David First and asked him if he had any idea what the numbers may represent.

"Sorry old man, I have not got an inkling. Unless..."

"Yes?"

"Well, you know Hermeez did a bit of work for us as an unofficial tipster. You know for the greyhound races. What with the Race Centre becoming such a feature of the town now, bringing in thousands of dollars investment and affluence to our humble town. It seemed a good idea to devote a bit more space to the races in the Casablanca Post. It was Hermeez's idea of course, but I saw the potential immediately. It worked as well, I'll tell you, we took a good few points back from the racers."

"How do you mean 'unofficial'?"

"Well, he wasn't named you see. He didn't want the limelight but was adamant that he knew his game. I don't know whether it was beginner's luck or of he really did have inside contacts, but he was very successful. Our tips by far exceeded any of the so-called experts in other rags."

"Did he tell you that, that he had 'contacts'?"

"Not at all, Black, that was just a figure of speech. I was just trying to illustrate how good at it he was. Oh no, we wouldn't tolerate any impropriety here at The Post."

"Of course, I'm sorry. But you think these numbers may be something to do with the predictions?"

"Could be. Certainly it is a possibility, but who knows. It could be his lottery numbers or simply a doodle."

I nodded, although how many people First knew that doodled sets of numbers was beyond me. And there was no Casablanca lottery.

"Is it still okay for me to take the box," I asked, packing it all up again.

"Of course. If there's anything that will help the investigation I want you to have it."

I stood up. "Well I guess it's time for me to be going." I shook hands again with David First. "Thanks again for your time, you've been very accommodating."

"Any time Black, keep in touch won't you."

Chapter Fourteen – Alison

Trowell Street was nicer than I imagined. This was from the old town, which would always be a pleasure to remember. The buildings were hundreds of years old and had been properly and tastefully maintained. Every piece of stone was restored to its ancient beauty and the uneven, cobbled roads had a certain character predating automobiles.

That said, it was a surprise to find a huge, new leisure and sauna club housed here. Although there was a small sign on a solid mahogany door, set within a solid stone archway, it would be easy to walk right past without realising it was there. There was no neon, no billboards, no advertising hoardings and no real sign of what was to come. It was bliss.

I had checked 'The Gajin Sauna and Leisure Club' out with John Wimpon, back at the station. It was apparently a legitimate club that specialised in corporate fitness classes and was a favourite for lunchtime sauna and Thai massage. The owner was again sketchy, although Wimpon speculated that a Mr Jevon Earl was the proprietor. I tried to check if Hermeez Wentz had been a member, but to no avail.

The reception area was classy; a compact, yet high-ceilinged room with white walls and potted topiary plants. The desk was like that of one of the finer hotels, it spanned the whole room.

Sitting behind it was a handsome, dark-haired woman of about forty, in a dark blue business suit. She had ample makeup, without over doing it, a red necktie, and a name tag, with 'Alison' printed on it. Next to her was a young girl with 'trainee' written on her badge, alongside her name, 'Traci'.

"Good morning, sir. Welcome to The Gajin. Would you like some information on Casablanca's foremost leisure club?"

"That would be lovely."

"If you would like to come this way, we can discuss membership details."

She turned to the girl, "Traci, can you mind the desk while I introduce Mr…"

"Black."

"…Mr Black to The Gajin's facilities."

We took a short tour of the club. There appeared to be no shortage of overweight, old men sweating and grunting on various types of fitness machine, all being encouraged by Oriental instructors. There were two swimming pools, a keep fit class was in progress and several doors had a sign on saying 'massage in progress'. All in all it looked just as it should have looked; a high class club for the corporate and business sector, where ageing executives could come for an hour over lunch and punish their bodies, before undoing all the good work in The Gajin Bar and Restaurant. I couldn't shake the feeling however, that there was a little more to it.

"Impressed?" asked Alison, over a fruit juice in the bar.

"Very," I nodded. "The Gajin certainly lives up to its reputation.

She smiled. "I like to think that we provide a worthwhile service here. Would you like to sample some of the facilities? A sauna, or a short workout, perhaps?" Her eyes lowered. "Not that you need it, you look in excellent shape. We have complimentary kits for all our guests."

I looked into her dark eyes and she smiled back warmly. It was time.

"I'm sorry, Alison. I'm afraid I'm here under false pretences." I pulled out my identification and put it on the table. She studied it and frowned.

"Bang goes my commission."

"I'll still join the club, if you want me to."

She sighed a heavy sigh and forced a smile. "Well, Mister Black, what do you want to ask me? I take it, that this is just an informal chat? I mean, I'm not under arrest or anything?"

"Why would you be under arrest?"

"Oh, come on Mr. Black…"

"Errol."

She looked hard at me. "Errol, I don't want to play games. This is about the murder of Hermeez Wentz, isn't it?"

I nodded grimly.

She closed her eyes and took a deep breath. "For a short while, Hermeez and I were seeing one another, okay? It was

93

nothing serious, although not for want of trying on my part. He was a beautiful man; kind, gentle, funny, sensitive. If you want to know the truth, I think I was in love with him, but…" She pursed her lips and a tear rolled down her cheek. I put my left hand on hers, softly and dabbed away the tear with the back of my right hand.

She took another deep breath and closed her eyes for a moment. When she opened them, she smiled again. Weakly, but determined.

"I'm sorry," she said. "Do you mind leaving your hand there for a moment? It's what Hermeez would have done."

"Not at all. Take your time."

"He never did tell me just what it was that he wanted. He told me he cared about me, he enjoyed my company, but it wasn't enough. I wanted him fully and unconditionally. I wanted to set up home together and maybe get married."

"But Hermeez had other ideas?"

"That was the really frustrating thing," she said through gritted teeth. "I don't really know what Hermeez wanted because he never told me. He was so secretive, so vague and sometimes so bloody distant. He never took me out with his friends and refused to come out with mine. It was like we couldn't share anything but each other."

"Were there other women?"

She took her hand away immediately and looked at me guardedly. "You know he kept a photograph?"

"A photograph?"

"Of a girl. Somebody from his past. She meant a great deal to him, whoever she was." She exhaled noisily. "A great deal more than I ever could."

Another tear rolled down her cheek. This time I left it, giving her time.

"There was another girl, a real one. She was very tall, red headed. Hermeez met her for lunch one day. I wasn't following him, honestly I wasn't. I thought maybe he was scouting restaurants to find a nice one that he would take me to at a later date. Because he did that, you know. He took me to the most wonderful restaurants."

94

"The girl?"

"Oh she was nobody. Hermeez told me she was nobody. Just a girl. I was his only 'woman'"

She said the last sentence assertively, maybe a little too assertively and then she carried on reminiscing about their time together.

"When we were together, we had the most amazing fun. It was so beautiful. I wish we could just put up the shutters around us, and close out the rest of the world. Hermeez was so caring, so considerate. He was funny and charming. At those times, I really did believe that he loved me."

She paused and I let the silence ride for a while. When she was ready she started again...

"I didn't kill him, Mr Black."

"I'm not suggesting for one moment, that you did, honey. But I am sure that you would want whoever did kill him brought to justice."

"Oh yes. Justice..." she sneered.

"And I will catch whoever did it."

She stopped looking out of the window and looked at me, wiping away the tears. She re-applied her makeup, keeping her big brown eyes focussed on me all the time.

"I'm sure you will, Mr Black. You look like a man who always does exactly what he says he's going to do."

"Why did you leave him, Alison? Did his indifference finally get too much?"

She never stopped looking at me, right in the eyes. The question hardly appeared to register.

"I had to move on," she eventually said. "I guess that I hoped, you know, that a little time apart would give him a jolt, make him sit up and realise that what we had was really special."

"But it didn't?"

"Clearly, Mr Black, it didn't. He's dead, isn't he?"

"Have you any idea who may have murdered him, Alison? Was he in trouble? Did he have any enemies? Anything, anything at all? The smallest thing may help me."

"It was a burglary. A burglary that went terribly wrong. Nobody would want to harm Hermeez, and..." she paused a moment, "…and even if they did he was too good. Nobody could harm Hermeez."

I looked surprised. "Too good?"

She looked down at her hands briefly and then back into my eyes.

"I'll tell you a story about Hermeez Wentz, Mr Black. It's from when he was in the army. He served in the war as a United States Officer. He held the rank of Lieutenant and was very highly regarded by soldiers and officers, alike. All his men looked up to him, they respected him and had the utmost confidence in every decision he made. If they had a problem, they took it to their Lieutenant and he would always give good advice. If they were scared about something, they confided in the Lieutenant, and he comforted them. Like he used to do with me. He made them feel good about themselves, proud to be who they were.

"His superior officers were always keen to have a line to Lieutenant Wentz. He was a long way short of being a tactical genius, like Patton, but he had an unerring ability to pick holes in dubious theories and alternatively add meat to a plan and turn it into a master plan!

"One particular mission towards the end of the War, when our boys were rampaging through the enemy, Lieutenant Wentz's troops found themselves isolated. They'd been given the wrong coordinates and were now surrounded by heavy enemy fire.

"Hermeez gathered all the men together to decide what they should do. The way the war was going they knew it would be won in a matter of weeks, so the obvious thing to do was to give themselves up as Prisoners of war, hope they would be treated well and released at the end of the conflict. But some of the boys were scared, they'd heard stories of troops being massacred as they raised the white flag. After all the enemy were sure to be defeated and no man is more volatile and dangerous than a defeated one.

"They were in Catch-22, as Heller would say. If they surrendered they were likely to be killed, or worse. And if they stayed and fought they were sure to be overrun and shot to death in the throes of battle."

"So what did they do, Alison?"

"They decided to have a vote. When Hermeez asked for a show of hands in favour of surrendering, they all stayed down. And for fighting on, they still remained down until Hermeez smiled and slowly raised his own. Within a minute every arm was in the air and the whole troop was full of smiles and chatter. Hermeez said there was a funny feeling that washed over him at the moment. Suddenly he felt indestructible and he knew they would get out alive!"

"And they did?"

"Sure they did. As they advanced towards the enemy fire, instead of it becoming closer and overpowering and circling them, it actually retreated. Turned out there were less of the enemy than they were told. There were plenty artillery pieces and heavy armour, but few men to operate it, so as soon as they took out the hardware they were safe.

"Every opposition soldier that they killed, Hermeez ensured got a proper burial. He was killed with honour, and had honour bestowed upon him at death. And every one of his own men that was killed was carried back to HQ, so as the body could be flown back home. It didn't matter if they were in the middle of a battle, if they were outnumbered, or if they were on the retreat, every soldier that was killed under Lieutenant Wentz's command would stay with the troop."

"A truly remarkable man," I said.

"Yes, yes he was." There were tears streaming down her cheeks. "I'm sorry, Mr Black, I must get back to work."

"Of course." I gave her my card. "Anything. Anything at all..."

"Of course, I'll call you right away." She stood up and kissed me on both cheeks. "You're a good listener, Errol."

She headed off back to the reception, but stopped and turned. "That story is true, by the way. I checked."

I nodded and watched her disappear.

"Oh yes," I said. "I was there."

Chapter Fifteen – The Diner

It was almost midday by the time I arrived at the diner on Jack Street. It was a small, typical greasy spoon with happy music playing in the background and bright coloured wallpaper. A tall, balding man with a thick, black moustache, stood at the far end of the long, narrow room. The only other occupant was an old bum on a barstool that was either dead or in a deep sleep.

The tall man looked at me briefly before returning his attention to the hot plate by his side. He tossed the sizzling eggs before breaking a couple more. I took a stool next to the old man as he let out a loud belch.

"I'll take a beer and one for the shamus."

The man nodded and left the hot plate. A large ugly cockroach scuttled out of the cupboard, but he didn't bat an eyelid. He returned with a pair of bottles of beer, wiped them down on his grubby apron and grinned a foul, toothless smile.

The grin disappeared when he picked the note from the counter. I took the photo back and stared right into his scared eyes. First reactions usually told a tale.

"What do you want fella?" he asked.

I sipped my beer and grinned. "What can you tell me?"

"You heat, are you?"

"You got that right, so there's nothing to worry about."

He wiped the back of his arm across his nose and looked at the door. The old boy was happily snoring away so he made for the other beer. I nodded, as if giving my approval and he took a long swig.

"There's not much to say. He comes in most days, has bacon and eggs… shit hold on a moment." He rushed over to the smoking hot plate and salvaged the burning eggs, throwing them on individual plates each with a slice of toast. When he returned he brought a plate but I politely refused.

"Like I was saying, he had breakfast with black coffee and spent twenty minutes studying the papers."

"The Post?"

"Sometimes. Usually the racers. All the time he spent here he barely spoke a word. He'd place his order, eat his fodder and pay his bill. Cash, always cash. I once offered him credit, with him being a regular but he insisted on cash."

"What was his name?"

"Hell, I don't even know that. I didn't need to know so I didn't ask."

"Did he ever meet anybody here?"

"Not so's I can remember. He always seemed a bit of a loner."

Another bum came through the door and parked himself at the far end of the room. The counterman excused himself again and shoved a plate of burnt eggs in front of him. He brought a couple more beers from the cupboard, treading on the cockroach as discreetly as he could. When he returned he shrugged.

"What's happening anyway, mister?" he asked. "I guessed there was something wrong when he stopped coming in. Has he made a complaint about my eggs?"

We laughed together.

"Nothing like that," I said. "He's been murdered."

There was a short silence, broken only by the old bum at the back chewing on his sandwich.

"I'm sorry about that," he said eventually. "I never knew. I just thought he'd deserted me for that club of his."

"Well now you do understand just how important it is for you to remember any scrap of information about him. Okay, so he sat alone, he never met anybody, so as you can remember. That right?"

"Ahem."

"Who sat across from him? Who sat on the table next to him?"

"He always sat in the corner."

"None of your regulars ever talked to him?"

"Don't reckon so."

He swilled his beer and again wiped the contents of his nose on the arm of his aprons. "Look, I'm sorry fella, I can't stay and talk all day I gotta restaurant to manage."

I looked around the place keeping my wisecrack to myself.

"Just one other thing," I said. "The Club, where would that be?"

He came in real close so as our noses almost touched. I coughed instinctively, the stench overpowering.

"It's the Plaza Club," he whispered. "You oughtta check it out. There's some real nice girls there. It's just around the corner on Osprey Boulevard."

I nodded and tipped my hat, leaving a couple of bucks on the counter.

Chapter Sixteen – Venice

We were on a vaporetta travelling down the Guidecca Canal towards the San Marco harbour. The sun was shining and there was a cool breeze whipping off the water. Hermeez was dressed as immaculately as ever in pale green suit, single-breasted, made from a very fine, silky material, white open-necked shirt and a suede hat to keep off the sun. I was also wearing a suit, not as light and therefore hotter. Whilst Hermeez gave off the appearance of a man calm, cool and collected, I looked like I had just run a marathon.

"Rolly, you look hot, let's stop at the square and take a beer."

I agreed, wiping the sweat from my brow with a handkerchief.

We alighted the waterbus at stop sixteen and strolled through into St Mark's Square. Narrowly avoiding a huge dollop of pigeon shit, we found a table outside and ordered a couple of beers.

"That's better," I said, taking a long slurp and lighting up a Lucky Strike. I offered one to Hermeez.

"No thanks buddy, still going."

"How long's it been now?"

"Three days and counting."

I smiled and finished off the beer, ordering another from the young waitress.

"I remember when I tried giving up the booze. Leaves you very angry and agitated. Fruit juice doesn't compliment the smokes like a bottle of Yell."

"Booze aint the same. Contrary to what you may believe I am not addicted to alcohol."

"A couple more days and you'll be through it."

"Yeah, and I'll weigh three hundred pounds! Either that or I'll become a quivering wreck."

I laughed at the absurdity of it. "You look pretty cool to me."

The beers came and Hermeez signed the cheque. "Cheers. You're looking a little better yourself if you don't mind me saying, mate?"

A brass band burst into tune down the Piazzetta, filling the whole square with sound. My arm was almost fully healed now. Maybe I wouldn't be pitching for the Mets for a while, but my drinking action was unaffected. Other than that I was physically one hundred percent.

"Do you fancy a sandwich, Errol? There's a wonderful little shop around the corner?"

"Sure, why not?"

We finished our beers, left a handful of lira and headed along the Procuratie Vecchie towards the 5th Century clock tower. The beautiful, four-story building faces the sea, an elaborate collection of bronze figures and ornate decorations with a clock that not only tells the time, but also indicates the various phases of the moon and the zodiac. We then passed through an archway and into the spider's web of alleys and thoroughfares, which is the hallmark of Venice.

"Here we are in the romantic's home and both of us without a companion," said Hermeez as we ambled along the narrow passage, the colourful walls tall at either side of us. "Tonight we should visit the bars, roll dice in the casinos and feast in these wonderful eateries that we keep passing. And most important of all, we must find ourselves some lovely females."

I smiled. "We should. And I'll end up kissing the horse as usual."

Hermeez grinned a painfully handsome smile of perfect white teeth with flattering dimples in each cheek and gentle lines at the corners of his eyes. "You're probably right but hell buddy it's got to be better than a life of lonely bachelorhood."

There was a pause. For a moment I could sense my friend's unease; had he gone too far too soon. After all it was a dangerous line to cross and he knew I could easily relapse into a well of self-pity, but I could feel the concern and genuine feeling as he smiled. The moment soon passed.

"Sure," I said. "Let's give it a go"

A moment later we found the sandwich shop, a wonderful understated gem deep in the caverns of Venice's courtyards and snickets. We both ordered baguettes, one of ham and cheese, the other just of cheese and received generous fillings and snappy friendly conversation.

Chapter Seventeen – The Pimp

In most towns they don't start prowling the streets until after dark. Every town, no matter where it is, how perfect it may seem, or how beautiful it appears, has them. You just have to know where to look, or more importantly you have to know what you are looking for. I knew both.

Casablanca was awash with them. I didn't have to do much digging. A simple stroll through the bad part of town showed me more than enough. The myth goes that they are all smokes, but that is far from the truth. Pimping embraced multiculturalism far before any respectable body knew what it meant. There was no prejudice in this most lucrative of vocations, although they usually fit into a pattern.

Benny Jacobs was of Latin American origin. He had a long, pointed face with sharp, nervous eyes constantly on the move. He wore what was probably once a dapper tweed suit, which looked three sizes too big for his spindly frame. When he stood he kept switching the weight from one foot to the other and when seated he jigged his legs under the table like he was riding a bicycle.

Although Benny was a relatively small fry, the word was that he had connections to the top. He had a small stable of his own girls, but paid a percentage to the bosses, offering his services whenever they were sought. He also packed a gun and was suspected of a string of brutal beatings.

I found him exactly where the two girls had told me; in a seedy bar off Rockwell Street. He had a cigar the size of a javelin between his thin, greasy lips and a bottle of beer in his hand. I ordered a beer and pulled up a stool beside him.

"Hello Benny," I said, lighting up a Lucky.

He sucked on his cigar, desperately trying to keep it alight. "What can I do for you?" he asked, looking me up and down.

I sipped my beer. "I'm gonna ask you a couple of questions, Benny, and you are gonna answer them. Simple as that."

He laughed a hee hee laugh, spluttering on his javelin. "What you shittin' man. I'm a businessman, not a public information service. Get the fuck out of here."

"That firearm you're packing Benny. Would you have a licence for that?"

His eyes twitched nervously. "Who the fuck are you man?"

"I'm investigating a murder."

"What fuckin' murder?"

"You might have heard of him. His name was Wentz, Hermeez Wentz. I'm sure he knew you."

"Never heard of him. Now I've got things to be doing."

I slipped a hand under the table and gripped Benny's groin tightly, squeezing a little as he struggled. He spat out his cigar and reached for his piece, so I twisted my vice-like grip, drawing tears to the poor man's eyes.

"Not a good idea Benny, there's a lot of people in this joint."

"Okay, okay, okay," he said, twisting his oily face in agony. "What do you wanna know? I don't know nothing about no murder."

I loosened my grip and he took a couple of deep breaths.

"I want to know everything about Hermeez Wentz. Why did you meet him at the Canon Club last Thursday?"

"What you giving it man? I don't know any fuckin' Wentz, okay?"

"It's not okay, Benny. You want me to squeeze a little harder? You want me to make you squeal like a pig?"

A little spittle ran down his chin.

"Wentz?"

I nodded. "Wentz."

"What do you think I met him for?"

"A girl?"

"Shit, sure it was a girl. That's what I do and you fuckin' well know it."

"Which girl, Benny?"

He shook his head. "Can't tell you that, it'd break my code of confidentiality."

I laughed. "Who do you think you are, a fuckin' attorney of the state? You…" I prodded his chest with my other hand,"…are a piece of shit. The fuckin' scum of the fuckin' earth. Now don't give me no confidentiality shit and answer the question! Which girl?"

"I provide a service. That don't make me no piece of shit." He said it sulkily and I really think I had hurt his feelings.

"Which girl, Benny?"

He shook his head. "Never got that far."

"Come on, elaborate a little or you'll never get that far again."

He looked down at my hand nervously.

"You a friend of his or something? He came in here one night just like you, thought he could go roughing Benny up, throwing his fuckin' weight around."

I listened, deciding not to interrupt.

"He called me all kinds of names too, all kind of disgusting insults. Then, when he finished with all the abuse, he said he wants to meet me in some white pussy club."

"The Canon?"

"Shit, yeah, the fuckin' Canon."

"So you decided you were gonna teach him a lesson?"

"Maybe I did." He laughed his hee hee laugh once again. "Somebody beat me to it though, eh?"

I gritted my teeth. "What did you mean, 'It never got to that'?"

He shrugged. "After Thursday I never saw him again."

"Let me just recap a minute. Hermeez Wentz roughed you up a little, what night was this?"

He shrugged again. "I don't know, maybe Tuesday."

"Okay, say it was Tuesday. Then he agrees a meet with you on Thursday. Why? I mean why not just sort out the girl on Tuesday, why wait till Thursday?"

"He wanted a full run-down, you know of all my available bitches. Told me to bring photos if possible, although I told him I couldn't do that."

"Why, would it break your ethical code?" I sneered.

"Anyways we talk turkey on Thursday and he still can't decide. I told him to stop wasting my fuckin' time and walked out."

I smiled. "Not bad for someone you never met."

Benny chuckled. "Well you kind of good at refreshing memories, you know. Now are you gonna leave me the hell alone?"

"All in good time, Benny. All in good time."

"I want to know about a girl."

He sighed and gulped his beer. "Hey now you're talking my language. I knew we'd get there in the end. What's with the heavy treatment, heh?" He smiled. "Why don't you let go of the meat and veg and tell Uncle Benny just what kinda girl you're after?"

I didn't let go. "Not any girl, Benny, this girl's special."

"All my girls are special man. What you saying, you saying Benny don't deal in quality meat?"

"Hermeez Wentz once had her. She's tall with long, red hair. Can't remember her name, I'm sure you know who I mean."

His eyes widened and he twitched his cheek, "Wrong guy, buddy. I don't have no redhead, none above five foot two anyways, and I told you before I don't know no fuckin' Hermeez. All I know is what I've told you already."

He sighed. "I've got a couple of beautiful blondies though. They'll suit you right down to the ground."

I ordered another couple of beers and twisted my hand. Benny squealed quietly and a tear rolled down his cheek. The drinks arrived and he nearly missed his mouth.

"I don't think you're listening to me, Benny. I want the redhead. The tall one with the distinctive mole on her pretty little cheek, I'm sure you know the one I mean."

Another twist and he winced in agony.

He was slow in finding his voice. Licking his spittled lips nervously he picked his words with caution. "Listen pal, I'm being straight when I say I don't run no redhead. The last one left me fuckin' months ago." He took a deep breath. "To be honest I don't know many fuckin' redheads with moles…"

I tightened my grip.

106

"…but…but…fuckin' hell man. Okay, okay, okay. There is somebody answers you're description with a mole, but how do I know if it's the right one? Is this to do with the murder?"

"I don't think that is any of your concern. What is your concern is that I've had your tackle in my hand for five minutes and I'm getting pissed."

"Okay, okay, okay," he said and wiped the sweat from his brow. "Like I said there is this redhead with a mole, goes by the name of Leather. Maybe Leather and Hermeez were buddies?" He sighed deeply and grimaced. "But I don't know where to look and that's the gods honest truth, man. Leather's relatively new in town and does Leather's own thing."

I relinquished my grip, finished my drink, and left the bar. I didn't bother to thank Benny, leaving him in one piece was favour enough. Now maybe we were getting somewhere.

Scouring the bars in The Downtown took its toll on the feet, and what's more I found out very little. It was difficult digging for information on hostile territory. I much preferred to be on home ground. You can only play the tough guy for so long, after a while it wears a little thin and loses its effectiveness. I decided it was time to call Timmy and report back.

I found a call box on the corner so I dropped in a dime and asked for a New York City number. Timmy answered after only one ring.

"Timmy, it's Errol, things are moving."

"Errol, I've been having second thoughts ever since you jetted off."

"Put 'em aside buddy, it's started and I'm here until it's finished."

"Okay Errol, what you got?"

"You were right about the investigation. It's a sham. The coroner suggests burglary gone wrong and everybody's happy as pigs in mud. I'm as good as on my own."

"That's just how you like it, kid. Are you positive they're wrong?"

"The more I look into it the surer I become. I get the feeling Hermeez was a little more active than his retirement suggests."

"How do you mean, 'active'?" he asked.

I sighed. "I'm not sure, it's only a hunch but there's plenty to be going at. Now listen Timmy, I need a make on a hooker, at least I think she's a hooker. Don't have the real name, but she uses Leather."

"Leather?"

"Ahem. Tall, beautiful redhead with a distinctive mole on her left cheek. She's new in Casablanca. This is all on a hunch but I suspect she's something to do with all this."

"Have you checked with Peru?"

"No, not yet. I think I'm gonna be careful around Mr Peru. He wants me to think he's not interested but I'm not so sure."

"Okay, I'll do what I can, Errol. You'd do better keeping a low profile until the full autopsy report. You never know the crazed, drugged-up house robber could be all there is to it."

"Damn it, Timmy, you don't believe that. Hermeez was no punk and he was no fisherman either. Look, I gotta go. Find out about the broad and I'll call you tonight."

"Okay Errol, and be careful eh, buddy. Remember it's not your patch anymore. Everybody says Casablanca is not what it used to be."

"Same old town, Tim. Changed on the surface, but the magic's still here."

I left the phone booth and headed briskly to the parking lot where I had left my heap. It was time for a good feed and to put my feet up. I guessed Arthur Peru would want to be briefed but he could wait.

I passed the attendant who gave a slight nod and walked towards my car. It was parked in the far corner of the parking lot. The only sound was that of my own footsteps echoing in the otherwise silence. I suddenly got the feeling; the instinct that had kept me alive for so long, but it was a moment too late.

As I got my hand on the cold metal of my gun the first blow was struck. It was something heavy and sent me tumbling

108

flat on my face. My grip was lost and before I could move again the blows were raining in. I was smashed over the head, across my back, on my legs. I curled up into a foetal position and relaxed the best I could until the kicks and punches ceased.

Everything stopped almost as soon as it had begun, but I felt too groggy to move. So I just lay there, the pain washing over me in waves. I felt more pain at my stupidity than the cuts and bruises. It would return; that old feeling. It was coming, but was slow. The rust was still clogging the system. Maybe a good beating would provide the oil I required.

I slept a while.

It was the blinding rays of the sun that brought me round. Reflecting from the windscreens of the rows and rows of vehicles. Providing a welcome warmth that cleared the grogginess from my pounding head.

I lifted my face from the concrete floor and rested on two elbows. A quick check satisfied me that there was nothing broken. Everything felt sore and my left eye was swollen, but there was nothing more than cuts and bruises. Had this been a warning, but for what?

I rolled over and pulled myself into a sitting position. Sweat bathed my whole body, running down the side of my face and mixing with the blood from the open cuts. I looked across the lot and there was no blurred vision, only a heavy ache across my forehead. I noticed the cars were different. There must have been ten cars that were different to the ones before. Probably more than ten. They must have all seen me here in a crumpled heap. Like a drunken bum.

The chimes rang out from the old clock tower and I realised I had been out for over an hour. What a place to sleep, on the solid concrete of a dingy parking lot. A familiar smell filled my nostrils. I couldn't quite place it, but I had smelt it before.

I managed to find my feet and to my surprise I didn't fall over. Instead I got into my car, fired the engine and drove back to The Dockside.

Chapter Eighteen – Dinner at the Dockside

Back at The Dockside I received medical attention in the form of a damp cloth and a couple of band aids. They were applied by the beautiful, young red head receptionist, who claimed to be a qualified first aider. She completed her work by giving me a daughterly kiss on the forehead that did nothing for me but made me feel old.

I dined in The Dockside restaurant, enjoying a three-course meal of homemade minestrone soup, chicken supreme in white wine sauce with new potatoes, broccoli and carrots, and delicious profiteroles with hot chocolate sauce.

I was wiping the chocolate from my face when a handsome, middle-aged lady planted her plump backside on the chair opposite me.

She had bottle blonde hair, long and curly with dark roots coming through. A well worn face was tidily made up; the creases of oncoming old age were well hidden. Her lips were so red they looked bruised. She had a tiny nose and little pixie ears with a couple of rocks sparkling away. She was smiling warmly.

"You look like you've had a hard day," she said in a husky voice with a definite southern inflection. Her large, upstanding breasts wobbled as she spoke. They were barely concealed in a tight, red dress that had a plunging neckline and ended well above her knees.

I smiled back at her and pushed the plate aside. "I've had better and I've had much worse."

She laughed a chesty, attractive laugh. "I'm sure you have," she said, before thrusting out a hand; it was tiny and soft with each fingernail painted red. "Diane Ebrahim, pleased to meet you."

I took the hand in my own and kissed it gallantly. "Errol Black. Likewise. Tell me, are you staying at The Dockside?"

She nodded. "You could say that. I have the penthouse suite. In fact I live there."

"Ah, so you are the one I should be thanking."

She looked puzzled. "Thanking?"

"Yes, for maintaining the dignity and character of The Dockside in the midst of all this raging development. For keeping a nostalgic foot in the golden past as the rest of this wonderful town sells its soul."

"You surprise me, Mr Black. I didn't take you for an old romantic."

"Less of the old, please, and call me Errol. I insist. I'm not a romantic, I like a bit of class, that's all."

Her tomato red lips curled up voluptuously as she said, "Why thank you, Errol. You and me both. I do like to think of The Dockside as classy."

"It reflects its owner, Diane. I've only met you a moment ago and it's clear to me that you exude class."

"Oh you are a flatterer. Now tell me, Errol, who would hurt you?" She put a hand to my wounded face. "When you seem such a nice boy."

"Sorry to disappoint you, Diane. I'm afraid I'm not nice either. In fact I can be very bad, and there's a whole pile of people been queuing up to do something like this to me. They won't be doing it again, I can assure you of that."

She smiled.

"I hear that you're Arthur's little agent. I guess you federal boys are always getting into scrapes. Tell me Errol, how are you settling in? In Casablanca I mean."

She was teasing me and maybe fishing a little too. Arthur's little agent, ha? Word sure did get around fast. I wondered just how much the lovely Diane really knew.

"I'm settling in fine Diane, like a duck to water. I ought to after all, I've swum in this little pond many a time."

She raised her eyebrows, or at least the makeup that was in their place, and smiled an intrigued, curious smile.

"You got history?"

"Yup, I got history, but that's just what I want it to stay."

She nodded. "And the present?"

"The present I've got no problem with, only I bet you know all about that already."

She looked puzzled and then flashed those red lips at me again.

"You think that me and Arthur?"

I shrugged as Diane let out a hearty laugh.

"No, I'm afraid you have definitely got that one wrong. Arthur and I are good friends, extremely good friends, but nothing more. Similar creatures stick together in the social jungle."

"I'm sorry."

"Don't be. Arthur always attends my parties but always goes home afterwards."

I'd heard about The Dockside parties. They were gatherings for all the movers and shakers of the town. A place where a lot of business could be done. And a lot of information could be gleaned.

"I bet he has a veto on the guest list as well, am I right?"

"Sure, I help him out if that kind of thing is called for. That's what friends are for, but don't worry I'm not helping him out now if that's what you think." She produced a packet of cigarettes from a small purse, placed one in a gold holder and lit it up inhaling deeply. She offered one to me, but I refused.

"I thought all detectives smoked."

"They do," I said and lit up a Lucky. "I was being polite."

"Polite as well as charming, not to say ruggedly handsome. I wonder what other qualities do you possess?"

It was a rhetorical question, either that or an attempt to make me blush. I didn't do that, but I did give her an answer.

"I'm a good party guest. I keep the ladies charmed and feeling good about themselves and I keep the boys in drinks and scintillating conversation."

Again, she laughed heartily. "Okay Errol, you are on. Tomorrow evening, eight o clock, you are on the invite list. I'm afraid, now I really must go."

She stood up and a tall, handsome officer called Lloyd Stone appeared and kissed her hand. "As you can see my escort is here."

"Hello Lloyd," I said to the stubbled detective.

Stone nodded. "Not been here two minutes, Black, and already taken a beating, eh. You want to be more careful."

112

"Oh Lloyd, don't be so cruel." She tapped him playfully and he smiled at her, but as she turned away the smile became a sneer.

"Tomorrow, Mr Black, wear your best penguin suit. Must dash."

Chapter Nineteen – Crime Scene

The cab driver pushed the car into third and sailed through the mire. The street ahead was awash with flashing blue and red, so I figured I was heading in the right direction. I told him to follow the leaders and follow them good. He obliged without a spoken word, but made good of my humble request.

I got out of the cab, paid the fare and took in a deep breath of sea air. Solid ground felt great, so I stood still for a moment or two.

I found myself in one of the better areas of town. It looked like the heavenly suburbia that only exists on television. Rows of big, detached houses on spacious plots of land with double garages and colourful gardens. The highway was as wide as a car park and all the streetlights worked.

By now the red tape was in place and the mad cacophony of noise and activity indicated it was the scene of a crime. There were several police cars, an ambulance and the medical examiner's van. A small gathering of people pushed against the ribbon waiting for something to happen. Neighbours twitched their curtains, but dare not venture out to ask what had happened. A couple of uniforms were fighting off the press and any suspicious busybodies at the end of the gravel drive. I flashed my pass and went through into the interior of the house.

I walked through the hall and found myself in a large, open living area with huge windows looking over several acres of lawn at the back, expensive paintings on the wall and a lab man on his knees dusting everything down meticulously.

A corridor led out of the living room with several doors off it. Through the first of those doors I found what I was looking for.

Peru was stood over the body. I instantly recognised his enormous frame in the dim lighting of the washroom. Two older men, presumably the medical examiners, were knelt at either side of the corpse; plastic gloves on, poking and probing at the bloody mess in the shower.

"What the fuck happened to you?" spat Peru. "And what are you doing here?"

"Travers called," I said. "He dropped it discreetly into the conversation."

"Yeah right."

I peered over the big man's shoulder. The body was crumpled in a heap at the bottom of the shower cubicle. The glass of the door was shattered, leaving rather nasty shards all over the area. There was a great big hole in the man's chest, which was black with blood. The shower had been on and had swilled a lot of the claret away, but was now a mere dribble. The eyes of the dead man were wide open and staring.

"He knew who killed him," I said.

"What?"

"You can see it in his eyes."

Peru rubbed his forehead irritably. "Look, keep your opinions to yourself. At least for the moment, eh?"

He looked around the crowded room and down at the two MEs who were busily beavering away, oblivious to the world. "And seeing as you are here keep a low profile. I don't want to hear you and I don't want to see you! Okay? By the way, you look like shit."

I stepped away into the anonymous corners of the increasingly crowded room. So far the press were being held back, although the police photographers more than made up for it. The forensics too were out in force, crawling on their hands and knees, reaching out into every nook and cranny, busily brushing away covering everything in white powder.

I felt a familiar hand rest on my shoulder and turned to see the awkward smile of Jackson Travers. He pointed out the two homicide detectives that were currently embroiled in a heated discussion with Arthur Peru. Apparently they were reluctant to take on the investigation, preferring to hand it over to the bear-like Italian.

"He knew who killed him," I said again, this time to Travers.

"Maybe you're right, he doesn't look particularly surprised. Maybe his old lady popped him."

"Too professional, too cool."

"You don't know Mrs Kalac."

"Feisty lady?"

"Dangerous lady. She used to be a hooker until Tony took a liking to her and pulled her out of the gutter. Rumour has it she was reluctant to give up her day job."

"What, so one day she decides to shut up his whining for good?"

Travers shrugged. "She's out of the country at the moment, so I guess not."

He wandered out of the washroom and back into the living area with the views. I slipped out after him.

"You didn't call me out here for nothing," I said. "That body in there looks familiar wouldn't you say? Not your usual contract hit, too messy by far."

"And like you say, he knew who killed him."

"The same expression from the photographs in the Wentz file, the wounds are identical, the calibre looks the same, which will be confirmed soon enough. Even the same venue, the victim's house."

"There's no sign of forced entry."

I nodded. "And no robbery either."

"But you never did come around to the burglary theory did you?"

"You called me, remember."

Travers smiled a truly awful smile.

"Did you notice the imprint in the carpet by the body?"

"What kind of imprint?"

Travers made a circle with his forefinger and thumb. "About so big. A heel, perhaps?"

"Do you think it has any connection to Wentz?" I asked impatiently.

Jackson ignored the question, instead opting to take a stroll outside. I followed him out into the grounds at the back of the house. Here it was quieter, with just the odd investigator sweeping the edges of the property.

"Shall I take that as a no?" I pressed. "Or are you still sulking after losing your dinner money?"

He stared at my bruised face.

"Jarvis McSwarve is a big man in this town," is all he said, before characteristically producing his little tin. To both our surprise there was no smoke of any description inside the tin, so I offered him a Lucky Strike.

"Are you sure that you want to make an enemy of him?" he said, ignoring the packet I held out.

"And what makes you think I want to do that?" I asked cursing my loss of cool at the Racecourse. Travers was clearly a lot more perceptive than I gave him credit for.

"You went to The Penitence."

I nodded. "Sure, I went to The Penitence. That doesn't mean shit; most of the town would go if only they could get in. I was interested, that's all. He wasn't there anyway." I added as an afterthought.

"Impressed?"

I laughed. "The Club was okay, the food was excellent, the punters were of a certain pedigree, but the show…"

"Seen better Downtown, ha?"

"Yeah, something like that. Hardly golden ticket entertainment, a live sex show."

"Very popular."

"So are hookers."

"Yeah, but the makers and shakers like their hookers to be private. Whereas at The Penitence they can all be boys, and girls, together."

I nodded. That kind of made sense. I still held the Luckys.

He eventually relented and took a cigarette from the open packet. I did the same and lit them both, smiling broadly at my first score as Travers coughed heavily on the first pull. He recovered quickly to wipe the smile right off my tired face.

"I had a conversation with Bob the bookie after the meet. Seems the luck of your friend was not all bad."

My look of incredulity was lost on the weasel.

"Two days before he was killed he collected the second win of a hugely lucrative treble. Would have paid a good few ticks of McSwarve's tab, that's for sure."

"Did he collect the wedge?"

"No, he wanted to ride the wave and wait for the third. Hell of a break, it came in tonight against all odds. He would have been a rich man."

There was a chill wind in the air. It blew across the gardens with unerring ferocity. I ruffled the collar of my trench coat and shuffled my shoulders.

"It was Scamper, right?" I said, deadpan.

The weasel grinned. "He picked an impossible bet. A bet which, if it came off, would complete the most audacious treble."

Before I had a chance to digest this new twist, there was a sudden commotion ringing out from inside the house. A car had rolled up on the gravel drive moments ago, screeching to a halt with arrogant abandon. Now there were voices raised to a notch above shouting in what sounded like a heated argument.

Travers grabbed my arm and pulled me into the shadows as the group of irate men came stumbling out from the rear of the house. Peru was right there in the middle, waving both his arms about angrily. Two of his own lieutenants flanked him at either side, tentatively holding his flailing limbs.

I opened my mouth in preparation to speak, but Travers gently "shushed", holding a finger to his own twisted features. "The cavalry have arrived, you're better off out of it," he whispered, stubbing out both our cigarettes.

I didn't answer, instead watched silently as more men came out into the already crowded gardens. On the one side stood Peru, his own private army alongside him, facing up to a small bunch of black suited henchmen all hiding behind ridiculous sunshades. Uniformed officers were scattered amongst the multitude, looking as if they wished they weren't. It looked like a disturbance at a Mafia funeral and within minutes died down, resulting in a lot of shrugged shoulders, open palmed gestures and blank looks of innocence. As Peru lit up one of his cigarillos a tall figure emerged in the doorway and slowly ambled down the three steps towards the crowd.

Men on both sides parted like the red sea, and you almost expected someone to start bearing roses and a team of bowed heads. The tall man looked briefly at Peru and spat one sentence before staring directly right into my eyes. He then turned on his heels and left. The screech of the spinning tyres ran out, before they took grip and the big car disappeared.

Things quietened down for the next thirty minutes. I squeezed as much as I could from a pimply, fresh faced uniform before setting off to leave. By now I felt exhausted. On my way back through the crime scene I bumped into Arthur Peru. His face was scarlet, and he looked jaded.

"Mr. Peru, I don't appreciate freelancers in my town. That's what he said."

"I know, I heard him. Look, I'm tired, I'm going to bed."

"And then he told me to finish it."

"Finish it? That easy eh?"

"That's what the man wants."

"Call me in the morning." I smiled wryly. "Later, in the morning."

Chapter Twenty- Ishmail Ouzanti

I arrived back at The Dockside as the sun peeped its head over the horizon. Peru would demand some answers soon, and I would have to be able to find satisfactory ones. But first, I needed rest. My body ached with fatigue, every nerve and every sinew throbbed with tiredness.

I wasn't ready to deal with another ghost from the past, but my wandering mind wasn't giving me any choice. As I mounted the stairs and trudged slowly to my room, sleep was uppermost in my thoughts. But as soon as my clothes were off and my head hit the pillow, he kept coming back. The thick, black bearded face, eyes as cold as stone and as commanding as a hypnotist.

I poured a bourbon and lit up a Lucky, every movement made me more irritable and uncomfortable. Tomorrow, after seven hours sleep, then I would face up to it, not now, not now.

My sleep was fitful and sparse and I woke up with a stub burning my lips. The clock said it was nine thirty, but there was no give-away sunshine shining brightly through the gaps in the curtains. A half full cut glass of bourbon stood where it had been abandoned atop the headboard.

I wiped my eyes, downed the bourbon and stretched my arms out tentatively. Too many thoughts were occupying my shattered mind, too many invasions from the past. I yawned noisily and thought of Sarah. I felt sure I had dreamt of her, but failed to recall any detail. Then I remembered last night's altercation, and the presence of the big man. So commanding in his black three piece suit and colourful, silk turban.

Ishmail Ouzanti, Senator, priest and would be king of Casablanca. A tall, beast of a man with a thick, black beard, and a hand-crafted, silk turban. The dog collar around his neck not only indicated his allegiance to the Church, of which he had offered his services since his immigration. More importantly, it demanded the same allegiance and respect from his masses. The brave described Ouzanti as unorthodox, even eccentric, but a wider, more whispered opinion claimed he brought a hint of sinisterism to the place of peaceful worship. He had several unconfirmed links to shady figures, which was commonplace and generally expected in politics, but the Church should not be tarred with the same gutter speculation.

I remembered my first impression of Ouzanti; after witnessing one of his powerful, oratorically mesmerising sermons. One of wonder, how he could speak so passionately about anything he cared to do so. He appealed to the emotions and fears of his audience, feeding off the signals they gave, their dreams, and their hopes. Often repeating a statement over and over again, asking questions to which there was only one answer. It was an incredible experience, to some sensational, to others quite frightening, but never dull.

Here was a man of huge influence. Not only using the clergy to widen his base, but adding a political string to his bow. Curiously, he was openly scathing of other politicians, but then Casablanca was his only real concern. No further national, or international intentions surfaced. He appeared to single-handedly call the shots of the whole town, the business, religious and political shots. Unchallenged by anybody. The only pie his fingers would not breech was organised crime. But to truly believe that would be naive.

"Finish it," I said aloud, imagining how serious Ouzanti would have spoken it. To him it would seem simple. Everything in his life was simple. No problem that could not be overcome. It might take a good deal of log rolling, or bribing, or even down right threatening; but everyone has his weakness. The politicians are simply better at finding that weakness than the rest of us.

I remembered what else he said to Peru. There had been more than a brief recognition in his eyes, and I had no doubt it was me who he was talking about. That would give me even less time than I had envisaged. Unless I talked to Peru, came clean and told him everything. Slit my own wrist and wait for him to provide the medical assistance.

Chapter Twenty-One – Coming Back

I breakfasted alone in the all day bar at The Dockside. This place had not changed one little bit, probably wouldn't in the next hundred years. Sitting in the dimly lit watering hole, with nothing stronger than a cafetiere of Colombian coffee, I felt maudlin. I ordered pancakes with a thick serving of maple syrup, but ate very little, picking at the edges and pushing the remainder around the plate.

The death of Hermeez Wentz was now opening a whole can of worms that were most unwelcome. I got the impression that it wasn't just Errol Black that had an ulterior interest in getting to the bottom of the sticky pile. Too many relics from the past were popping up. A little too frequently to be written off as a coincidence, but closing quarters sufficiently to dispel any real speculation. I wondered just how much the murder of Wentz really mattered to them. Peru had already made it clear he was disinterested. Maybe now he would make himself take an interest.

When I decided to come back, my intentions were not clear. Did I come back to avenge a former friend, to seek vengeance for the cutting short of such an unfulfilled life? Or did I simply yearn for a return to my daring days of private investigation. See the opportunity of a real good film noir mystery to sink my teeth into. Timmy Matthews waved the carrot under my nose, giving much more assistance than an officer of the law ever should. Maybe it was just too good a chance to refuse?

As I gratefully accepted my first drink of the day the familiar sensation warmed my belly and the thirst for answers grew more and more intense. I sighed in resignation. There was no hiding from it, however much I danced over the romance of renovated memories. I simply had to come back. Casablanca was a whole shopping list of unfinished business. It would never go away; eating away at the subconscious like a trapped moth. Hidden in the darkness of the packed, untidy wardrobe; caged within the confines of any escape route. So it would forever stay, nibbling away, at first slowly but as more clothes were crammed in, pushing it further to the back, it got more and more hungry. Skewing mercilessly through a life of mundane trivialities, with a single minded desire to be noticed.

In a perverse kind of way, I always wanted to come back. In moments of drunken anger, to come back and get revenge. To clear out all the old scars with ruthless abandon. In times of foolish weakness, I would come back with an olive branch and a Samaritans handshake. Make peace with the history and start again, a better person for it. Neither were compatible with reality, more distortions of a catalogue of jumbled memories.

But it wouldn't let go. Always chewing away, strangling any sense of detachment or refreshment my life took. I had to come back. Exorcise the demons and clear the cupboard. Hermeez was just a good excuse.

Laying on the cold slab was not the way I would want to remember him. There he looked so alone, so vulnerable, and so weak. He was not the man who had stood shoulder to shoulder with me in the war, the man who had been my childhood friend and my adult accomplice, not even the man who had suddenly disappeared five years ago.

The feeling came back instantly. The empty, hollow sensation cutting deep inside, poisoning my whole body. Snakes wriggled inside my belly, chewing and spitting fire with a frenzy. I fought it off and gritted my teeth, but the wound was reopened and blood was spilled.

Somebody had put a tune on and it drifted around the bar sweetly. Too distant for the words to be clear, though loud enough to seep deep into the soul. There was a steady buzz of conversation, the atmosphere dark and smoky kept the memories flowing.

I sauntered over to the leather sofas by the main bar. The dark, oak bar was lined with zinc, as were the tables, engraved with the words 'The Dockside'. Scented candle lamps burned away providing scant lighting and willowy shadows.

Chapter Twenty-Two – George Field

"What do you think about revenge Eezy?" asked Hermeez, as we sat out looking over the Giudecca Canal.

The sky had darkened and filled up with heavy, imposing clouds, which made the air chillier and the waters choppier. Around us were a thousand yachts, all with hundred feet masts, hauntingly swaying in the evening breeze. The relative silence of the canal contributing to the eerie atmosphere. Distant gondolas soundlessly drifted by.

"Do you think that it is always a nasty, filthy business, one for gangsters and honourless thieves, or do you think that it is sometimes…you know… sometimes acceptable, a wrong put right?"

I pondered the question.

"I guess the word itself is the difficulty," I replied, thinking philosophically. *"'Revenge' is a word forever associated with the bad, however there must be a situation in which the concept of revenge becomes acceptable. Circumstances are the key, obviously, but there are cases where revenge can be justified."*

"You are right, of course, but only in a human sense. To the justified avenger revenge has now become something other than revenge, don't you think? It is now justice by definition, or divine retribution, or some such cop out."

"I suppose I believe that what goes around comes around, you know? It's only how you deal with it yourself that language comes into play."

I lit up a Lucky and looked out over the city. From here you could see the distinctive buildings of the Square, The Doge's Palace, the Marciana Library and the Basilica. Relics of a bygone world of beautiful architecture and culture, of romance and passion.

"Anyway, what's with the deep conversation?" I asked. *"You'll put the ladies off."*

I chuckled. The ladies in question were a stunning pair of Italian waitresses that we had stumbled across in one of the Rialto's many bars. Very Latin in appearance, they both had dark, tanned skin, strong, fit bodies and jet black, silky hair. Maria had taken a liking to Hermeez, giggling like a teenager, which she wasn't far from, as he entertained the locals with his saxophone playing, bringing a taste of East Harlem to the joint. Teresa, on the other hand, was more straight, much less animated in her emotions. She preferred to talk. I listened as she tore into her elder brothers, complained about her strict parents and spoke of her desire to see and probably conquer the world.

"I don't think so, my friend," said Hermeez, loosening his tie. "Conversation appears to be Teresa's strong point."

"Unlike Maria?" I probed.

Hermeez smiled. "Maybe."

The silence was broken by the two girls returning from the yacht club, a hundred yards to our right. Each carried a drink with an umbrella in the right hand and a beer in the left. Teresa looked at me and smiled a sweet smile as she got closer. Perching herself on my knee and giving me a long kiss, which I instinctively returned.

Hermeez winked as he got similar treatment from Maria.

Later we slipped back into another obscure discussion. What was the nature of good and bad? What possibly made people bad and what were the real solutions? Neither of us were church goers and therefore we looked at the problems from a secular viewpoint, which made our conclusions all the more bizarre. How could we possibly balance the assertion that there was a great deal of innate badness in this world, a lot of which we were convinced we had personally witnessed, yet not give the option of an omnipotent battle between good and evil, or even a God?

Hermeez signed off for the night with a vicious diatribe at all things that were wrong. He was rarely in such a reflective mood and although I enjoyed the meat and drink of the debate he was quite scary.

I felt a hand on my shoulder. It was a soft grip, not threatening. I turned around and did a double-take. Looking back at me was the smiling face of George Field.

"Errol Black. What the hell are you doing here?"

I stood up and took his hand in my own. He put his other arm around my side and patted me on the back. "I could tell you, George, but I'd have to kill you!"

Field laughed a boyish chuckle and we both sat down. He was dressed in grey, pinstripe pants, with an open-neck, yellow shirt. He had a navy blue tank top over the shirt with an old school coat of arms emblazoned on the chest. He was as British as they come.

A tall man, standing a touch over six foot, he had an awkward, clumsy stance. He was slightly overweight, although not fat, with a double-chin, stubbled with a day old, black growth like the rest of his face. Jet black hair was combed back, but stuck out at odd angles. Looking out from the boyish face were piercing brown eyes about a bauble nose and a deep cleft below his nostrils.

Despite his scruffy appearance, George Field was one of the most intelligent men I had ever met.

"I'll tell you what, Errol. How about we trade? I'll tell you what I'm doing here and then I'll tell you what you're doing here!"

I smiled and we both sat down.

"Okay, George. You have a deal."

It was five years since I had last seen George Field. In that time he had kept his reputation as one of America's foremost mystery novelists intact. He only ever wrote a novel in which the subject was steeped in fact. His research and ability to dig out the details from history was legendary. And he did it all without an editorial team behind him.

I suppose George was as much a loner as I was. He moulded himself effortlessly into many other worlds, depicting eras, locations and people with such gritty reality you would have thought he was there. The story he wrote about me, a short story entitled The Gift, he was there. It was a commercial disaster, although gained good critical acclaim and was loosely based on my last days in Casablanca, through the eyes of a fictional private eye. The way he wrote with such passion about the sudden collapse of a man's world, many people suspected it was autobiographical. I suppose it almost was, we had spent many sessions soul searching together, with Hermeez re-filling the glasses.

"You are still drinking that Deep South liquor, I see," he said, nodding towards my bourbon.

"I got a liking for it. So did you, if I remember correctly."

George chuckled. "Makes people think I'm a private eye. I much prefer a good stout, or a gin and tonic, but I have got to check the scenery to make sure none of the branches move. My publishers are very particular, you know."

I took a long drink, letting the bourbon slowly burn my throat, before making the long journey of warmth down to my stomach.

"Who's the publishers this time, George? That is why you're here, isn't it?"

George smiles enigmatically.

"It's not a follow up to The Gift, surely. Not unless you've taken up vanity publishing."

"Better than that, Eezy. With this one, I hope I won't have to change the ending."

"Do tell."

He looked from side to side and leaned in towards me. "I'm freelance."

"Freelance. For who?"

"Hearst."

"Hearst!" I nearly choked. "You always did fall for thirty pieces of silver!"

I took another drink. "Not fiction then?"

"Nope."

"Come on, George. You were gonna spill, remember?"

He pulled out a bag of tobacco from his pants pocket and rolled a couple of cigarettes. "Here, take this. They're good."

He was right. They were.

"Apart from you, Eezy, who does this town have to offer? Who is there that would be worth the time and the effort of more than a couple of sentences?"

"There's crime and mystery everywhere. You told me that, buddy."

George exhaled a stream, of blue smoke. "But I'm not writing crime mystery here. I told you, it's not fiction."

I looked at George. He looked back, his face expressionless.

"It's not…"

"Of course it is, the old dog himself."

He remained silent for a moment to let it sink in.

"I wondered whether I'd be bumping into you when I accepted the assignment. I had one of those strange feelings. I didn't honestly think that I would, but here you are."

I gratefully accepted another drink from the waiter and held it, clinking the ice.

"It's uncooperative, I take it?"

"Of course. A real hush hush, unauthorised biography of the old maestro. I tell you, Eezy, this guy is worth a break from fiction. You couldn't make it up, he's got more history than Joe Kennedy!"

"And more connections. Be careful, George."

He smiled and sipped his stout, which formed a white moustache in the cleft about his thin lips.

"Twice he ran for Governor and each time the vote came down to a couple of percent. He's served as State District Attorney, Attorney General and now, for the last thirty-five years, as Senator and unofficial kingmaker. He's a politician, Errol. Okay, a politician with more colour than Huey Long, and more clout than your average mafia don, but that's what he is. So far I've had a lot of cooperation."

"Be careful, George. Ishmail Ouzanti is not a man to cross. Whoever is backing you."

"You'd know about that."

I nodded. "Am I right in thinking when he took over as AG, it was because the existing officer died suddenly?"

George shrugged. "Same thing happened all over the country. I've checked it out, there was no foul play."

I stared hard at my old buddy.

"Look, I'm not suggesting the Uncle is squeaky clean, but he's not going to go having his biographer knocked off, is he?"

I sighed and patted George on the shoulder. "You're right. Maybe I'm being paranoid. It's just being back here."

"I understand. Have you seen her yet?"

I nodded.

"And?"

"And what? She's married now. She's got nothing to do with the present. She's the past."

For a moment or two there was silence, as we both contemplated just how hollow that sounded. George kept a silly grin on his face, but didn't say anything. It was strange seeing him again after such a long time, and even stranger to be sitting here in The Dockside breakfast room, just like old times.

George Field was merely a fledgling writer in the old days. He was painfully intelligent, but whereas he could put down anything on paper and make it sound poetic, he struggled to communicate as smoothly with people face to face. He was a homosexual as well, which not only was illegal, but was very, very dangerous if you weren't discreet.

It was his homosexuality that led to our first meeting. George was taking a beating from a huge, tattooed skinhead in one of the back alleys down by the docks. Not because he'd wrongly made a pass, simply because the skinhead was also a homosexual and thought that gave him the right to have sex with George. If I hadn't have stepped in, he would have raped him.

I sent the skinhead packing with a thick lip and took George back to The Dockside for a drink and to clean up. We hit it off immediately and talked for the rest of the night, draining a full bottle of Jim Beam in the process.

Hermeez had just left town and I had started seeing Sarah. George was fascinated with a life that really did brush with crime and mystery. I told him stories, cases I had investigated, characters I had come across, places I had been. And I told him about Sarah; sweet, beautiful Sarah.

He listened.

He told me stories, most of which were made up, but seemed every bit as real as the ones I told him. He described people, fictional people but with much more clarity and vividness than I could ever describe someone real to him.

Over the months we often went out. We had meals, went to the races and got very drunk. George grew to like Sarah, and her him. We became pals.

His writing was taking off and it was soon to take him away from Casablanca. But not before my own exile would begin. He warned me that Ishmail Ouzanti had found out about his god-daughter and me. He was concerned that she was

129

heading in the wrong direction, going off the rails, being led astray. I can't remember just how he put it, but he had decreed he would put a stop to it. Mixing with gangsters and criminals was no behaviour for a lady. Only for a Senator. He would put things right and straighten her out. I, too, would be straightened out!

"Anyway, Errol. It's your turn. After everything that happened, you came back. Do you want to tell me why?"

"I thought you were going to tell me."

George didn't say anything for a moment and then he lit up another cigarette.

"If it's not Sarah, then it must be Hermeez."

I wasn't surprised. George could dig out any information. The papers may have been quiet, but little got past George Field. I told him all I knew about the death of Hermeez Wentz.

"Are you official?" he asked. "Because if you're not, it's you that needs to be careful."

I showed him my badge.

He whistled and smiled. "Does Hoover know that you're carrying that around?"

I told him all about my arrangement and my investigation so far.

"Good reason to come back. Very honourable."

He looked at his watch and grimaced.

"Look, I'm sorry, Errol. I'm going to have to skedaddle right now, but we'll meet up for a meal."

"Sure thing. Tomorrow night?"

"Tomorrow, eight o'clock. I'll meet you here."

His eyes flickered to the door. I looked over my shoulder. He kept looking at his watch as if it might stop and start going around the other way.

"I really am going to have to go, but I will bring my notes tomorrow. I might have something that could help you."

He was on his feet, apologetically shrugging his shoulders. And then he was gone, into the throng in the reception amongst the crowds.

Chapter Twenty-Three – The Club

He was right. The Plaza Club was definitely worth checking out.

The girl on the hat counter gave me a sweet smile and a ticket. I gave her ten dollars, blew her a kiss and wandered on through.

The first thing I saw was a pair of huge breasts bouncing happily up and down. They belonged to a short, dark haired girl, who was sitting with her back arched and arms in the air, on the lap of a well dressed suit and tie. She kept licking her fingers, rubbing her nipples with them and then stroking the man's elated face, who didn't know where to put his hands. Whenever they got close to touching, she discreetly slid them back down to his sides without losing the huge, fake grin, or look of ecstasy she was wearing.

I realized I had been stood staring, when someone bumped into me from behind. I apologized and walked through the room, which was full of similar sights. There was a small bar on my left, which appeared to sell only bottled beer at a buck a bottle. The rest of the room was filled with chairs and padded benches, most of which were taken by all kinds of men. The only thing they all had in common was the look on their faces, like the little boy in the toyshop.

I ordered a beer and took a stroll around the dingy bar. There were ten girls in all, who were working this side of the bar. All were extremely pretty, with larger than average breasts and beautiful, shapely bodies. When they were not dancing, the girls were clad in a variety of seductive and revealing lingerie, leaving little to the imagination. The only other item of clothing they wore was a pair of boots, or an ankle suspender belt, which was usually packed heavily with notes.

"Have you had a dance yet?"

I turned around.

She was young; early twenties, with dark brown hair and an innocent smile that made her look vulnerable. There were faint traces of a mottled complexion from her youth, although this was well disguised with make-up and surprisingly didn't deter from her attractiveness at all. Her face may have looked young and vulnerable, but her body was entirely different. She had the full curves of a woman; big pert breasts barely concealed in a one piece, black lacy body. If my eyes had lowered, which they did, it would have been impossible not to see her large, brown nipples through the flimsy material and, lower still, the faint trace of black, pubic hair.

I smiled. "No."

"Would you like me to dance for you? All you need to do is give me the gold ticket for a five minute dance. I get a dollar for the ticket. Anything else you want to give me is up to you. You are under no obligation."

She smiled. Her voice was also that of a girl. She struggled with the word 'obligation' but reeled off the spiel like she was auditioning for a movie.

I sipped my drink and sighed. "I'm sorry. I think I might just hang onto my ticket for the time being."

"That's no problem. If you change your mind I'll be just over there." She pointed to an alcove where a group of men were sat looking restless and nervous.

I watched her head over to the alcove, wiggling her hips, as she walked. She sat next to a black fellow in cowboy gear, who had a smile the size of the Mississippi and whispered in his ear. He pulled out his wallet and handed over a couple of notes. She shook her head, but he insisted and eventually she relented with a shrug putting the money down her boot.

As soon as the current tune ended, she stood up facing the excited cowboy and began a slow, sexy dance. She pushed his legs apart as far as they would go, casually put his arms at his sides and stepped into the space, swaying sexily to the music.

She was smiling as she danced, looking right into the cowboy's eyes, although if you looked closer she was actually looking right through him. Sometimes the smile would be replaced be a look of desire, or pleasure, not unlike the facial expressions of budding young models in certain underground publications, but mostly she just smiled.

As the act progressed she would go through a series of provocative moves; rubbing herself right across the cowboy's groin, turning around and shoving her shapely ass an inch from his lusting face and fondling herself in the most outrageous way. By the time she peeled off her lacy body down to her trim waist, revealing the most beautiful pair of breasts, with big, dark brown nipples like brass nickels, the cowboy's friends had all edged nearer to get a closer look.

I must admit, although aware of the absurdity of it all, I was faintly embarrassed with myself for enjoying the performance as much as I did. It had more effect on me that I would like to admit and was much more erotic than the show at The Penitence the other night; so much more understated so that you could almost feel the rampant urge to touch that every male participant was desperately fighting. I could tell the cowboy was seriously weighing up in his head, whether it would be worth a little flick of the tongue, lizard-like, when she next rubbed her nipples a hair's breadth from his face, even though he would be sure to be forcibly ejected.

The dance finished with no more than her breasts on show, although I noticed some of the other girls were keen to pull their g-string aside for just a second, probably feeling even more power by offering a quick flash of their pussy, or by pulling their own buttocks apart, affording a similar anguished response from the client. I smiled inwardly as the young brunette simply pulled up her body and took a drink from a passing waitress, waiting for the next punter willing to throw his money at her.

I found a table in the corner by a potted cactus. I ordered a cognac from a passing waitress and to my surprise they actually had it. The bleached blonde waitress brought my drink and took a seat at my table.

I dropped a buck on her tray and smiled.

"You're new here?" she said, pocketing the buck. "Are you enjoying yourself?"

"I'm trying. Take a drink with me."

"I don't mind if I do. I'll have a Manhattan."

She returned with her drink a moment later, and gave me a big smile from her red, red lips.

"What happened to your face?" she asked, watching me.

"I fell in the shower."

I lit up a Lucky and put it to her lips. She sucked it and sat back patiently as I lit another.

"Are you going to dance for me?"

She shook her head. "I'm not a dancer. I leave that to the professionals."

I nodded. "So what do you do?"

She smiled. "I serve drinks and provide scintillating conversation to the punters. Sometimes the punters are shy and like to talk. You're not shy so why are you on your own?"

"Was Hermeez Wentz shy? You remember Hermeez Wentz, don't you?"

She took a sip from her drink, leaving a bright red mark around the glass. "I'm aware he came here," she said. "I never spoke to him myself." She leaned over the table and whispered, "You know he's dead don't you?"

"Yeah, I know."

"Was he a friend of yours?"

"A friend no, a debtor yes. I hear there were others?"

"I'm sorry, I wouldn't know about that."

"How about the other girls, would they be able to tell me anything?"

She smiled. "About his taste in underwear, maybe. From what I hear, he liked his women."

"That's why he came here?" I asked grinning a wolfish grin.

"It's not that kind of club."

"Oh no?" I said. "So tell me, what kind of club is The Plaza?"

The waitress smiled. "It's classy. Yeah The Plaza is classy, it's a place where gentlemen can come and relax and enjoy a bit of company. Without any strings or anything heavy."

I found myself liking her. She spoke with a passion and a certain verve that most waitresses wouldn't relate to.

"Tell me," I said. "Just what happens if one of your gentlemen takes a shine to the company that is provided for him? What if he wants more than a pretty smile and a keen drinks waiter?"

She shrugged. "Well, I guess that is up to the person in question. Your friend, Wentz, never had a problem persuading certain ladies to take their duties elsewhere. Although with his looks and charm, I doubt very much if it was his wallet that they were after."

"After all, it's not that kind of club."

She put her drink down and put her hand to my face, brushing her fingertips down the wound gently. "I'm a waitress, nothing more. I wait on. I'm not for sale."

"I bet you get lots of offers."

"Listen fella, I get offers walking the street. It's not for me, y'hear? Every girl can make her own decision, but this is a club and not a pick-up joint, okay?"

"I'm sorry. Take another drink, will you? We'll start again?"

She took our glasses and flounced off to the bar. To my surprise, she returned a moment later, the wonderful smile restored to her face. We talked for half an hour and killed another few drinks. Eventually she stood up.

"Look sweetheart, I'm gonna have to go. My manager is over there and I'm gonna have to spread myself a little thinner. You know what I mean?"

I looked over my shoulder. A small, stocky man with a full beard quickly looked away.

"I understand, honey. Just do something for me will you?"

"I'll try."

"Ask a few questions about Wentz. Anything you can, you never know it may be a help."

I slipped a couple of bucks down her cleavage. "I promise I'll make it worth your while."

She smiled an all too red smile, bent over and kissed me softly on the nose. "I'll try. Look, I'll be finished here at 2 o'clock. Meet me downstairs and we'll compare notes. Deal?"

"Deal."

I smiled and left The Plaza. Maybe it was that kind of club after all.

Chapter Twenty-Four – Arthur Peru

I met Peru outside The Dockside and we drove to the east side of town. The rain had stopped and the mist moved in swirls. We found an take out eatery and Peru ordered a steak and three vegetables, a pile of creamed potatoes and four chocolate bagels. I settled for a steak sandwich and a fresh packet of Luckys.

"I don't like the way that this is turning out, Black. I don't mind you knowing that," he said in between mouthfuls of food. "People like Kalac should not get shot whilst taking a shower. This sort of thing does not happen to blokes like that in Casablanca."

He polished off his main course, wasting no time in munching the bagels. I said nothing, watching Peru like you watch a gecko that's just devoured its partner. Travers appeared with a steaming mug of black coffee.

"It looks like it's linked to the Wentz chill. Either that or it's supposed to look that way. The old reverse gambit." He chuckled throatily before chasing a dissolving lump of sugar around the cup.

"Who owned Kalac?" I asked. "He did have a partner, right?"

"Same boss as everybody else," Peru screwed up his paper bag and tossed it expertly in one of the open garbage sacks. "There's only one boss in this town."

I waited.

He shrugged. "Jevon Earl."

It was a name I had heard earlier. I was expecting maybe one of the McSwarve brothers, possibly even Ishmail Ouzanti. Somebody I could easily draw an unhealthy dislike for. Somebody from the past. Somebody associated with Sarah. I was not expecting Jevon Earl.

Jackson Travers threw down his whole cup of coffee in one gulp before enlightening me about the local big man.

"Jevon Earl is a man not to cross. Runs most of what's bad in this town. He's not fussy, prostitution, labour rackets and gambling, even a little money lending, kidnapping and protection.

Wherever there's a buck to be made you can bet Jevon Earl is taking a cut somewhere along the line."

"And massage clubs," I said.

Travers smiled and said. "You catch on quick."

"I've done a little digging, that's all."

"Well yeah, massage parlours too, but that's not exactly high crimes and misdemeanours."

"Could be a front."

"For what? Jevon Earl doesn't need any fronts. He wants to do something he does it."

Peru wandered back to the van and returned a moment later with a huge hot dog. "Ouzanti and the politicians publicly write him and his bandits off as robbers, petty thieves. That way they can deny any presence of organised crime, and continue to reap the cream of private enterprise.

"We simply play baby-sitter and make sure they contain their business to the right end of town. Can't have them upsetting the high rollers or shooting the wrong people."

"What's Jevon Earl like?" I asked.

Peru smiled. "He's black."

"And he's mean," chipped in Travers.

"Snappy dresser, got a liking for the nice vehicles, always got a looker on his arm, you know the sort? But don't let him fool you, he's not one of your gentry wiseguys, who has a button man by his side. He likes to kill and he likes it up close and personal."

"Sounds a lot like organised crime," I said. "Casablanca aint supposed to be no mob town."

Peru laughed. "That's right. According to the dailies it isn't."

"For a long, long time Casablanca was totally clean, but like in Philly it gradually started heading down the bad road," said Travers. "It all came down to the killing of an attorney, high profile mob assassination."

Peru patted Travers on the shoulder. "I've been teaching my boys some history."

"This caused an almighty stink. The G boys were immediately dispatched."

"And as a result of their failure I got my big break."

"It took one hell of an effort, but we flushed them out. Most of them, anyway. It was like the old Wild West for a time, but we won the gunfight. Capone stayed clear, Lansky wasn't interested and Luciano got deported."

"And then in comes Earl."

"Mystery man from the deep south. Slowly but surely got a foothold, buying a piece of one thing and a share of another. Before you know where you are, he's the man. Did all his own jobs in the early days, you see. Hell of a lot bigger risk, but if you show a clean pair of heels there's no-one to drop you in the shit."

"Rumour has it he moved from Harlem. Once upon a time East Harlem was a Jewish stronghold, but all this changed with the assassination of Dutch Schultz and the Sicilians and Negros took over the whole place. Seems Jevon Earl was one of those two-bit hoodlums."

"Then why come to Casablanca?"

"Who knows? Never did get to ask him that one. Something happened, that's for sure. Whether he got fed up with being a small fish in a big pond, or was ostracised for some misdeed, nobody seems to know. Whatever the real reason was, he holed up here in Casablanca and that's when things started turning bad again."

"Then why not hit him with everything you got? If you did it before with the big boys, why not again with the pretender?"

Peru and Travers exchanged glances.

"One reason," began Peru, "is that Jevon Earl has been a gentleman gangster. Okay, so he arrived in a blaze of glory, leaving a trail of destruction wherever he went, but that was simply a means to an end. He needed to eliminate all rivals to attain overall control."

"Only nobody controls this town but Ishmail Ouzanti."

"That's right. In a way Earl helped us in cleaning out all the petty gangs, nipped them in the bud before they got a chance to grow. Ouzanti figured it was better to have one enemy than a thousand would-be enemies. That way you can deny there's a mob presence, after all it's the tit for tat executions, buckwheats

138

and machine gun fights that draw people's attention. Earl kept all of that out of Casablanca."

"So when it's all been cleaned up for you, you hit him right between the eyes when he least expects it."

"That's exactly what we did," he said. "We waited and waited, patience being the thing. And when the time was right we got the green light and went after him."

"We used every man we could get hold of, raided the brothels, shut down the illegal gambling dens, picketed the strikes, followed every known man in his stable morning, noon and night. You know what we got him on?"

Before I could answer Peru continued, "Jack shit, that's what we got on Earl personally. Everything we could close we fuckin' closed. Lots of his guys were put away for a long time."

"But nothing you could get him with personally?"

Peru shrugged. "You want to know what we were left with?"

"Don't tell me."

"Yup, tax evasion. The whole department worked around the clock for three weeks and the only thing that would stick was his greed in not giving Uncle Sam his fair share."

I chuckled. "Puts him in rather illustrious company."

"Sure does, only Earl didn't do time."

"Neither did he go fuckin' nuts with syphilis nibbling his brain."

"What happened?" I asked, but Peru shrugged it off.

"Nothing we had could be certain of personally implicating Earl. He may have been a cold-blooded murderer, but he was a fuckin' clever one."

"Or his accountant was," chipped in Travers.

"Yeah, or his fuckin' accountant was." He sighed. "Numbers geeks ha, supposed to be the dullest of professions in the world, yet most of them wouldn't sneeze at keeping a made man's books in order and his ass out of jail."

"Tax evasion's a complicated business, if you don't have everything in black and white."

"And you didn't?"

Peru shrugged again. "Needles and haystacks."

"We could find no written records of the transactions. For the complicated system they used there must have been a ledger, a book, probably in code or something."

"Without that we were always up against it. All the skimmed money, the profits from the ill gotten gains, the dirty money, all of it just disappeared. We got several bag men from various establishments linked to Earl, but nothing that directly led to the top…"

"They were all washing it at various little banks around the State, sometimes using a positively baffling pyramid system of deposit. Some of them went down, some escaped the net but every single fall guy stayed loyal and kept Earl's name out of it."

"The ones that got off disappeared, the ones that went down quietly did their time. Nobody was turned which left us scratching our heads and questioning our own minds. Was Jevon Earl not really the man he was supposed to be?"

"But."

"Oh, he was in charge alright. When the dust settled and he was finally cleared he sent me a case of champagne."

"Cheeky son of a bitch."

Peru grunted.

"Couple of days later I got the call to cool off. Things have generally run smoothly since then. Earl's so good he don't need to kill people anymore. The crime rate is low, therefore our jobs are a whole lot easier."

"Until now."

He smiled. "Until now."

Peru polished off the hot dog and wiped the mustard from his face with the back of his hand. "One thing is for sure," he said. "If Jevon Earl is involved in this thing – which he now fucking is whether he likes it or not – then it's gonna be messy. We're gonna have to wade waist high through shit."

"You think your men can now find their motivation?" I asked, but did not wait for an answer.

Peru strolled on down the wide sidewalk. The far East side of town was one of the better areas, but still showed little resemblance to the Casablanca of old. Tall, sixty-foot palms towered over the wide boulevard, but the olde worlde architecture was replaced by a network of cellar joints and flaring night spots, flashing with neon. Traffic was heavy and the constant hum of a busy city purred out.

"I think it's time to lay a few cards on the table, Black," he said. "Straighten a few things out."

I flared up a Lucky, offering the light to Peru as he squeezed a cigarillo between his lips. "Maybe you're right," I agreed.

"Tell me, what was it you did to upset our benevolent Uncle Ishmail?"

"From what I remember, Ouzanti is anything but benevolent."

Peru smiled. "You just took a right turn, Black. I thought we were gonna play a little."

"It'll come," I said honestly, catching Travers oily smirk. "Let's take a drink, I've got half an hour."

The nearest bar was called The Crow and was doing plenty of business. There was no shortage of atmosphere, cigar smoke obscuring any visibility of the decor. The three of us found a table and a waitress took our orders. She returned a minute later with the drinks and then disappeared into the smog. A small orchestra were playing somewhere in the background.

"Tell me more about Ouzanti," I said. "Does he still rule Casablanca with an iron fist?"

Peru studied me slowly for a moment before answering. "Ishmail Ouzanti does what he thinks is right. He has no compunctions in attaining that end. Have you ever heard one of his sermons?"

"Oh yes."

"Incredible don't you think? I go when I feel like packing it all in. I'm yet to find God or offer my services for doorstep collections, but it sure makes you feel like trying again. You leave that church with a hell of a lot more purpose than when you went in, and that's got fuck all to do with religion and love they neighbour. It's the power of the spoken word."

I nodded. "He still gives Huey Long a run for his money?"

Peru sipped his beer, before putting the bottle on the table. "And to answer your question, yes and no. Uncle Ishmail has been the top man in this town for as long as anyone can remember. As you've probably noticed by now, things have changed. Everywhere changes, but not at the top."

"There aint a fruit machine drops a dime without Uncle Ishmail knowing about it. He knows the hookers and their mothers, the dealers, the petty thieves and all the would be wideboys."

"And so do you, right?"

"I'm learning, that's for sure, but Ouzanti is the man. He grinds the grapes and makes the wine."

"What about the rumours. Is there anything in them?"

"You've heard them too, eh?" He shook his head. "No, Ishmail Ouzanti is many things, but I don't think a criminal is one of them. Breaking the law is below him. He prefers to stand above it."

"Sounds to me like he did a deal with Jevon Earl. Maybe he's not as benevolent as he'd like us all to think."

Peru and Travers said nothing.

"Come on guys, something happened. Capone had Cermak in his pocket, maybe it's the same with Earl and Senator Ouzanti."

"You're dreaming, Black. If you knew him, you wouldn't believe a word of it. Ishmail Ouzanti is in nobody's pocket, that's a fact."

I wasn't sure. For a man with such a wide base of power he had remained remarkably clean. Maybe he'd had Kalac killed. I suggested as much but Peru brushed it aside.

"Why on earth would he do that? As you've already noticed, Casablanca has lost a good deal of its natural charm and beauty since the good old days. Love him or hate him, Uncle Ishmail is slowing that decline. The CRC are running the town like a Roman Empire and a lot of people like the way they're going about it. That's got to be good. He's not into murder. This kind of thing only blows up bad."

"I read the papers," I said. "Not a word."

"Ah, but the press can only be silenced for so long. Burglars and thieves rather than gangsters and killers. But soon enough, his pocket will not be big enough. Favours are one thing, but like anything else, they run out."

I admitted there was little point in that theory. And Peru was right, the media would soon rediscover their freedom. I decided to pursue another question.

"Who's behind the developments?" I asked. "The dog centre, the casino, they're popping up everywhere. Is that Ouzanti too, or McSwarve, or Earl?"

Peru jiggled the ice in his drink and lit up another cigarillo. "This give and take session seems a tad one sided, Black. I'm on my home park, yet I get the feeling I'm playing blind. Come on boy, we've had the pleasantries, we've done the stand off, now are we gonna shake hands or have a shoot-out?"

"I'm just trying to fill some gaps. There's plenty to go at. I need background on all the maybes, the possibilities and the no ways."

He held up both hands like he was shouting house. "Woe, woe. I don't think you're listening. I'm done with answers. I got a few questions first."

I nodded. "Okay."

"You've been acting the tough guy ever since you got here. Mean sonofabitch, who only works alone and all that bullshit. That's fine, maybe that's who you are, but I'll tell you somebody you're not. And that's the fresh faced tourist."

He smiled. "You've got a history in this town, Black, and I don't know if it's Uncle Ishmail, or McSwarve or even Wentz. But there's a story and I wanna hear it."

"I don't know who I can trust, that's all."

"Neither do I, least of all you, but I don't seem to have a choice."

A brief silence followed.

I sucked a deep breath of smoke and exhaled.

"I remember Ishmail from years back. I was only a young man then. A fresh faced kid, new to the game. I didn't think he'd remember, but I should have known better. The man's a great white elephant."

He smiled a sardonic smile.

"I had a fling with his god daughter, the apple of his eye. Things didn't work out and that was that; eternal damnation from the Uncle. I don't know if you know her. She's still around, I think."

The orchestra stopped and there was a wild round of applause. Arthur Peru and Jackson Travers didn't clap. They stayed frozen to the spot, without moving and inch. Eventually it was Travers that found his voice.

"You had a fling with the lovely Sarah? How long ago was this?"

"Long enough for me to forget her second name. It was no big deal, only Ishmail had her down as his own Virgin Mary."

"So you left town." It was Peru, the glazed look on his face clearing.

"It was one of the reasons. There were others. Tonight he was probably as shocked as I was. Two blows to his authority in one night. He'll get over it."

"I doubt it. He wants this thing over, and fast."

"You better keep your distance," said Peru. "At least don't make a scene. The girl's married now, and I don't need a scandal right now. You got that?"

"Sure," I lied. "Whatever you think."

"What else you keeping?" asked Peru, placated a little. "Tell me about Wentz."

"Nothing to tell. We were friends from way back. Did a little business together, swapped girlfriends, that sort of thing." I finished my drink and ordered another. "We lost touch about five years ago. I only found out he'd wound up in Casablanca when he was going cold on the block."

"How do you remember him?" he persisted.

I sucked the life out of the butt and stubbed it out. Brushing over the truth was one thing, raking up the long buried past was another.

"He was a good man. Natural lady-killer; tall, dark, handsome, with the charm to go with it. He wasn't a bad detective either, but tended to prefer the small meat."

"Did he gamble?"

"Sure he did. Don't we all? But he rarely lost. Had good contacts in every field. Hermeez was a walking yellow pages."

"Which obviously helps, in this line of business."

"Sure, but he wasn't practising here, right? Not in Casablanca?"

Peru and Travers swapped glances.

"Because he was retired, right?"

Peru shrugged. "Okay, I'll square with you."

My heart skipped a beat.

"No, he wasn't practising. That's what we think, but then he wasn't part of our regular script and he had no reason to be."

"But?"

"But," sighed Peru deeply. "He did occasionally pop up on surveillance tapes, covert photographs, that sort of thing. There was nothing wrong, or even out of the ordinary, but he did enjoy both Jarvis McSwarve's and Jevon Earl's company. Even Uncle Ishmail went to dinner with him."

"And?"

"And nothing. That's it. He was a face and now he's a dead face."

"Come on, where's all this leading?"

Peru looked at Travers who shrugged. "Did you enjoy yourself at the dogs the other night?"

I smiled ruefully. "I would have enjoyed it a lot more if I had a pony on that thirty threes outsider in the last."

"Like Wentz, you mean?"

"Like Wentz, yeah. Especially if it was on a treble with several thousand dollars riding on it."

"The Racing Commission have launched an enquiry. Until it is finished all bets are suspended."

"I see. You think that maybe this ties in with the killings? Fuckin' dog racing leading to two guys getting shot to death in their own pads?"

"I'm trying to draw up an angle, that's all. First, Wentz is chilled, then Tony Kalac goes in a similar way."

"And not only are they both shot to death they both would have won a lot of money if they weren't shot to death," chipped in Travers. "Money they both needed, because they both owed people."

Peru sighed. "Maybe there's something in Jackson's theory, maybe not. I'm just trying to draw up an angle, that's all"

"You should have thought about your angle when he was killed in the first place."

Peru didn't rise.

The waitress returned with another round of drinks. I graciously accepted and she turned and went away. I watched her tight, round ass all the way through the bar.

"Let's get back to the suspects, the players in this game. What about Jarvis McSwarve? He's involved in both the race and in Hermeez Wentz's money situation."

Peru chuckled. "You're reaching in the dark, Black. Why is that?"

Travers interjected. "McSwarve's got as much of a vested interest in this as Ouzanti. There's no reason for him to rock the boat. You want to be careful saying things like that about Jarvis McSwarve."

"Come on boys," I protested. "What's going on here? McSwarve is right there in the middle of this, and yet you continually warn me off. First, it was don't go to The Penitence, now it's don't even mention his name."

"Which you ignored," said Peru sternly.

"I was curious. I still am. Jarvis McSwarve is an interesting guy and whether you like it or not he is linked to Wentz."

"He's clean," said Peru. "In fact he's cleaner than clean and you're just going to have to trust me on this one. I don't want you wandering in on his setup, especially now that I know you had a thing with his wife."

"That's history," I lied.

"Good. Keep it that way!"

There was a short pause. Peru interrupted it, "No," he said. "If we are looking for names it's difficult to look past Jevon Earl. We're just gonna have to figure out why."

"What's the CRC? What's it all about?"

Peru paused and I could see he was debating himself whether to tell me. Finally he did.

"It's no big secret, Errol."

I smiled in acceptance of first name recognition. Maybe I would call the big man Arthur.

"The Casablanca Regeneration Committee are doing just that, regenerating this old town of ours. They're the good to Jevon Earl's bad."

I felt like protesting, but kept my mouth shut. Maybe now he was really ready to talk. Quibbles about the Yellow Brick Road could come later, he didn't need that pointing out now. What I really wanted to know was who was on this band of Roman Emperors.

"The developments you mentioned. That's all down to the CRC. The greyhound centre, the casino, a fleet of high-class clubs and diners. They also run programs, extensive training and education schedules for future high flyers.

"But that's not all. Using the CRC as his base, Uncle Ishmail has cut the town down the middle. You've probably noticed the stark differences. Believe me they are not all bad. Take a walk down the Trimbles and you'll think you're back with that old lover you wished you'd never left. That old feeling will grip you again and every desire will be catered for in triplicate.

"You see to begin with he tried the clear out. The old Communist method of banning the church, executing the academia, only in reverse. It didn't take long to see that it would never work. The scum are a lot more difficult to flush out than the cream. So he just built a wall, an invisible wall, that is policed not only by me, but by the very people he despised."

"A side of good and one of evil."

"Add the religion to it all and yeah, you're not far from the truth. But to the most it's simply a system of class or caste. There's nothing new here."

I looked at my watch. It was nearly nine, so I set off to leave. "Just one more question before I gotta go."

"The names? Come to the office tomorrow morning. I'll give you a list. Now I'm gonna get some sleep."

"Okay."

"And Errol…" he stood up and offered a chubby paw. I shook it and turned to go. "No scandal, you hear me? No fuckin' scandal."

When the mist cleared, the moon pushed its way though and shone brightly over a troubled town. Looking up into the dark sky, illuminated by a beautiful array of sparkling stars, it was easy to be lost in another world. Away from bloody corpses, and drive through gun battles. Where the Jevon Earls of the world had no place.

Chapter Twenty-Five – The Ranch

It was past nine when I set off for the vineyard. The sun was a massive red orb, slowly descending behind the horizon. A race against the sun was one I didn't mind losing. The elements could happily keep a secret. I reached the old stone bridge that ties the huge vineyard to the outskirts of Casablanca, just as the night was taking over.

I crossed the bridge and the trees disappeared. As I drove over the rim of the Earth, the tall, spindly vines took over. For miles around, there was nothing but grape vines. The narrow, gravel drive wove in and out through the huge hundred acre plantations.

There were no streetlights on the road to the ranch, but the sun would soon be replaced with the moon. It tempted the insects, fauna and forest life to one last odyssey, before disappearing for another night. Within seconds, night had fallen and another world had taken over. And then it was dark.

The ranch stood at the end of the track. A large, wooden structure, ghost-like in the moonlight, surrounded by several garages, dwarf conifers and yards of landscaped garden. At the foot of the garden was another building, primarily for the hired hands and workers, but more suited as a luxury holiday home. Dog kennels and rabbit hutches were to the side of the small, square pool. Leaves floated on the surface of the water, which glistened in the moonlight.

Past feelings, long since disposed of, came swimming back.

I parked the car outside the first double garage and got out. The air was warm and sticky, and I found myself wiping my brow. Somewhere in the distance the ocean was crashing over the pebbled beach.

I remembered this as such a happy place. We would all sit together on the patio, sipping wine under a scorching sun. The two lively dogs would playfully wrestle each other, whilst keeping a keen eye on the barbeque. Any stray sausage would be hungrily devoured, and any hint of a tickle would be gleefully accepted.

I took out my weapon and put it into the trunk of the car. A solitary bird was singing a melancholy love song. I took the gun out of the trunk and put it back in my shoulder holster. A strange feeling of guilt washed over me, as I edged around the house towards the seaward porch. My cheeks were burning and it was a feeling that was difficult to shake.

Looking over the ocean was the white, square porch. It was adjoined to the main house by a long, narrow corridor with the walls and ceiling made entirely of glass. Thick shrubbery covered the translucent walls, giving it the feeling of a greenhouse. I walked down towards it, listening to the rustle of leaves underfoot.

Unsure if I was ready for this, I fumbled in my coat pocket for the comforting packet of Luckys. Before I had one between my lips, I remembered the old rules. There would be no smoking inside of the ranch. Sarah's uncle decreed this as the only definitive house rule. He was the owner, although infrequent lodger, of the whole vineyard, and was a grand old man. In the old days we talked and talked and talked. A strict, moral man with an unerring sense of family loyalty.

A shiver rolled down my spine. I was ready.

She was standing just outside the porch, facing the black of the ocean. Although her back was to me, I knew her eyes were shut. Her head was tilted slightly back as she exercised her own memories.

A gentle tune from the past began ringing in my ears, and at first I wasn't sure if it was actually playing aloud or just in the tainted past. A few more steps and I was standing only a couple of feet behind her. She must have sensed a presence and turned around.

Frozen in time, like an angel, she was crowned by the glint of the moon. Her blue, oval eyes looked startled and innocent. Time had forgotten to move on, leaving Sarah as beautiful and regal as I will always remember her. The scant light from the moon silhouetted her trim legs neatly etched behind a cotton skirt that rested just above her knees.

She smiled nervously and held out her arms. I instinctively took her hands in my own. The haze of the night seeped in through my pores, a mist of unreality filling me with worry. Her soft, warm hands felt good, but I could feel the trouble they

150

exuded. All the hate, the misery and the death knell of history would never leave me.

"Oh Errol," she whispered huskily, as the music upped a tempo in my head.

She eased closer towards me and I found her in my arms, clinging on like a frightened puppy.

The wind skimmed off the ocean, blowing hauntingly all around us. Her golden hair was swirling, whipping over my shoulders, covering and uncovering her perfect face.

As the shadows shielded her in flashes, I was well and truly in the past. Her scent, her warmth, her energy.

She gently moved against me. Her breasts heaving in the soft, cotton blouse brushed menacingly against my chest. Fingers fluttered down the back of my neck, delicate like a butterfly. I felt a shiver, a pang of desire, of need, which had become alien in my life since before.

But now was not before.

She took a step back, and in the blink of an eye the clothes were gone. A heap dropped to the floor and she gracefully stepped away.

Naked.

Beautiful.

I smoothed my hands slowly over the swell of her buttocks, pulling her towards me. She responded, hooking her arms around my neck, rocking gently side to side. I was immediately rock hard and becoming desperate to be relieved of my clothes. She duly obliged, fumbling awkwardly, eventually unfastening my belt and pushing the hurdles away.

"Errol, I've missed you so much. Where have you been?"

"Where you sent me, honey. Where you sent me," I thought, but before the bitterness returned she reached down and caressed me.

I released my grip and let my hand slip down the back of her thigh. The anticipation was building up tremendously, as I opened out my hand and trailed a finger back up sensitively. She murmured, urging herself forcefully against it. Pushing a little further, I could feel her warmth and she clamped together trapping my hand in the moist within.

As I eased her gently to the cushioned floor a hot, heady feeling of sheer intensity engulfed me. It was a feeling I had not experienced for some years, but welcomed with open arms. I was now in the land of the never. Nothing else existed, or ever likely would, ever again. No guns, no bodies, no heavies, no Casablanca. Together we ascended to another dimension, electricity charging through us like a thunderbolt.

I looked at her face; so soft, unblemished, so innocent, so beautiful. Her eyes were tightly shut and she held her arms out at her sides, her hands folded into fists, with white knuckles. She arched her back and bit her lip as I teased her, running my fingers around her breasts, circling the nipples slowly before brushing down further towards her warmth. As I reached lower, she thrust roughly against me and pulled me down so our bodies were pressing together tightly. Our mouths met and our tongues lashed wildly.

I moved my hand further, and she began to tremble, urging me on, groping with her hands, sucking with her mouth. I lowered my mouth to her breasts, one then the other, kissing, sucking, licking, as she grasped me roughly and tugged back and forth.

Crying out she pushed away my hand and pulled me gently into her. I slid in first time, plunging deep into her intimate domain. So smooth and warm, I felt totally engulfed as we drove on together, whimpering and crying as one.

As we came there was nothing else. Nothing.

But it all came back.

One night cannot change a lifetime. A thought I had clung to throughout it all. In dreams, or fantasies maybe. There it had all been different and things evened out; became good again.

Chapter Twenty-Six – After

Lying back in post-coital satisfaction, I failed to stop the memories flood my brain. The sound of the sea lapping wildly against the rocks proved a good catalyst. As did the soft, warm, beautiful figure in my arms. I suddenly realised that I had a desperate need to know the truth. I had got so far, surviving on bitterness, on scant theories and circumstantial evidence, but I needed to know. To hear it from her own sweet lips.

I looked down at her flustered face. She was nestled tightly against my breast, breathing gently and peacefully. Never did I think the opportunity would arise, but then had it really done so? She failed to utter any explanation in the past, scurrying away into a hidden world. Why would things be different now?

I wanted to shake her. To awaken her and interrogate her like a prisoner. To find out why she left me, why she abandoned me, and why she tried to have me killed. But when her eyes opened with a start and then she smiled a wonderful smile, I didn't. I simply kissed her softly and pulled the blanket snug over our naked bodies.

"Why did you come, Errol?" she asked.

"You asked me to, honey."

She wrinkled her nose and yawned a sleepy yawn. "Is that the only reason?"

"No, but it's a good one. And better than saying I missed you since the day we parted. That I needed to see you again, to feel you, touch you and do what we just did together."

"That's why I left the note and I don't mind admitting it."

I ran a hand through her silky hair. Running my rough fingers through all that history.

"And does your husband mind you admitting it?"

She looked out into the ocean, as if searching for an answer in its dark midst. She found one.

"All I know is that my husband is away for a couple of days. He's away most evenings, not that that is an excuse. The only excuse I need is that I have missed you so very much. I loved you then and I have loved you ever since. I know we don't have much of a future together but I guessed you're gonna be in town for a while."

"And while I'm here you thought you'd rekindle an old romance?"

"Is that so bad, Errol? What's wrong with a little romance?"

What indeed? I pondered her suggestion and immediately wondered just whether she really meant it. Would it be possible to simply go back and pick up the past as easily as all that? Become that young naive, optimistic man I was before. We could hold hands as we walked the beach, we could go dancing on an evening and feed each other oysters and ice cream. Maybe I would pack in the weed and start drinking dry white wine again. For a brief moment it all seemed like a good idea. Plausible and most very attractive. But the moment passed.

I would never be that man again. And I ventured Sarah would never be that little girl that found me so daring and attractive. Too much water, too many bridges and all that. I was here for a job, but when I reminded myself of the fact I got annoyed. Wherever I tread land mines scattered the field, there were side-tracks at every point along the way. But when I looked at her perfect face my heart still missed that beat. I revelled in the moment when our bodies became one and the warm afterglow, but eventually the reality crept up and woke me up.

I decided that tonight was gonna be a one off. Husbands tend to get in the way of sweeping romances. And Jarvis McSwarve was no ordinary husband. I released her suddenly and began gathering my clothes together.

She twisted around and looked up at me. "How long are you staying, Errol?"

"As long as it takes. A good friend of mine has been murdered. When it's finished I will be leaving."

"I hope it takes a long time," she said, looking at me as I began to dress. "Who was he?"

"That doesn't matter sweetheart. Look I gotta go."

She sat up, leaning naked against the side, her pert breasts outlined by the fading moon. "I'll be here on Wednesday, the same time," she whispered. "We've a lot of catching up to do."

154

The warm feeling in my belly was now burning deep. I needed to hear her side of the story, but it sounded like she was reading a different book.

"You will come back won't you, Errol?" she whispered again, more desperately than before and placed a velvet hand on my chest.

I shrugged. "Maybe I shouldn't have come back in the first place."

"How can you even think that?"

Tears welled in her eyes. "When I saw you yesterday on Waterside I nearly died. You were watching me too weren't you? You didn't think I was looking. And then at the dogs, it all flooded back again. All those feelings, all those memories they just hit me like a big wave." She rubbed her hands up and down over my half dressed body. "You feel it too, Errol, I know you do."

The anger sneaked up on me before I had a chance to recognise it.

"Don't play games with me, Sarah. Not after all these years. You left remember?" I said bitterly.

"But I didn't want to. I loved you."

My hand instantly went to my shoulder and I rubbed the scar. Her eyes followed my hand and she quickly looked away. She picked up her cotton blouse and fumbled with it clumsily. I waited, but it seemed the subject was closed.

The telephone started ringing, drowning out the sound of the waves.

"Are you going to answer that?" I asked, fastening my shirt up.

"I better, it'll probably be Jarvis," she said, smiling at me sheepishly. "Promise you won't go, Errol. Not just yet. We need to talk. I'll be right back." She wrapped herself in the blanket and set off for the door. "I wanted to visit you there, I promise I did."

I slipped out of the back entrance before she returned. Tonight had been one big mistake, but already I knew that wasn't true. Pangs of regret were all over me before I reached the bridge. I stopped the car and sat staring into the night.

Chapter Twenty-Seven -Where it all began

By the time I got back to town, the sky had blackened over and the rain returned. I had a couple of hours to kill so I found a bar with an empty chair and enjoyed a beer. Then another, and another. I should have felt good; having just left the bed of a beautiful woman I was awaiting the invitation to that of another. But as I sat back, letting the cold nectar trickle down my throat a most grisly feeling overcame me.

I thought of Hermeez. His death was definitely no burglary gone wrong. I was certain of that much. There was a whole lot more to it, and I was gonna be the one to find out what. Arthur Peru would be a lot more useful with Uncle Ishmail on his back. But when it came down to it, it had to be me, nobody else's version would suffice. Only when I knew for sure, could the ghost be laid to rest.

I called Timmy, but he wasn't there so I left a message for him to catch me at The Dockside. He would have other things to do, but his mind would not be fully focused. Like me, Hermeez and Timmy had been buddies. He was as curious to find out the truth as I was.

The night I took the call was now a blur. It was only two weeks ago but the whole evening was a blur...

It had been a bitterly cold New York night. There was snow coming down hard, making a snug blanket over most of the City. It had taken me twenty minutes to get home from Joe's, but at least the chains did their job. When I arrived, the telephone was going bananas.

I slung my wet clothes in the laundry and poured myself a large Remy, as the phone rang out. Tired and cold, I almost left it to itself and turned in for the night. Instead I poured myself another large one and picked up the receiver.

"Errol, where the hell have you been? Listen, I've got some bad news, Hermeez is dead."

It was Timmy, the new police Captain of homicide. He sounded upset and tired. He told me all he knew, which wasn't much. Hermeez was dead, that is all that mattered. We talked and talked as we drank ourselves silly over the telephone. Reminiscing had never been a strong point for either of us, and death was a regular associate, but for some reason Hermeez's death took us both off guard. He was less likely to die than either of us and so we were unprepared. A lot of things go through your mind when you lose one of your own. It drives it ever closer to home that we are all expendable. One day there will be a bullet with your name on and there's nothing you can do about it, so you might as well accept it. It happened so often in the lives of us all, so to feel upset and actually mourn is no longer a natural reaction. With Hermeez, we made an exception.

Death dehumanises us all. Sometimes to the point of becoming unimportant, and therefore superfluous. But with the good guys you can usually reach it again, the bygone of emotions and feelings. Circumstances may give you a leg up or an extra urge to just reach out that extra inch, and then you wish you hadn't bothered. Wouldn't it be easier if we could just shrug our shoulders and get on with it. Catch the bad guys and pump them full of lead in return. I said as much to Timmy but he threw it all back in my face.

"That's what sets us apart," he said. "We're allowed to feel emotions."

I think maybe Timmy cried, although he denied it ever since.

Hell so did I, but I'm dammed if I can explain it.

Hermeez had wound up in Casablanca. Timmy was concerned that the police there would sweep it under the carpet. There were already indications that they were gonna do just that. He was concerned that our buddy had been murdered, but would be remembered as a cheap no good punk, shot down by amateurs. He didn't believe that was true. Neither did I.

That's how it all began. I knew Casablanca from way back. I would be perfect to go down there, as a federal agent and find out what really happened. I had done a considerable amount of work for the Government during the War and was still on their books. So had Hermeez. It wouldn't be too difficult to arrange, I would be going freelance but with semi-official status. Timmy Matthews, well respected police captain, would fix it with the locals and act as my controller.

I finished my beer and left that bar. Well Timmy, maybe it's just too big for you to control. A shiver went down my spine. I lifted my collar and strode out.

157

Chapter Twenty-Eight – Liona

I spotted the hostess at just after two and she hopped in.

"I thought maybe you had a better offer for the night," she said.

"I did."

"You were gonna be nice to me," she said, showing her innocent face.

I smiled. "Where to?"

"Keep going straight ahead, I have an apartment looking over the bay."

I kept driving until she told me to stop, then pulled into the kerb and killed the engine. She was out before I could open the door for her and skipping towards the apartment block. The apartment was small, but homely with no illusions of grandeur. The elevator took an age, and creaked like a haunted house, but eventually took us to the third floor.

She fumbled in her purse until she found her key. I flicked on the light switch and took a seat.

I threw my hat on a stand in the corner and the hostess brought over a pair of drinks.

"Maybe we should introduce ourselves. I'm Liona, humble, but happy club hostess."

"Errol Black. Pleased to meet you, Liona. I chase bad guys."

She threw her head back and smiled. "I thought as much, and I bet you don't carry a badge either."

"That's right." I lit a Lucky and handed it to Liona. She repaid the favour.

"Was Hermeez Wentz a bad guy?" she asked, putting on that all too innocent face again.

"Depends on which side of the fence you're sitting. What do you think? I believe that it was you and your friends that attended to his needs?"

She blew a pair of perfectly round smoke rings and put on a thoughtful look. "He always seemed the perfect gentleman to me. Kind, generous, charming. He came to the club frequently, had a few drinks, watched the show and most nights then

158

disappeared into the back room. He always had a girl as company. Sometimes one of ours, but not always. I don't think buying girls drinks makes him a bad guy."

"What's in the back room, Liona?"

"Usual thing. Roulette wheel, blackjack, backgammon you know. Only for the inner circle."

She moved closer and hooked her arm into mine.

"Did you drink with him?"

"No, I never got the opportunity. I brought over his order a few times, but never got any further than that. Did he really owe you money, Errol, only he never struck me as short of a few dollars."

"No he didn't owe me honey," I said crunching the ice from my empty glass. "But there are plenty"

She replenished the drinks and sat back down. "Is that your assignment, finding money for all the sharks. Isn't it enough that he was killed?"

"Wrong again sweetheart. I want to know just who it was that pumped a slug into him. And why."

Now she looked puzzled. "It said in the papers it was a house robbery. He just got in the way. You don't believe it, eh?"

"Who owns the club honey, and why did Hermeez disappear most nights?"

She shrugged. "A slime ball called Clyde Gabriel. I'm sorry, Errol, I'm not much help, am I?"

"You're plenty help honey," I said. "Tell me a little about Clyde Gabriel."

She shrugged. "What's to tell? You saw him; he's small, fat and disgustingly ugly. He's tried it on with nearly all of the girls and the biggest shame is that most of them think it's a ticket to a better life."

"Not you though, honey?"

She pulled a face like she was sucking a lemon.

"Were Clyde and Hermeez pals? Did they talk ever?"

She shrugged. "A little."

I edged closer to Liona, put my hand to her cheek and put on my most reassuring face. "Listen, Liona. Hermeez Wentz was

159

not just a guy who got killed. He's not just another investigation, do you hear me?"

She nodded.

"And you're right, he was not a bad guy. He was not a bad guy at all. He was a friend, and a damn good one at that." I softened my voice an octave, "If you did find out anything, anything at all, you're better off telling me about it right now. I'll make sure you're safe, I promise."

"Errol, you don't know what Clyde is like. He can be very scary, that's why none of the girls cross him."

"Did Hermeez cross him?"

She didn't say anything for a full minute. I didn't want to push her any further, not just yet. She had something to say, but was too frightened to say it.

"You can trust me, Liona. Hell, we've been here in your flat for a good half an hour and I haven't even tried to kiss you yet."

"Maybe you should," she said, but her eyes weren't smiling.

I did.

She tasted good; a little smoky but it was nice.

"There's a rumour going around the girls."

"A rumour, what about?"

"A couple of weeks ago one of the dancers, Francoise, disappeared, did a moonlight flit. Emptied her apartment and just vanished into thin air."

"Maybe she got tired of the life."

Liona nodded. "Maybe, only the day before she left she paid a month's advance on her rent. Why would she do that if she knew she was going to up and leave?"

"I don't know. Do you?"

She shook her head. "No, but tonight when I ask around about Hermeez Wentz everybody clams up as if they never heard of him, when I know that they did. All except one girl, Brandi with an 'i'. She tells me the rumour."

I waited.

"She says that Francoise was instructed by Clyde to go to Hermeez Wentz's flat. He gave her the address. She was to go there and wait for Wentz to return."

"Why not pick him up and go with him?"

"Apparently Hermeez would not go for it, so she was to wait and enter the apartment when he arrived home. Get him a little drunk, seduce him a little and…"

"And what?"

"And drug him. She was given some pills by Clyde."

"And then what?"

She shook her head. "Nothing. Just leave the flat with the door unlocked. Oh, Errol, you don't think that this has anything to do with the murder do you?"

"Probably not, but you were right to tell me. Now what happened? Did Francoise do what Gabriel instructed her, did she drug him and leave the door open?"

She shook her head. "She waited outside for him, but he put her in a cab and sent her home. Now Francoise has disappeared and Brandi is worried that something has happened to her. She's leaving tomorrow."

"Does Clyde know that you know this? Did he hear you ask any of the girls?"

She shook her head. "Clyde heard nothing. I made out that I was curious about Francoise, and then they just told me to leave it. I don't think that they were suspicious. Do you think that I am in danger?"

I gently kissed her forehead. "The only danger you are in, is of making out with an old punk like me."

This time she smiled and kissed me again. "You're not a punk, Errol."

She stood up again and headed for the kitchen. When she returned she had a fresh bottle. She reached over and put it on the table, the thin nylon of her dress enhancing the firmness of her breasts. As she passed close I reached out and stopped her. She looked into my eyes and before I knew it she was in my arms, her mouth exploring mine. I pulled her close so I could feel every part of her delicious body rubbing against mine. She pushed my head back and kissed my neck, my shoulders and lips.

Just as I was getting lost in the pleasure of it all, I felt a pang of guilt. Guilt over what, I wasn't quite sure, but it was unmistaken. It just crept up and hit me right between the eyes.

Liona sensed it immediately and stopped.

"What is it, Errol?"

"It's nothing honey," I lied, trying to focus on her, but Sarah kept getting in the way.

"You're not…married are you?" she asked, pronouncing the union as if it were a felony.

"Would it matter if I were?"

She smiled. "Not at all." And she continued to plant little kisses on my neck and face.

But all the time she was there. Where Liona kissed me it felt like Sarah, when she looked up, it was Sarah's beautiful blue eyes piercing me.

Tonight I had seen her again after many, long years of pain and already she had cast a spell over me. It made me angry, hell did it make me angry. I must have slept with a dozen different women since her and I was damned if I was gonna be dictated to by her again. She was history, she was goddammned rotten history, whereas Liona was real. Liona was young and clean and fresh and real.

I kissed her anxiously, feeling her all over, trying desperately to extinguish Sarah from my mind. By now, I should have exorcised all the demons. I had returned to Sarah's bed and walked away. For some reason this did not appear to be enough. The satisfaction I had envisaged was not there. The feeling of smug superiority had failed to materialize and I realised I needed to do it again.

Liona pulled away and kissed my nose gently.

When I let go of her she smiled a sultry smile and stood up. Her deep blue eyes were embers ready to ignite. Her lips glistened and I wanted to kiss them again, but before I could she turned around and left the room.

"Won't be a moment Errol, promise."

I smiled, poured myself a drink from the fresh bottle on the table, closed my eyes and sat back comfortably. She was rummaging around in a drawer in what I assumed was the bedroom. My head was pumping hard with anticipation and my body was a nerve end. I gulped the drink and lit a Lucky as the

162

noise next door stopped. The zipping or unzipping of a garment made my grin wider. The ensuing silence made my mouth dry.

Liona had done well in a short space of time. It was a pity that this girl, Francoise, had done a runner, but I must talk to Brandi before she went the same way. Clyde Gabriel was another matter. I would approach him a little more carefully. Maybe Peru would fill me in a little. I smiled. Maybe this was the lead I had been looking for.

The silence continued deafeningly. I suddenly got a bad feeling.

Two guys killed.

One good, one bad.

Maybe both bad, but one not so bad.

Burglary gone wrong.

Hell, something was wrong here.

Footsteps pattered from the bedroom and stopped maybe a yard in front of me. I opened my eyes, half expecting to see a killer with a loaded gun. Pointed right at my head and a finger on the trigger. Or maybe my chest.

What I did see was not Liona. In so much as she didn't look the same as when she left. The dress was gone. She had an above the knee, clinging, satin robe. And nothing else. A cigarette glowed from between her lips.

"What do you think, Errol? Good?"

"On you, sweetheart. Yeah"

She stubbed out the cigarette and glided towards me. "You think it might look better on the floor?"

I tried to smile, but my eyes betrayed me. They hung heavy and tired from all the smoke and my body felt warm from the alcohol. I felt a warm tongue in my ear and edged away.

"A man is dead, Liona," I said. "Two men are dead, and soon there's gonna be more. Burglars don't kill in Casablanca, not with a .33 to the chest. So that makes it murder. Two murders."

Liona frowned and folded her arms.

"Now you're a beautiful girl, Liona, and I'm just the punk that's gonna find the murderer. An ageing punk with no money, who drinks and smokes too much."

"You aren't a punk, Errol."

"Oh believe me sweetheart, I am."

She moved towards me and before I could move away she straddled me, the robe riding her rounded thighs.

I tried to ignore her.

"I don't care what you say, Errol. I think that you are nice and I want to show you just how nice I am. You just shout out if you want to leave but I don't think that you're gonna do that are you?"

I sighed. "Just tell me something, honey. Why does a beautiful, young lady, who can probably have scores of men much younger, richer and nicer than me…"

She put a finger to my mouth and shushed me. Her breath was warm on my face. My hands were folded behind my head, supporting my neck and I didn't move as she slowly pulled open the robe and lowered it down her body. The material disappeared around my knees and she just sat there, her breasts gently wobbling in my face. She stayed silent now, a kind of nervous smile on her face, as I soaked up the view.

My curiosity was temporarily put on ice.

Chapter Twenty-Nine – Buddies

I was back at the station house by eight thirty the following morning. Clean shaven and wearing a freshly laundered shirt and trousers, with creases you could cut your finger on. For some reason I was cheerful. Liona thought I was nice. Rich and young, maybe not, but I was nice. I showed her just how damn nice.

Arthur Peru arrived soon after. He came in stomping his heavy boots that were covered in mud. He appeared to be wearing the same clothes as the last time I saw him, and the same expression, but he soon lightened up. He shed his heavy overcoat and pushed my feet off the desk with his briefcase.

"What the fuck are you so creamy about?"

"The sun, it's shining out there. What's with all the mud?"

"Oh that," he waved his paws as if swatting at a lion. "I've been watering the garden."

I nodded. "The garden."

"We had a good talk last night, Black. It's good to lay a few cards on the table," said Peru, opening his briefcase and pulling out a file of papers. "Maybe we can work together after all."

"That's all I ever wanted. Pulling in the same direction."

Peru looked at me hard and nodded. "Okay," he said. "Fill me in a little. Give me a progress report"

So I did.

I told him about Janice Crouter and the hoodlums. I told him about the diner, about Alison and about The Plaza Club. I went into great detail about The Casablanca Post, how there was little interest apart from the numbers in the diary.

He listened intently to all of it, but didn't interrupt. I went through the timetable of forty-eight, point by point, crossing off irrelevances and highlighting possible clues.

I told him a lot and I felt better for it. But I missed a lot out. I neglected to mention the mysterious redhead, or my run in with Benny Jacobs. And I said nothing of my information from Liona about Clyde Gabriel. Maybe I still didn't trust him, or maybe I wanted the case to be easy. I wasn't really sure, but for the moment my gut was telling me to hold a little back.

When I finished, Peru let out a little laugh.

"You know, Black. I think you are for real. Either that or Uncle Ishmail really did pick you off the theatre circuit."

"I told you, I'm not Ouzanti's boy. Hell, he wouldn't use me if Edgar offered him the Presidency."

Peru nodded. "Out at Kalac's pad I wasn't so sure. That little scene could have been choreographed."

"It was a bit melodramatic," I agreed.

"Melodrama is what the Senator likes. I don't need to tell you, he's an entertainer, but no, I think you might be on the level."

He continued to stare at me hard.

"It has been done before. Senator Ouzanti has placed a couple of federal agents in my care before today. Plants to report back to him and him only. Before now, they've been easy to sniff out, but you…you were different."

"Probably because I'm not a plant."

Peru nodded. "Probably, but you understand my caution? I run this squad whether the Senator likes it or not…"

"I thought you were a fan."

"Oh, I am. I think the man is brilliant. Right up there with Alexander The Great! But this is my show." He sighed. "He needs to learn a little compartmentalization."

"So where's the conflict?"

Peru shrugged. "Ouzanti doesn't like the look of some of our movements. He thinks we're going back after Jevon Earl."

"And are you?"

Peru laughed. "Who knows where the camel goes? It looks a distinct possibility, wouldn't you say?"

"You want to fill me in a little more?"

Peru's eyes widened. "You want more? Fuck, I think we pretty much got down to it last night. And this morning you want me to fuck you again?"

Peru's mood had soon become ebullient. He poured us both a cup of coffee and opened the window to his office, letting in the sound of downtown Casablanca and stifling the sound of any bugged conversation surviving the background noise. It had taken a while, but I think I now had the backing of the Police Captain.

"You never really thought it was a burglary, did you?"

"That was always the favourite outcome," he said cautiously, "but there was always going to be other more likely possibilities."

"And now?"

"We will have to see what happens. Things are likely to move fast. I think you may well get the adventure you came for."

He clinked my coffee cup.

"That is, if you are still planning on sticking around?"

"You bet."

He looked over his papers and gave the faintest hint of a smile. It was gone immediately. "Good. You'll be wanting these then," he said, handing me a couple of sheets of paper. "Kalac's autopsy report should be out this morning. Let's hope it turns up something new."

He pulled out a pencil from his inside pocket and lit it up. I did the same with a Lucky.

"Don't worry, I'll keep you posted."

I nodded. I believed he would.

"I'm gonna be here most of the day. If you're gonna stay on this thing, I want regular progress reports. Okay?"

"Okay."

"I've put a twenty-four hour tail on Jevon Earl and all his known shooters. It makes fuck all sense to me, icing your main powder man, but who knows what goes through these wacko's heads? If it is Earl that's doing the killing, and we now appear to have a reason to suggest it is, then it could be a double-cross."

"Money."

"Perhaps."

"Maybe he's restructuring the business. Putting more of the loot in his own bank account, and less in the minions."

Peru grunted and killed the pencil. "Risky," he said. "Ever since he crossed the Uncle, back in '42, he's kept to the rules. Earl may be a ruthless, nasty sonofabitch but he's not stupid. He knows Uncle Ishmail has more eyes and ears than Big Brother. Any alteration to the status quo would not be appreciated. Upsets the apple cart and then nobody gets a piece of the pie."

"So what's the motive?" I asked, expectantly.

167

"That's what we gotta find out. If it is Earl there's got to be a reason. A big fuckin reason, and we're gonna be right there in the ringside seats when the curtain falls. And if it's not Earl there's gonna be a blood bath. This has been his town for going on five years now. Half his town anyway, as long as he sticks to the rules, which he has, meticulously. So if somebody's peeking their nose through the door and testing the water for a coup, Jevon Earl is gonna cut it off. And his mother's, his father's and all his children's too, 'cause that's what he's like."

I grinned a wide toothy grin and stood up. "And I thought I was here catching burglars."

Peru didn't smile. "Officially you still are. Don't go making waves, okay. Wentz is still your baby, not Kalac. There's no proven link...yet. And maybe there's not gonna be. You wanted the local talent, it's all there for you," he pointed at the papers he had given me, "but remember what I told you. Jevon Earl is the only bandit that counts. Every name on that list answers to him."

"I think I got the picture."

"Good. Let's hope my peeping Toms turn something up. It usually happens."

"Sure."

"If you need anymore," he nodded at the papers in my hand. "I'll see what I can do. Read, but don't think. I'm serious when I tell you the CRC are good for this town. Believe it, okay?"

He clicked shut the briefcase and pulled out a huge baguette brimming with all kinds of meat. "Now excuse me if you will, Black. Oh," he paused mid munch and it seemed an age till he cleared his mouth, "Jackson Travers wants a word. He'll be at the Drum in half an hour."

Chapter Thirty – The Drum

The Drum was a twenty four hour cellar joint. There was little on the outside to advertise the fact that a bar existed down below. Just a small, conservative sign with a sketched drawing of a big bass drum. Down a flight of shabby wooden stairs was where it all happened.

I took a seat on a stool by the bar and waited for the weasel to appear. There was two rooms, the main one a long, narrow corridor of a room with the bar running the length of it. The wall across was mirrored from floor to ceiling. The other room was smaller and squarer with a couple of pool tables, a dart board and nothing else. The music was loud and bad for the ears and the locals were shifty and uneasy in the presence of strangers. I could see Jackson Travers fitting in swell.

Drinking a cafetiere of Colombian coffee, I felt like a leper, as the locals inched away. My change sat untouched on the bar where I left it. I was almost relieved when Jackson Travers appeared, swapped friendly conversation with the bartender and sat down beside me.

"You okay?" he asked.

"I was till I came here. What's the attraction?"

The weasel smiled a sickly smile. His black, droopy moustache hung over his awkward shaped mouth at both ends. Again he wore an oversized cloth cap, although this one was navy blue, and shabby jeans covered by a long, camel coat.

"The Drum has character," he said cryptically. "That's all that's bothering you?"

"Sure, I'm fine, why the concern?"

"I thought maybe you got the blues. You look like maybe you got the blues."

"I'm fine. In fact I'm quite happy. Today I thought I'd try happy, okay?"

He looked at himself in the mirror. "I brought a witness here once who had the blues. Seemed all right at first, then his eyes all sort of misted over. Sat staring at himself in that there mirror." he nodded at cracked segment. "Wouldn't move for hours. Just staring there. And then he took out a gun, calm as you like, put it in his mouth and swallowed a metal sleeping pill."

"Well, that's a very nice little story, but I'm fine, okay."

"Good. I'm glad. It was pretty messy, I can tell you."

I pulled out a packet of butts and lit one up. Sucking it deep into my lungs until they burned. Jackson ordered a beer and a chaser and took out his tin. A whole five minutes of silence passed between us.

"Your face is looking better. Healing quite nicely," he said eventually.

I laughed. "Thanks."

"Teach you to be more careful in the shower." He took a swig of the beer and threw down the spirit. "I've been doing some digging."

I smiled even wider and looked into the weasel's eyes. "Did you find treasure?"

"A few rough gems. Not worth a dime, right now, but with a bit of work who knows? Could be a gold mine." He stood up and walked to the music box. Five minutes later he returned.

I ordered a beer and finished it in one go. I slammed it on the bar and took another.

"Okay, I'm tired with riddles. You play the enigma like a professional, but I've got a busy day ahead. Say your piece, Jackson."

The weasel rubbed his moustache, evening the edges out with his fingers. When he was satisfied he took out a tape and put it on the table.

"I have myself a taped recording of a conversation."

I said nothing.

He smiled.

"I got a friend you see that works a few wire tricks for me. What he can't do with a little microphone and a receiving device aint worth knowing."

I was intrigued, but tried not to show it. "So you been taping private conversations. Who's on the tape?"

"There in lies the problem. I only half know. I was hoping you may be able to clear that little problem up for me. You see my friend swears blind it's not one of our names. And if it's not one of your names there's not a lot we can do with it. Without making it public."

"Which you don't want to do, because it isn't quite legal and above board."

Jackson smiled. "You want to hear it?"

"Sure. Who's the other voice?"

"Don't you want to have a guess?"

My instinct to say McSwarve was overwhelming, but I managed to withhold. Still, my heart was pumping hard as I asked again who the other voice was.

"I took it from his house last night."

"Tony Kalac?"

"That's right, and it's hot stuff. Not as clear as I would have liked, but then they never stand in the right places, do they?"

I sipped my beer and considered the story. If Jackson Travers suspicions were correct then the link between Hermeez and Tony Kalac was established. What first seemed like two isolated killings, even more so after the disappointment of the autopsy report, were brought together. It seemed too impossible to be a simple coincidence. My instincts had been right all along.

But that wasn't it. This tape had the potential to go a lot further than establish a link. What did they say together? Just what were they discussing to make Traver's smile so permanent. It had to be about the dog races. That was his little conspiracy theory after all and so he would be vindicated by any confirmation.

I put my beer down and realised I was shaking.

"You want to tell me the crux of the conversation?" I asked.

"I don't want to spoil it for you. Come on, I've got a machine in the car."

I left my beer and followed Travers out the door. I must have looked like a nodding dog, chasing him out with my tongue hanging out, but until I had heard the tape I didn't care.

Chapter Thirty One – The Tape

"Okay, you ready?" said Travers, his finger hovering over the play button.

I didn't answer, instead pressing my own finger on top of his, activating the tape player.

Instantly the hollow sound of a recording rang out. There was music playing somewhere in the background and the shuffling around of a body, maybe two bodies, but no voices.

Jackson gave an expression of patience as the near silence continued for three whole minutes longer. Then there was muffled voices from far away and a door opening. The voices stopped and there was a sound of a lighter and drinks being poured, followed by a meow.

Suddenly an audible voice:

"I told you there was nothing to worry about. The big J is cool. Everything is cool."

I didn't recognise the voice. Jackson mouthed K-A-L-A-C and pointed to his ear.

"You better be right. If he finds out what we have done, he'll kill us both. You know he will."

It was Hermeez. He sounded different, very different, but it was him, there was no doubt.

"He won't find out. The numbers add up. He's getting his fair share. He don't need the money like we do. Like I said, relax. It's gonna be fine."

"I hope you are right. Today was easy, it's the next one that matters. And the one after that. That trainer is a real bastard."

"Relax. By Friday you'll be out of jail. We'll both be out of jail. It's all sorted, we can't lose."

There was laughter. "Yeah, you're right Tony. I'm sorry. I get a little tense. It would be a hell of coup, a hell of a coup."

"Don't worry, my friend. It's in the bag. All we gotta do is keep smiling and spend the money. Now are we gonna take that dip now?"

"Sure thing."

There was a sound of glasses being put on a table and then footsteps moving further away. A door opened, then closed and the tape stopped.

Jackson Travers sat grinning at me. "You like it?" he asked.

"That's it?" I asked, looking at the tape machine hopefully.

Travers grin dropped ever so slightly. "What do you mean, is that it? This tape is dynamite. It establishes a clear link between the two deceased. Not only that but it gives us the identity of the big man, the big J."

I lit up a Lucky and rewound the cassette. We both sat through the whole episode again in silence. I could feel the confidence slipping away from Jackson Travers by the minute. He was desperate to hear my confirmation of his name, but pride prevented him from asking.

"What's wrong with you, Black? This could help you get your killer. Yesterday you were obsessed with Jarvis McSwarve, but failed to provide a scrap of evidence. There was nothing a court would even listen to that disproved 'burglary gone wrong'. Now you've got a link and not only that but a starting place. Beats searching blind alleys."

I sighed and shook my head slowly. "I wish you were right, Jackson but there's only a link if the voice on that tape is Hermeez Wentz..."

Travers's face dropped. The grin, which had become a semi-permanent fixture during the last hour was nowhere to be seen. Instead his weasel features were a picture of brooding. He played nervously with his moustache, rolling the edges between finger and thumb, and stared blankly into space.

I was on my third Lucky before he moved his view line and looked over to my smiling face. A big grin transformed into a gentle chuckle, which metamorphasised into an out and out chortle. Travers, at first, looked puzzled then angry and finally he cracked and joined in with the laugher.

We had our link.

Hermeez appeared above deck in a thick, cotton bathrobe. His masses of dark chest hair, poking out of the neckline. He had a frown on his handsome face and looked at me like a disapproving father.

173

"What the hell did you do to Teresa? The poor girl is sobbing her heart out down there!"

I sighed a heavy sigh and filled two glasses with wine. The sun was slowly descending behind the tree line of the island of Burano, casting an effect of deep lacerations across the darkening sky. Once white puffy clouds, were now red and bleeding down onto the horizon.

And I was bleeding inside.

"She asks too many damn questions," I blurted. "Always Casablanca. Why did I leave? Will I go back? What really happened back there? Always why why why!"

Hermeez looked at me cupping the glass in his hands. For a second I thought he was going to hit me, but all he did was shake his head.

"She's a curious girl, that's all. Interested in you, Errol, because she likes you. She just likes you, that's all."

"Well she has no damn right in liking me! And certainly no right in being interested."

"Is that what you told her?"

"Yeah. That's what I told her. And if she doesn't like it she knows what she can do…"

This time Hermeez did hit me, with an open palm across the cheeks, like a mother would admonish a naughty child. His face was contorted in anguish. I wasn't sure whether it was for me or Teresa.

"You shouldn't have said that, Errol, and you know it. Teresa is only a girl, a sweet, innocent girl. If you are going to break her heart, do it by fucking some other broad, but don't let her get in here." He patted his chest. "Don't let her in here and then piss all over her! It's not fuckin' right!"

He was right. I knew he was right and he knew that I knew he was right! We'd been in Venice for the best part of a month, touring around on our own little gondola, come yacht. Teresa and Maria had never been far away, showing us the real Venezia as they said. Although to most this would usually mean more than the inside of a tiny, two-man cabin with plastic curtains. And we enjoyed ourselves immensely. The arm was as good as new and the nights were becoming less and less like a black shirt torture camp. I was more relaxed that I had been in months. A lot of this was down to Hermeez, but most of it was Teresa.

She was every little bit the perfect, little Italian girl. Tall and slim and fit, with a beautiful young face of typically dark features. Her eyes were deep pools of knowledge, with a stare to make your body melt. Her eyebrows

174

were thick and dark, but well-shaped and fitting her face. Her lips were full and voluptuous and usually painted deep red. Her nose was small and slender, with a little button on the end. When she smiled it made you think the Gods were happy. Her body was lithe and well tanned, with big, firm breasts and taut, supple thighs. Body hair was well-pruned, except between her legs, which was a thick, dark forest of wiry, pubic hair. Unlike Sarah's soft, wispy tufts.

We talked for hours about Italy's culture; the beautiful architecture, the opera, the sensational food, the great wines and vineyards. We discussed the Romans and the Vatican. All the time, we laughed and we sang and we frequently stopped to make passionate love.

When we did make love, that too, was the most wonderful fun. For such a young, innocent Catholic girl, Teresa was not in the least bit inhibited. We experimented with different positions and different games, we fucked and we kissed each other all over for hours on end. She, and I too, were generally insatiable. Quite often when we'd finished, we went up above deck for a cigarette and found ourselves listening to Hermeez and Maria fucking downstairs. It made us feel naughty and wicked, but was the most incredible turn on, and we usually ended up naked again and fucked in the open air with the sea breeze on our backs.

Sometimes we liked to play chess, a game I had always admired and wanted to like, but one I could never really get into. Every time, Teresa won, usually declaring checkmate within twenty moves, but never did she tire of explaining her secrets and teaching me how to improve. I don't think I actually did, but luckily she never tired of beating me over and over again, either.

This wonderful few weeks with Teresa and Hermeez and Maria, was a real catharsis for me. I had entered Italy a broken man, with only a tough, cynical shell for protection, but I had found a way to relax and to enjoy myself. Never far away was my eternal buddy, Hermeez Wentz. For him I would always be naked, he had stripped me bare and played poker with my soul. For him there would never again be pretence or false facades. But for Teresa, however much she had done for me, however much I liked her, or however much I knew she was falling deeper and deeper in love with me, the shell simply had to be unbreakable.

I couldn't allow myself to be shot at again!

"I'll apologise."

175

Hermeez nodded. *"You do that, Eezy. You tell her you are real sorry and give her a big kiss. She'll understand, in time."*

"You think?"

"Oh yeah, I'm sure she will. She'll lay on the third degree, just don't spank her arse every time she has a little relapse, okay?"

I laughed and refilled our glasses.

Hermeez held out his arms and gave me a bear-hug, patting my back like a baby's I looked out into the black of the sea his hand drumming my shoulders. The other boats on the gentle water were bobbing up and down. The moon was dull tonight, not yet breaking clear of the burnt clouds, making it eerily dark. It was all quiet below deck.

"You want to do it now?"

I nodded. "Yeah, I think I will. Listen, buddy, I appreciate everything, you know. Everything."

He smiled that handsome smile.

"You know I'll never let you down. I'll always be there."

He was still smiling as I descended the steps below.

Chapter Thirty-Two – Being followed

I watched the green Olds in my rear view mirror. It had been tailing me several blocks, keeping a respectable distance away. I didn't try to lose it, just keeping a steady pace and the Olds did the same. It followed me the whole way home.

The Dockside car park was thankfully busy as I parked the car, so I got out before the Olds appeared. Instead of entering the hotel, I slipped into the narrow alley that leads to the kitchens. Out got a regular sized guy and sauntered towards the entrance. He was dressed smartly in a black three piece suit without a hat. His face was solid and square with a short, thick moustache defying his baby features.

He strolled past the alleyway and entered the lobby, nodding at the doorman who let him in. I got into step behind him and followed him into the elevator, pushing my weapon into his back as the doors closed.

He turned his head and grimaced. "What the hell…"

I stuck out my tongue and rammed the metal into his kidneys.

The elevator began to ascend and I reached out an arm and pressed the stop button. It juddered to a halt. A look of fear flickered across the man's face.

"For the last ten minutes you've been up my ass," I rasped. "And I'm not that kind of boy."

"What are you talking about," he whined. "Let me go!"

He reached for the control panel so I chopped him between the shoulder blades, dropping him to his knees.

I reached inside his jacket and pulled out a wallet and a handgun. I emptied the breech before returning the gun and searching the wallet. There was fifty in cash, a slip of paper, but nothing else. I pocketed the wallet.

"Give that back! I…" protested the man, trailing off as I grabbed him by the scruff of his neck and pulled him back to his feet.

"What's your name?" I demanded.

He paused briefly before sighing resignedly. "Dave Peters."

"And what's in room sixty-four, Dave?" I asked eyeing his bland face.

He looked puzzled. "You are."

"Weren't you ever told that it's dangerous to commit plans to paper Dave? Keep everything in the head, it keeps the detection in detective work."

Again he looked puzzled before smiling nervously. "Hey I'm here to talk, man. Nothing else."

"Of course," I said. "So why the piece?"

He shrugged. "Everybody has a gun in Casablanca."

Visions of halcyon days flickered past. Of picnics down by the beach, with the sun shining and the sea raging, when you needed nothing more than your hamper full of cold meats and salads and a surfboard under your arm. When pretty women played volleyball in skimpy bikinis and the fellas wore nothing more than uncomplimentary swimming trunks.

I shoved him against the wall and shook my head.

"Look are you going to listen, or not? It's you who is waving the shooter around, I just wanna talk."

"Let's talk downstairs," I said, and pressed the ground floor button.

"I don't think that's a good idea, Mr. Black," the man said, stopping the elevator again. "My man don't want us to be seen together. He says you're the latest double-bill."

"And just who is your man, Dave?" I asked.

He gave me a look of incredulity before answering. "Who do you think my man is? Who do you think is the only man in this shabby town."

"The Big J?" I asked.

Peters smiled. "You could call him that, but most people prefer Mister Earl."

"And why does Mister Earl want a meet with me?"

"That's between you and him. I'm just the messenger," he said, putting the edge back in his voice.

"You know that messengers have a nasty habit of getting shot."

He scowled. "Look, most people get an invite from Mister Earl they don't ask questions, okay. You wanna play the wise guy,

178

don't wanna listen to what the man has to say, then fine. I'll be on my way."

I put him down and thought about it for a minute or so. Meeting Jevon Earl was a very tempting offer. I felt like snapping his hand off, but that was more my curiosity making a play. Why would the Big J want a meet with me? It could be a setup. I considered it, although why would he want to set me up? Maybe he was gonna make me number three.

No, if that was the case he would have already done it. There would be no messing about. He would have me taken down a dark alley and I would know nothing about the whole thing.

A cold thought crept over me, making me shiver. It sounded too stupid to be true, but lingered in my brain, refusing to be dismissed. Just maybe Jevon Earl was scared. I almost laughed as the theory developed in my mind, but it wasn't funny. Maybe, just maybe, Jevon Earl was worrying that it was him that would be number three, and was planning for me to be his shield.

"Where does he want to meet?"

Peters opened his palms. "You tell me, and I'll tell him. It's your ball, man. The only condition is that it's not in front of paying guests, if you get what I mean."

"One on one?"

"One on one."

"Okay. You tell Mister Earl he's got himself a deal. Friday."

"Sounds reasonable. You wanna choose a venue, or shall I make a suggestion?"

"Why don't you make a suggestion."

"That's all it is, mind, but I think you'll agree it's a sensible choice."

I nodded.

"You familiar with Honeycomb Island?"

"Down by Samui Bay?"

"That's right. Mister Earl has a small fishing hut down there. The whole Isle is only the size of a football pitch. It's quiet and very private, no hiding places, if you know what I mean."

I smiled.

179

"The hut is more of a cabin. Lovely views over the bay, and a good place to discuss business. You happy with that?"

"I'm happy. You tell Mister Earl I'll be there at seven. We can take breakfast together. And Dave, no gorillas, okay? There'll be two generals on the Isle, both with backup nearby, but they want to discuss this alone. You got that?"

"You're the boss."

Chapter Thirty-Three – Theory

When I got back to the Dockside there was a message from Timmy Matthews. I went up to my room and took a beer from the refrigerator. Sitting comfortably on the couch I called Timmy at his office, was told he'd not come in yet, then caught him at home. I gave him everything except the meeting at the Ranch.

Even so he guessed there was something more. "Is everything okay, Errol? You've not told me everything?"

"Sure I have. It's all opening up nicely."

He dropped it. "And how are your partners in blue shaping up? Any favours?"

"At least they're taking the case seriously now. They know as well as I do that Hermeez was not killed by an over-zealous burglar, but it's gonna take time for them to like it.

"And Peru, is he looking after you?"

"Peru does a good job in difficult circumstances. The police are not the power source they need to be in this town."

"It's sinking in, Errol, you're learning."

"I even kinda like Travers. Weird sonofabitch, but useful. Likes to play stupid games, but he's the only one that wants to play with me."

"Sounds like you're fitting in swell, kid. How's the face wearing?"

"It's healing. I got a feeling it was some of Benny Jacobs pals. When I was doing the rounds, asking a few questions here and there, I must have aroused some unhealthy interest."

"So why did they wait?"

"They wanted to find out what I was after. Scooted on ahead, knowing I'd catch up with Benny sooner or later. And after I did they decided to teach me a lesson."

Timmy cottoned on. "So that's why it was only a playground tiff. You're lucky, Errol, if it had been the big boys you'd have got a lot worse."

I felt my face and sighed. "I know but I won't be slow again. They've had their chance."

There was a short pause and a shuffling of papers. Timmy then said, "About your hooker. I've been doing a lot of digging."

"Go on."

"Well, at first there was nothing. I called up all my sources and nobody knew of a redhead by the name of Leather. Plenty of redheads in Casablanca, plenty redheads on the game, but no moles and none by that name."

His voice betrayed him. A twang of excitement told me that wasn't the end of it. "But?"

"Well it just so happened I was talking to Billy Fisher last night."

"The prison attendant?"

"Yeah, we had a couple of beers and I somehow managed to drop the name Leather into the conversation."

"A couple of beers, eh." I laughed. "Did Billy know her?"

This time Timmy laughed. "Well he didn't know *her* no, but he had a full dossier on *him*."

"Him?"

"A real nasty, sicko sonofabitch, who's just done a ten stretch. Not a hooker but a male for hire, with bright red hair and the most distinctive mole. His real name is Vernon Carberry but he's known affectionately as Leather."

"I don't believe this."

"Believe it, Errol. Our Vernon is a perverted sadist. Form as long as your arm, usually sex offences on both men and women. When he got out, four weeks ago, he was heading in your direction."

My mind was buzzing and I was getting too wound up to talk. I needed to do some pretty serious thinking. Timmy gave me a more detailed description of Vernon Carberry and cut it short. He sensed I'd talked enough, so I told him I'd call back later and hung up the phone.

Chapter Thirty-Four – The CRC

I flicked through the notes Arthur Peru had provided for me. It stuck firmly to Ishmail Ouzanti's view on things; on the one side stood the CRC, guardians of all things good, and on the other were the bad guys, headed by Jevon Earl. To my disappointment Jarvis McSwarve was filed with the angels, alongside Uncle Ishmail himself, the Trade Unions President Pat Berry, the President of Casablanca Bank Jim Jacobs, the Police Commissioner Murray Andrews and the Congressman Raymond Charters. A real motley crew in shining white suits.

Jevon Earl was the big bad guy and there were names of five of his chief lieutenants, including Tony Kalac. I tossed the notes down on the table and rubbed my forehead. There was no mention of Leather anywhere.

I wrote the names down on a pad of paper and drew lines joining any I knew to be linked. McSwarve and Ouzanti. Wentz and Carberry. Earl and Kalac. Ideas came into my head and then evaporated before I could unwrap them. I sat there smoking one cigarette after another, trying to figure it all out. The tape was a definite lead. Both Hermeez and Kalac murdered. Was it the same killer? It had to be, but where did Carberry fit in? And the organiser, the Big J. I printed out 'The Big J' in capital letters and a question mark. Who was it? Surely, Jevon Earl?

I grabbed a beer from the refrigerator and sipped it slowly, until the bottle was empty. I sat there for over an hour thinking, letting my mind wander over the facts at hand and the conjecture, which was in plentiful supply. Everything came back to the Big J, Jevon Earl. But for some reason I was less inclined to accept this as fact. Jackson Travers and Arthur Peru would both take this for granted. The tape was their warrant to pin it all on the only 'usual suspect'. But maybe the Big J was someone else?

I drew a line form Jarvis McSwarve to the Big J. There was a faint link in that he owned the Racecourse and was head of the Racing Commission. This was a link that I was anxious to highlight, and the sick feeling in my guts returned. But he was also owed a substantial sum of money by Hermeez so why would he cut him in on a scam. There was no answer to that so I decided to leave that angle and get another beer.

I thought of Vernon Carberry. A nasty, homosexual gunslinger. Timmy painted a pretty vile picture of him; a man with few virtues. I wondered what Hermeez would be doing with a man like that. He wasn't gay, so it must have been business. But what business could you do with a man like Leather?

When I called Arthur Peru it was midday. He was buzzing with the news from Jackson Travers, seemed ready to swallow his theory about the race fix whole. What with the circumstantial evidence, the numbers from the diary, the tape and now the autopsy report, he seemed convinced Earl was the killer.

I quizzed him again on motive. It might have been enough for the new, amenable Arthur Peru, but a flimsy theory on race fixing was not sufficient to satisfy a cynical punk like me, or a county judge for that matter.

He said he had witnesses who'd swear on oath that Earl and Kalac were not getting on, and had been acting out a mini turf war for a while. He had it on good authority that the race inquiry would come up with a dirty verdict. Added to what we had on the tape, he was going for a murder rap on Earl, whether he personally carried it out or not. For the record, he thought he did!

Kalac had branched out into race fixing, with the heavily in debt Wentz as his ally, and had in effect railroaded Earl into breaking his deal. Either that, or he had cut Earl out of the deal, which amounted to the same thing. In Outfit land there was only one outcome – the big sleep.

As soon as the inquiry was finished, he would pull in Dragapetto, who would swear to serious wrongdoing and point the finger at Earl. In the meantime his force were closing their tentacles around Jevon Earl's empire, tapping phones, following associates and making a hell of an effort to find the weapon.

I asked him about Ouzanti, about the deal. What would he think about taking on Earl again? Peru brushed it off. "Leave Uncle Ishmail to me," is all he said.

184

I agonised whether to tell him about the conversation with Peters and the proposed meet with Earl, deciding that could wait. Instead I pumped him on Vernon Carberry.

"Oh, I've heard of Carberry," he said. "A real nasty, sicko, sonofabtich. The Vice Squad have a whole dossier on him."

"Give me the details," I said.

"The details? Think of the most perverted, sadistic, fucked-up bastard you've ever come across and I promise you he's not a patch on our Leather."

"I have reason to believe he's back in Casablanca."

"Is that right? I thought we'd got rid of the scumbag for good. Rumour has it he was raped by his priest in the confessional box. Now I'm sure that sort of thing has an effect on an impressionable seven year old. It's bound to, but that don't give you no fuckin' right to go torturing and fuckin' anything you please."

"What's he doing out so soon?" I asked. "Surely if the file is so damning he should still be inside?"

"He should have fried like the rest of the bad eggs," spat Peru. "But there was another great American justice story. Carberry had a good team behind him. He's always had money and lots of it. He put it to good use. Played the mitigating circumstances card to the hilt. Dredged out all the old family and friends who pledged their life on him being good at heart. Just misguided, you know the sort?"

I said I did.

"It never fails to amaze me just how far a sympathetic jury let their liberal feelings override their power of justice. Okay, so the kid had a bad upbringing. Too bad, so do half the kids in this shitty world, but he's a killer and he chose to be a killer. No amount of hardship moulds you into what Carberry is, I just don't buy it."

"What did he serve?" I asked, a little taken aback by Peru's outburst.

"Let me think. He did a couple of short terms for sexual abuse and battery. All those demons stored up in his sick head told him to snatch a classroom of kids and fuck their lives up a little like that priest did to him.

"Spent most of it in the nuthouse, undergoing intensive testing and psychological examinations. When he got out he graduated up to not just playing with lives, but taking them. My man in the Vice reckons the numbers could be anything between one and a dozen. They only got him on one, when he broke down in tears in the box, poor dear.

"I think he served, that's right, it was seven years. Seven poxy years and then a pat on the back and a licence to do it all again. Makes me fuckin' cry."

I thanked Peru and then there was a short silence.

"What's all this about, Black?" he eventually asked. "The presence of Vernon Carberry in Casablanca is most unfortunate, but what has it got to do with you, and what's it got to do with Wentz?"

I thought carefully before answering. The black and white world of Arthur Peru had no place for hunch following and I could hear the regret in his voice for being so forward. Complications were cropping up all over this case and Peru simply wanted to end it. So did I, but not this way.

"I think maybe he has connections to the murders," I said, awaiting the explosion.

I could feel the steam coming from Peru's ears and the phone line crackled with tension. He took a couple of deep breaths and then said, "Talk."

I told him about Alison. How she had seen a red head and Wentz together, about Benny Jacobs who confirmed the identity. Listening to myself reel it all off over the telephone made me less and less sure, but I continued nevertheless. I told him I had doubts about Jevon Earl, that the tape was not enough.

Peru listened a hell of a lot more calmly than I expected. He agreed the redhead in question was almost certainly Vernon Carberry, but refused to see it as any more than coincidence. Whereas the link with Leather was scant, the tape provided a concrete case against the Big J, which could be backed up with a shit load of circumstantial evidence. He had no time for hunches and no time for complications. Uncle Ishmail was restless, the case had to be closed and Jevon Earl was the man. He gave me twenty four hours to come up with something.

So I told him about Dave Peters's proposition.

Chapter Thirty-Five – Clyde Gabriel

Down by the park there was a row of public telephone booths. There were four directories for Casablanca and to my surprise they were all there. I picked the first one from the rack and began thumbing through it. I did the same with the next one and then the next. So far no luck, but it was the last directory, the one for The Trimbles that would change that.

Fifteen minutes later I parked my heap in the only municipal parking lot in The Trimbles. The attendant didn't even attempt to hide his look of distaste. I grinned wolfishly, and squeezed between a shiny blue Chrysler and a red Cadillac.

As I strolled from the lot, I lit up a Lucky and took in the beautiful surroundings. The Trimbles had always been one of the better residential areas of town and things had not changed a bit. I sucked the smoke deep into my lungs, a little off put by all this alien fresh air. Birds singing and insects buzzing were the dominant sounds, rather than roaring engines and the constant hiss of the downtown. Lot after lot of acre square land was filled with lavish detached garages. Forty foot trees swayed gently in the breeze, and well-pruned gardens housed enthusiastic hounds or inquisitive felines.

I stopped outside number nineteen and admired the red Dodge parked on the football pitch sized forecourt. There was a large, shiny knocker on the door which bore the initials CG in gold type. Just as I was about to head up the driveway and use that knocker, the door opened. I slipped unseen behind a row of large conifers and observed.

The man I took to be Clyde Gabriel stood in the doorway nodding his head like a puppy. He was a small, stocky man. Portly around the waistline, which was highlighted by the stretched suit he was wearing. His head was devoid of any hair, unlike his stubbled, flabby face.

The man who was leaving was a different proposition. He was tall, well-built with every muscle alive and alert. He was attired in an immaculate three piece suit with the creases firmly in the right places. He wore a suede hat on his head and had a well trimmed goatee beard. He was speaking but I couldn't hear the words. Gabriel carried on nodding, the fear in his eyes evident.

I stepped a couple of paces back as the man turned around and got in the Dodge. The grin I wore betrayed the way I really felt as the car fired and roared off, disturbing the idyllic peace. It was a real, nasty, smug grin. The kind that only Jarvis McSwarve could arouse.

Chapter Thirty-Six – Shooting

Curiosity had always been my failing. When all around you are putting their feet up and having a beer, patting each other on the back and accepting the plaudits, why not follow a hunch? The problem being, hunches get you into trouble nearly every time. And the more hunches you follow, the deeper trouble you create.

Like Vernon Carberry, Clyde Gabriel was becoming more and more of a loose end. At first, it was one of many loose threads. Nine out of ten lead nowhere, but at first you follow them all up and then cross them off the list one by one. Only I was having trouble crossing any of them off. More and more threads were interlinking and causing a whole heap of mess.

I was pondering all this as I made my way back to the parking lot. The birds were still singing and the sun shining so I stopped at a bar for a quick beer. When I came out there was only a couple of hundred or so yards to go. I pulled a full packet of Luckys out and hunched against the wall, cupping my hands around the flame to light one.

At first I thought one of the bums inside had dropped a drink, as there was a loud crashing of glass. People immediately came out of the door and stared at the window as it splintered to the floor. I shrugged and walked on, as the proprietor began clearing up the mess. Usually, windows required a chair or a body thrown through them before they disintegrated.

When I reached the lot I paid the attendant, fired up my heap and headed back to The Dockside. Clyde Gabriel would wait a little longer. I didn't want to frighten him off by going charging in. He wasn't going to go anywhere in a hurry. I needed to figure out what to do next.

When I got back I ran a hot bath and had a good, long soak. I lay back in the tub, steam filling the room and stared blankly at the creaking ceiling fan. As if I didn't have enough to think about I was again joined by the ghosts of the past. Memories came back to me, at first disjointed faces and voices, then slowly they materialised into some sort of sense. No longer

190

blurred by old romance and sentimentality, one face dominated like a demon.

It was Jarvis.

I remembered Jarvis McSwarve as an amiable businessman with a good eye for a deal. He had a reputation for being fiercely ambitious to the point of being ruthless, but he always appeared to be polite and charming.

On the opening night of his new club, The Penitence, he went against the grain by wearing a casual beige suit without a tie. I was there accompanying Sarah, who was naturally invited as the god-daughter of the great Ishmail Ouzanti. Uncle Ishmail was there too, but we managed to keep our distance. It wasn't that he had anything against me personally, Sarah assured me, it was private eyes in general.

More than once during the party, I found Jarvis looking at me in distaste. From right across the room he stared a cold, steely look, but then turned away as he realised that I was looking back. At the time I shrugged it off, it didn't seem the slightest bit important. By then, I was quite used to other men looking angrily at me, no doubt jealous of the beautiful girl on my arm. It made me a little proud.

Now I was the jealous one, looking at another man's wife in exactly the same way.

I only spoke to Jarvis once and that was when Sarah introduced us. Taking my hand in hers, she pulled me across the room before drifting off towards the Uncle. Jarvis shook my hand, a strong, solid shake, and smiled warmly.

"You have a lovely lady there," he said, his voice like velvet.

"Thank you," I replied, smiling back.

"Is she happy?"

My smile weakened. "I think so," I said, my voice not as commanding as it should have been.

"I hope so."

And he was gone, moved on to another guest.

That was it, a poor exchange which at the time only contributed to make me mad enough to get drunk, cling possessively to Sarah all night, and then insist upon fucking her twice when we got home. Looking back on the brief moment I often wondered whether there had been anything between them at the time. It was a ridiculous notion, but the thought was now cutting into me like a knife. There was absolutely no evidence of Sarah ever cheating on me, and it was actually another eight months before I left Casablanca. Most of that time was happy, but I couldn't help but wonder. Now it was me that had done the cheating, and ashamed though I was, I loved it.

I got out of the bath tub and dried off. Lying down on the bed I closed my eyes and began to cool off. Questions kept popping into my head; how long had they been married; did they have children; did she enjoy it with him as much as she did with me; did she love him; did she love me? Stupid questions. How in the hell could she love me, after all these years? Hell, why not, I could easily love her.

Did she ever love me?

Seeing Jarvis today with Clyde Gabriel was another line I used to join the names. Why did it seem so damn important? Gabriel had something to do with it all, I was convinced of that. Although what a humble club owner could have to do with all this, I could not even guess. What had Jarvis told him? Why was he so scared?

They kept on coming. Questions with no apparent answers.

All of a sudden, I sat bolt upright. The hairs on my chest were all standing all on end and I felt a chill down my back. The room fell deadly silent, the only sound was my breathing. Listening to my own heavy breath a thought formed in my head. A terrible, sickening thought.

Nobody had touched that window. Not with a glass or a chair or a body. The cracks had appeared all over it seemingly on their own, before it disintegrated into tiny pieces. I re-lived that brief moment. The only thing that went through that window was a bullet. That's why it ended up splashed all over the sidewalk.

The thought had dragged me from my memories, but it was soon returning. As I sat in the darkness, my suspicions were again being stirred.

The only reason a bullet had pierced that window was because it had missed its intended target. My eyes tightened and I creased my nose as the anger came over me in waves. I had been used as a target before and I didn't like it. I was damned if I was gonna be shot at again.

I tried to think back to the moment just before the window was hit. Faces that were in the street, cars that went by, out of the ordinary noises, but there was nothing. It was in the middle of the day, in The Trimbles, for Christ's sake. You don't go popping off cheap shots in a smart residential area in broad daylight. Not unless you're a crazy sonofabitch, or a cool, confident, professional, or desperate. I preferred the former.

I composed myself the best I could and called Timmy's number. He answered on the second ring.

"Errol, what's wrong?"

I told him.

"You know what this means?"

"It means somebody thinks I'm important. Important enough, to go risk shooting cheap shots in broad daylight. Hell, I didn't even sense a tail."

"I don't suppose you saw anything?"

"Not a garden gnome out of place."

"It must have been silenced. That, at least shortens the odds. Maybe this was a warning."

"Yeah, a second warning. Three strikes and you're out. I'll tell you something, buddy, there's not gonna be a third time."

I told him about Jarvis McSwarve coming out of Clyde Gabriel's pad. I told him that his was the last face that I saw. I told him there was something going on, I could smell it. When I finished talking my hands were shaking.

"Be careful, Errol. Don't let this blur your judgement, pal. I understand that Jarvis brings some pretty bad memories. I don't want you on a murder rap."

I agreed and hung up.

Chapter Thirty-Seven – The Party

I didn't much feel like a party, and I didn't much feel like wearing a tuxedo. But there was a whole stack of loose ends piling up and I figured I may be able to tie some of them up in the company of the lovely Diane Ebrahim.

She was dressed as stunningly as ever. A tight, figure-hugging, black dress that could have been painted on, served only to accentuate her already buxom bosom. Her lipstick was darkest red and she sparkled and jangled with every footstep.

Hanging off her arm was Trades Union man, Pat Berry. He was wearing a suit two sizes too small and puffing on a cigar as big as my wrist.

"Evening, Pat."

"Have we met, Mr…"

"Black. Errol, Black. I saw you the other day at The Penitence. You had had a tough day at the docks."

His eyes narrowed.

"All that settled down now?"

He nodded. "Everything is peachy, thanks," is what he said, but it might well have been, "Fuck you, asshole!"

"No more seals broken?"

He said nothing.

"Hope not. My pal in the border patrol would do his fuckin' nut if he heard about that. There would be import and export guys swarming all over this place. You would be lucky to stay out of jail, never mind lead a body of men. Anyway, must dash."

I left Pat Berry staring daggers at me as I walked away and grabbed a champagne flute from a willing waitress. Diane must have left too, because the next thing I knew she was pulling on my arm.

"My my, Errol. You really are a card. I thought you were going to be my charming young man."

"Berry's an asshole," I said.

She sighed. "And he has shot people a second asshole for what you just said to him."

And then she kissed me flush on the lips. Her tongue searched out mine and we explored each other's mouths.

"Miss Ebrahim, people will talk."

"Oh, I hope so."

She giggled and planted a big kiss on my cheek, no doubt leaving a bright, red lipstick mark. Before I could protest she skipped off to join Congressman, Raymond Charters, winking at me as she left.

"Diane has made herself known, I see," said Dan Vincent, one of Peru's boys.

I nodded and sipped my champagne.

"Peru not here tonight, Dan?"

He shook his head, "Nope. He's got a meeting with Uncle Ishmail."

I failed to react, but ants were loose in my belly. "To fill him in on the case?"

Vincent sneered and threw back his champagne in one. "I'm sure Wentz will figure somewhere, but don't flatter yourself, buddy. About page twelve of the report, I reckon."

"Just above your appraisal then, Dan."

I didn't wait for a response. I had caught sight of a few other faces in the room. My old pal, Jeremy Darcheville was there. I pumped him on the activity at the docks. There was no more trouble. McSwarve had stepped in and smoothed things over. I asked where Jarvis was, but he didn't know.

Jim Jacobs was there, the President of the Casablanca Bank. He was a typical banker – sharp of suit, scintillating conversation and intolerant of lowlifes like me. He gave me short shrift when I mentioned Hermeez Wentz, but he did know that Jarvis McSwarve was not present. I asked where he was and Jacobs simply walked away.

The next hour was spent doing the rounds. I was true to my word to Diane, and was charm personified. Three glasses of champagne and a stack of canapes later, I was tired of small talk and tired of small minds. Most people in this room would not piss on me if I was on fire. I was, therefore, delighted to see my old buddy George Field enter the hotel lobby and head up the main staircase. I excused myself from the beautiful, but empty-headed, blonde I was schmoozing and followed him up the stairs.

George spotted me coming and rushed into the corridor. Seconds later we were both in his room, glass of bourbon in hand and stern looks on our faces.

He was looking very different from the other night. All signs of mischief and fun had evaporated and his face was now lined with worry.

"I'm sorry, Errol, but I've got to go. Hearst has sacked me and cleared out my office back in LA. I have been getting threatening telephone calls every hour for the last two days and just now I got a message – Martin has had a car accident."

Martin was George's younger brother; the absolute polar opposite of George, but his only living relative.

"He's okay. A broken leg and cuts and bruises, but I've got the message."

"Who's behind it, George?"

He shrugged and slung back his bourbon, pouring another immediately.

"I knew it would be like this, but I figured I would always have Randall to fall back on. I didn't figure even Ishmail held such sway. If indeed it is the Uncle."

I put a hand on his shoulder. "You got me, buddy. I will look after you."

He looked me straight in the eyes and smiled. "Just like old times, ha?" he said, before shaking his head. "No. Sorry, Errol. I am leaving tonight, and I strongly recommend you do the same. This town is rotten to the core and we are both better off without it. Let's go find us a beautiful redhead for you and a butch sailor for me and go have us some fun!"

That was more like my old pal, although I knew it was just a swansong. He was physically shaking as he said it and he knew I was going nowhere, and he would never pursue it.

He picked up a stack of papers from his desk, deposited them in a wallet and handed it to me.

"Here are some notes that you might find useful. I would love to talk them over with you, but I really am going right now."

I stood up and embraced my friend. He held on tight, like I was providing him a lifeline, patting me heavily on the back. After a few moments we parted, looked each other in the eye and he left, shutting the door behind him.

I opened up the zip file, but was interrupted by a hammering on the door before I got a chance to read it. A sneering John Wimpon pushed his way in to the room and poured himself a brandy.

"Where's the nonce? Has he gone already?" he asked.

I didn't reply.

Not verbally, anyway. Instead I gave him a right hook and sent him sprawling onto the carpet, splitting his lip in the process. Wimpon licked the blood and laughed.

"You will fuckin' regret that, Black," he growled, and he attempted to regain his footing.

I didn't. Instead I kicked him hard between the legs and stamped on his right hand, before he could reach his piece. As he scrambled around on the floor, groaning, I grabbed him tight around the collar and slammed him into the wall.

"Who did this, John? Was it the Uncle?"

"Fuck you!"

I rammed him into the wall again and his eyes momentarily rolled.

"Who…"

He spat at me, a mixture of blood and snot and saliva. I dropped him to the floor, kicked him again in the stomach and left the room, tucking the zip file inside my jacket.

I was still shaking with anger when I made it back downstairs. John Wimpon was one of Peru's boys, but I was doubtful he was acting only on the policeman's orders. If Ouzanti wanted to put the frighteners on, there was nobody better than the tall, thin, psychopathic lawman. Dirty stories had followed him wherever he had been and it was only Peru's unorthodox methods that had got the best out of him. Now he would be gunning for me, but I would be harder to scare off.

I was back in the throng before I realised I had blood on my white jacket, and I could see the shock on some of the faces there. Diane rushed up and held my hand tightly. I told her what happened and she kissed me softly on the cheek.

"Go to my room, Errol. Take a bath, relax. I will get away as soon as I can."

I smiled and kissed her back, taking the key and putting it in my pocket. But instead of going to her room I took the back exit and headed for my car.

Chapter Thirty-Eight – Address

She was wearing make up this time. Bright red lipstick, darkened eyes and rouge on her pale cheeks. I found her sitting alone in a booth with a bottle of red, for company.

I edged into the booth, lit a cigarette and handed it to her, before lighting one for myself.

"Quiet drink?" I asked.

She looked hard at me and shrugged.

"Half right. Not that it is any of your business, Mr Black, but I am meeting someone."

I looked at my watch and smiled. "I won't keep you then, honey. I just wanted to check a couple of things."

"I think I said enough, the other day." She sighed deeply. "I need to move on."

I poured myself a glass and took a slug, before re-filling Alison's glass.

"The redhead."

Her eyes narrowed.

"Where does she live?"

"How the…"

I interrupted her, "Save us both some time, darling. You want to move on, and that is swell. I want to catch a killer, so let's not play hardball here. I am tired and don't have the energy."

I took another drink of the wine and continued, "You followed them to bars, and to restaurants." I held up my hands. "I know, I know. You were just being curious and had every right to be. But, you know, I was thinking. A curious girl like you, would need more. Am I right?"

She necked the wine and pulled deeply on the cigarette. Tears were once again forming in the corner of her blackened eyes. She nodded her head slowly.

"So you followed them to her apartment. They both entered and that was probably enough for you. Hell, it would have been for me too. I would have probably thrown a trash can through the window."

The tears were now running freely down her rouged cheeks and she was still sucking on a dead cigarette.

"All I need is the address, Alison. And then I will leave you to pick up whichever young man it is tonight and take him back and fuck him, pretending it is my old buddy, Hermeez Wentz. And while you are taking it up the ass, or whatever you and Hermeez got up to, I will be hunting down his killer. Because whether you are ready to admit it or not, we both want that, don't we?"

She stamped out the butt on the table and pulled a purse from the seat at her side. Just when I thought she might pull out a handgun and shoot me down, she instead took out a piece of paper and a pen. She wrote an address down, screwed up the paper and threw it at me.

"Please kill her, Mr Black. Whether it was her that shot him, or not."

I picked up the balled up paper and stood up. Bending down slowly, I let my lips brush hers gently and then left the bar.

I called Arthur Peru from a call box. I was about to tell him I had the address for Carberry's apartment, but he had news for me.

Dragapetto had been pulled in and was backing up the story about a Kalac race fix. He had been coerced into the deal by my dead friend and was now seeking witness protection to save him from a vengeance seeking Jevon Earl. Meanwhile, two more of Earl's henchmen had been found dead, although this was being kept under wraps for the time being.

He failed to mention Wimpon. So did I.

I asked if one of the dead was Clyde Gabriel, and Peru shouted down the phone, demanding everything I knew about Gabriel. When I clammed up, he calmed a little and told me about the pimp. He told me about a nasty killer, who had controlled Earl's women and had a lucrative sideline of his own, in the form of a brothel posing as a massage parlour.

When he asked me again why Gabriel's name had come up, I told him about Liona and the missing girl. I told him about the plan to drug Hermeez Wentz. He laughed out loud. This was even more evidence to finish Earl. He told me I had done a good job and that I should leave Clyde Gabriel to him. He would send Dan Vincent and Lloyd Stone to pick him up.

I put down the phone, wondering just why I had not told him about Gabriel and Jarvis McSwarve. I didn't want him to tell me again to quit badgering McSwarve and I didn't want him to bring up Sarah.

I would get an answer myself.

Chapter Thirty-Nine – Rubber Truncheon

I was standing in the shadows at the end of a dark alley watching the old house on Trowell Street. The gaudy neon sign flashed on and off casting a seedy punk image across the old building. The rain was now a steady pour and the street was deadly quiet. I waited a moment longer, until I was sure the street was empty, before swiftly crossing over the tarmac towards the solid looking mahogany door.

Behind the shiny mahogany was a neatly manicured garden with an aisle of cherry trees which led to the house. The garden was so immaculately pruned that it looked like felt, with every piece of bright pink blossom neatly brushed away. Curving through the twenty foot lawn ran a gentle flowing stream. Colourful fish glided the water towards the old stone house. Walls lined the boundaries of the garden at all sides.

I pushed the open door and silently moved around the undergrowth to the side of the house. Upon reaching the building I stood still with my back to the wall as my eyes grew accustomed to the dark. The soft trickling of the stream was the only sound through the constant rain.

The windows were clouded so you could not see through from the outside. Even the garish red glow from inside was dulled. At the far end of the wall was a door, slightly ajar.

The last window was cracked, the artificial coating had peeled away in a corner, leaving it barely see through. A musky scent of incense and marijuana escaped from the small crack in the glass, drifting up gently into the black night sky.

I smoked a cigarette silently before taking a look through the transparent gap.

The room was small, and reasonably comfortable. Its floor was made of polished wood, and was covered with an Oriental rug. In the corner was an oval bath tub, made of dark wood, which was big enough for two or three people. On the massage table lay a naked man, face down on a bed of feathers.

A young, oriental lady, in a kimino robe, stood over the table, which housed a selection of urns and bottles full of oils and lotions. Somewhere in the corner, burned a stack of incense

202

sticks and a pipe stuffed with weed. The only light was a dull, red ceiling lamp.

I eased myself through the door, along the corridor and stood silently by the opening. Feeling inside my jacket, I felt the cold metal of my weapon. Curling my fingers around the butt of the gun, I held it firmly and peered in.

The man was now in the bath tub, up to his chest in huge, white bubbles. Steam rose from the water and mixed with the vapour of the burning oils. The woman was leant over the man, breathing softly over him, brushing her lips gently over his neck, ears and back. The air was thick with the smoke of marijuana.

The robe slipped down the girl's shoulders, exposing her huge breasts, which dangled over the man's back. He turned around slowly, with his eyes closed. The silly grin that was plastered on his scarred face was soon replaced with a look of pleasure. He sucked hard on her large, brown nipples, and in that act, a sadistic killer was reduced to nothing more than a new born baby.

As I entered the room silently, the girl edged aside. He opened his mouth even wider, in anticipation of what was next to be enveloped. My Colt .45 was a perfect fit.

"Keep your hands where I can see them," I snarled. "And you," I pointed at the girl, "get dressed and get the fuck out of here!"

She turned around and ran for the door.

Clyde Gabriel's eyes bulged in anger, and then fear. I cuffed him round the back of the head with my left fist and took a step back. He immediately stood up and I kicked him hard between the legs. He winced in pain and held his naked genitals.

"Don't kill me. Please, don't kill me."

I could barely believe it. Here was Earl's number one shooter. One tap on the head and he was crying like a baby.

"Let's hope I don't have to."

He eyed my gun with wide, mad eyes as I slowly put it back in my holster and pulled out a ten inch rubber truncheon. I whipped him viciously around the head, knocking him to the floor. Blood rolled down his cheek.

"I'm gonna give you ten minutes, Clyde. Ten minutes. And if I'm not happy, then I am gonna change back."

"Who the fuck are you?"

I whacked him hard across the right shoulder with the truncheon. He grimaced, but stayed silent.

"That's better, Clyde. I'll do the questions, you do the answers."

He shuffled around, resting his weight on his right elbow. I kicked it away, knocking his head to the soft floor and he groaned.

"Hermeez Wentz. Who pulled the trigger, Clyde? Was it you?"

"You are gonna regret this!"

I smiled and hit him on the shins. He screamed.

"Fuck you, whoever you are," he shouted, making an attempt to regain his footing.

I hit him again, across the left shoulder. This time he howled in agony.

"Was it you, Clyde? Did Earl send you round?"

He looked at me, puzzled. "I don't know what you're talking about," he spat, tears rolling down his cheeks.

"The net is closing, Clyde. Earl is finished. You're gonna have to spill soon, or you can fry with him!"

I cracked him real hard on the left thigh with the truncheon.

He cried out a muffled choking sound and coughed heavily. I stood over him, the toes of my boots resting on his finger ends. He pulled his hands away so I reached down and grabbed his neck with an iron grip. He looked up into my eyes, his face a picture of fear. Blood and snot mixed on his chin.

"I didn't do it, you gotta believe me. I didn't do it!"

I lifted the truncheon.

"No, don't hit me again. I don't know anything."

I hit him again. In the midriff.

"I will decide what I believe," I said and hit him across the left bicep.

204

I waited a whole five minutes before I uttered another word. All the time, Gabriel sat back, crying, his eyes squeezed tightly shut, his face covered in sweat and tears.

"Why did you send the girl, Clyde?"

His eyes widened further and he cowered back.

"Why were you drugging Wentz?"

I dropped the truncheon and pulled out my handgun.

"This is big," he whimpered. "He'll kill us both."

"I told you, Earl's finished. You want to worry more about me killing you, than a washed up hoodlum, whose days are gone."

"Don't ever let Jevon Earl hear you talking like that," he warned.

"But you didn't mean Earl, did you?"

I checked the breech of my gun, clicking it out, spinning it around and then slamming it back into place. I raised it slowly and put it on Clyde Gabriel's forehead.

"Why did you meet Jarvis McSwarve yesterday, Clyde?"

He never did answer me.

Before he could move his lips the door was knocked clean off its hinges and wood splintered all over the floor. I was sent tumbling into a heap on the soft carpet and lost the grip of my gun. Before I could get up, Gabriel had the gun and was now aiming it at my chest.

Before he got chance to fire, two small, red holes appeared in the centre of his forehead, which blackened quickly and he slumped down in a pool of his own blood, dead.

Behind me, stood a smiling Lloyd Stone, smoking gun in hand. At his side was Dan Vincent, who was puffing on a huge cigar. He let out a whoop and pulled me to my feet.

"The boss said that sooner or later we would be saving your bacon. Looks like he was right."

I threw as hard a right hook as I could manage and knocked the cigar right out of his grinning mouth. Stone grabbed me before I could kick the bastard to death and pushed me towards the door.

"The boss wants to see you," he said. "Leave this to us."

He took my gun from Gabriel's dead hands, emptied the breech and handed it over. I snatched the weapon and stormed out.

Chapter Forty – Vernon Carberry

I found the apartment and parked two blocks away. It was cool tonight, with a harsh frost in the air. I huddled up my coat collar and walked back on foot, keeping my head down as the cars sailed by.

Picking the lock would be easy. A couple of jiggles with the pick and the lock snapped. I put it back in my pocket and entered the apartment, gun first, closing the door behind me.

It was cold and dark, with a musty, uninhabited feel to it. I found the light switch, but stopped myself from pressing it. Surprise would be better. I reminded myself I was dealing with a killer. It would be better if he didn't return, gun in hand, spitting pellets at anything that moved.

I got out a pen light and scanned the apartment. I was in one large room, which acted as bedroom, kitchenette and office. There was a small compact cooking area on the far wall, complete with cooker, refrigerator and wine-rack. To my left, was a desk with bookshelves all around, and three locked drawers. The rest of the room was dominated by a huge, king-size bed with an intricate metal framework and a blood-red cover.

There was a telephone on the desk, with a book beside it. I flicked through the pages, which was full of names and addresses. I went straight to M, then E, then W. No McSwarve, no Earl, no Wentz. I checked Clyde Gabriel and Benny Jacobs. Neither were there. There was a number listed under Travers.

I closed the book and checked the drawers. Holding the light in my mouth as I picked the lock, something caught my eye. The pen light had illuminated the bookshelf to my right. It was filled with Nazi literature and books depicting homosexual art. I flicked through a couple of the books. There were pictures of homosexual positions, showing full penetrative sodomy, in every possible way imaginable. The participants all had a look of extreme pleasure, or pain, it was difficult to tell. Most of the writing was in German, but I couldn't read it. I put the books back and returned my attention to the drawers.

207

The first one contained a loaded .45 with spare clips. I inspected the breech, emptied the clip and smelt the stock. The gun was cold and well oiled. I doubted whether it had been fired recently. I popped it into my bag and continued the search.

The second drawer was full of pills, a large bag of cannabis and several rolls of Benzedrine. I left that drawer alone.

The third drawer was crammed full of dildoes, cut-throats, handcuffs, a nailed whip and several jars of water-based jelly. I closed the drawers and inspected the rest of the apartment.

At first sight, it was an ordinary, everyday apartment. The bed was neatly made-up, all the pots and pans were washed and put on their shelf, and the carpet was vacuumed. Even the ash trays were empty and washed. But as I turned it over, looking in every cupboard, every drawer, every shelf and every corner, it told a different story. This was not the flat of a reasonable, well-adjusted individual.

I found more knives, a sawn-off shotgun, a selection of poisons in the kitchen cupboard and throughout the whole apartment there were a selection of photographs. Each snap was of a different child, usually between five and twelve. there was nothing illegal about the shots, the kiddies were fully clothed and most of them were smiling at the camera, but it left me feeling cold.

There was a sinister impression to them. Hell, they were under his pillow, in his underwear drawer. There was one next to his shotgun.

I heard a key being shoved in the lock. The lock turned and the door opened as I switched off the penlight and hugged the wall behind the door.

I had my gun ready, as a figure walked into the apartment, closed the door and switched on the lights.

The sight of Vernon Carberry made me hesitate. Before me, stood a beautiful, red-haired woman in her thirties. About six feet tall and dressed in a tight, black leather dress, with a shoulder bag, Her face was heavily made up, with bright red lipstick complimenting her long, flame coloured locks, that hung down free. To the left of her mouth, was a large, yet not ungainly, mole, which served only to compliment her beauty.

Only it wasn't a 'her' at all. It was a 'he', a goddamned killer 'he', that pulled a nasty looking flick knife from his purse and slashed wildly at my face.

I recovered my senses just in time, ducking out of the way of the knife and feigning a blow with my left, before spinning her round, jamming my thumb into her neck and slamming her pretty face into the carpet.

She didn't squeal, or grunt, just dropped the knife and coughed. As I loosened the grip, I cocked my gun and put it to the back of Carberry's neck.

"Get up slowly. Make us both a drink and sit down. Any sudden movements and I won't hesitate in shooting you in the head. You understand?"

Carberry nodded.

"Good, then move!"

Carberry got up and moved slowly to the liquor table, poured two glasses of brandy and sat down on the bed. I picked up one of the glasses and sat facing him.

"Have you forgotten that gun is empty?" asked Carberry in a tough voice, totally inappropriate to his womanly looks.

I looked at the gun and he smiled.

"Don't worry. Drink your drink. We should talk."

All kinds of thoughts were buzzing through my mind. Carberry knew about the gun, which meant Carberry had been at the brothel. Or at least close enough to see what had happened. It hit me like a hammer blow.

The smell. Pungent, sweet, familiar.

It had been at the car lot when I was left with a bloodied nose. It had been at the Trimbles, when the glass shattered before my eyes. It had been in Kalac's apartment.

It was here!

Carberry sat back on the bed and lit up a cigarette. He offered me one and I accepted. The knife was back in its sheaf and my gun was holstered. I was figuring out just how I was gonna kill this bastard when he began...

"What's your weakness, Black? Alcohol, tobacco, heroin?"

I sipped my drink and shrugged. "Women."

"You honest bastard. Can't keep away from the lovely Sarah, hey? No matter what she did, no matter what she is doing, you just can't help yourself. One little sniff of that sweet, little pussy and you go all psycho, right?"

I said nothing.

"For me, it's children. Boys, girls – makes no difference. I love children."

I tensed and gripped the glass in my hand tightly. A notch more pressure and it would shatter in my hand.

"Don't go getting yourself upset, Black. I control it." He reached into his pocket and pulled out a pack of cinnamon sticks.

The smell.

"I use these when I feel 'Leather' coming back," he said, chewing on a stick. "I get these urges, you see. I guess it all comes down to being sodomised repeatedly and made to eat cock as a four year old. It changes your outlook on the world."

"You are just as bad, Carberry. You have killed, abused and maimed…"

I wasn't expecting the head butt. It came so fast and before I could react, he had his hand at my throat. Blood ran freely from my nose.

"They're coming now." He loosened the grip on my throat and munched another cinnamon stick. "If I were you, I would sit back and listen."

I relaxed and he did the same.

"I cannot deny, I have done bad things. Not everyone I have killed has deserved it, not everyone I have…" he hesitated, "…hurt, has deserved it. But these urges, Black. They are uncontrollable, man. The cinnamon helps, but sometimes, I just have to kill.

"You are a very lucky, man. You have had the best of me. I have saved your life…let me think…one, two, maybe three times. If it hadn't been for me, Black, you would have gone the same way as your buddy Wentz."

"You killed him!" I shouted.

He shook his head and laughed. "You are so off the mark, pal. You call yourself a detective?"

"Then correct me."

He rubbed his mole irritably.

"Hermeez said you were a good guy. I guess he was right. You tried saving the girl. You do try to do the right thing."

The girl. Who did he mean? I remained silent and let him talk. It was like I was no longer there and he was talking to himself. He had to say this, and I had to hear it.

"Hermeez told me he would be killed. I didn't want to believe it. I told him I could help him, but he knew the urges would take me away. He told me an old buddy would come on the scene to avenge his death. An old detective posing as a federal agent, with a gold-plated ticket that even Mr Ouzanti or Mr Peru would not be able to squash.

"An old detective that had once been a most treasured and loved friend," he looked at me hard in the eyes, "but who had betrayed him and left him forever a shell of the man he used to be."

Still, I said nothing.

"I promised him I would be your guardian angel. I would watch over you and help you wherever I could. He was close to the end, but he knew that the war would only really begin once he was dead. Then the detective would appear and would need to be assisted. Prowling the mean streets, with Peru's shooters on one side, Earl's killers on the other, and the biggest wolf of all right in front of you."

He continued to hold my gaze as he spoke.

"Does Jarvis know you fucked his missus the other night, do you think? You're still breathing, so I guess he can't."

"What was Hermeez doing here? He was supposed to be retired!" I shouted.

"Hmm, that's right. He was supposed to be retired. Only Casablanca don't really accommodate retired detectives. Not of the calibre of Hermeez Wentz. He saved my life once, you know. Without blinking an eye, he saved my sorry ass from getting the mother of all poundings. One that even Leather would not have been able to recover from. He came round once a week, he practically forced these damn cinnamon sticks down my throat, which repulsive though I find them are still favourable to a stinking, filthy cock!"

211

Carberry smiled, refilled both our glasses and continued…

"You want to know who killed him. I am afraid I cannot tell you that, Mister Black. I have a damn good idea, but I was otherwise engaged, a crime for which I am still paying every waking hour. Take a punt from Arthur Peru, or any one of his goons, Jevon Earl, Jarvis McSwarve, Ishmail Ouzanti or one of a hundred hoodlums that answer to those men."

He coughed a hacking cough and spat on the floor.

"Don't rule out your precious Sarah. You know better than most just what she is capable of. Hermeez fucked her for no better reason than to avenge your misdeeds, but she knows more than he thought."

I wiped it away quickly, but he saw it and he laughed.

"Aww, Errol, did that touch a nerve, buddy? You thought she had been keeping herself all white and virginal for your return? You thought she was reading slushy novels and drinking cocoa before bed? C'mon man, once a whore always a whore!"

This time I did move before he saw it. I moved my whole body right on top of him and I directed my fist into his face over and over and over. His right eye was turning into a bloody pulp beneath me but I hit him again and again. His body didn't fight it, simply went limp and accepted the blows. I stopped almost as quickly as I pounced and was now looking into the eyes of a killer.

"What was he doing here?" I rasped.

Carberry spat blood and tooth fragments on the floor.

"You wanna know who's been taking pot shots at you? That's where you go next, pal. That might answer your question."

"I would like to know that," came a rich, gravelly voice from the now open doorway. "I would like to know that very much!"

We both turned around to see guns pointing in our direction. In the open doorway stood Arthur Peru, cigarillo hanging out of his mouth. To his left stood Jackson Travers, who winked at me and smiled.

Chapter Forty-One – Fifty-Fifty

During the car journey to the station-house I struggled to keep awake. In fact, I'm fairly sure I closed my eyes a few times and slept fitfully. I was desperate not to succumb, to the point of smoking cigarette after cigarette. The second time I awoke with a jerk, with a burning sensation in my left arm, I gave that up.

I had barely slept over the last forty-eight hours and suddenly felt absolutely exhausted. It had been a long day and the incident with Clyde Gabriel now seemed a long time ago. I also had a feeling of events taking over. I wished I could stop the car and call Timmy. I really needed to speak to a friendly voice; a voice that I could trust. If I had to offer odds on my surviving much longer than this very night, I would have offered no more than fifty-fifty.

Carberry had hinted that Jarvis McSwarve was as dirty as Earl. Hell, he had even suggested Arthur Peru was dirty. Right then, as I sat in the passenger seat of Peru's sedan watching the midnight traffic blur past, gently rocking with the motion, I couldn't decide just who was a bad guy and who wasn't. Every damn resident of this town came wrapped up in riddle, mystery and death! What was clear, was that there was no longer any black and white. I would have to be ready for any eventuality. In which case I had to sleep.

Travers had bundled Carberry in the other vehicle and I travelled with Peru. He drove slowly and carefully, stopping for every red light and giving way at every junction. He also spent as long with his eyes on me, as he did with them on the road. His face was impassive, unreadable and he didn't utter a word, only to tell me to rest, that I would need to be alert soon enough.

When we arrived, Peru hoisted his immense frame out of the driver's seat, danced around the car and guided me into the building. I was led to a small room with a cot and collapsed in a heap, sleep coming within seconds.

A steaming mug of coffee welcomed me back into the waking world. And a smiling face of Arthur Peru loomed behind it, Jackson Travers alongside him.

"Welcome back," is all he said.

I picked up the cup, took a sip which burnt my tongue, blew it and drank some more.

"Where's Carberry?"

Peru smiled and pulled out a cigarillo. "On his way back to New York City. Hopefully, that's the last we will see of him. Let the City authorities fight over him. How are you feeling?"

I shook my head. To my surprise it didn't ache half as bad as I feared. "Peachy."

"That's good. Today is a big day. I will be back to brief you soon enough. For now, I have to go and report to the Uncle. Jackson here will fill you in."

And he left, leaving a Peru shaped cloud of smoke behind him.

"Is it bad?" I asked Travers, who grinned his toothy grin.

"Seven homicides in the last twenty-four hours..."

He told me about the crazy day, that resembled a bad thirties gangster movie. He looked genuinely upset as he described finding the two whores, naked and mutilated on wasteland in Blue Hills. Throats cut, breasts sliced and sexual organs violated. He didn't need to tell me that they were Liona and Francoise, I just knew. I couldn't prevent the tears rolling down my cheeks, but nor did I want to.

He told me about Peru's anger with Lloyd Stone and Dan Vincent for killing Clyde Gabriel, and how they would be busted down to traffic duties as soon as this was all over. But he held nothing back in describing the role of Gabriel in enforcing Jevon Earl's empire and his hands-on responsibility in controlling and terrorising women under his wing. He suggested it was probably Gabriel that had killed the girls. I doubted whether this was the case.

Jevon Earl had now gone to ground. So had Jarvis McSwarve. For an elite force, who had lots of surveillance experience, what he told me was pitiful. Earl had managed to escape his shadows by switching cars, using friendly locations, and basic movements. It smacked of amateurism or lack of effort. Which was it? McSwarve, of course, had never been under surveillance, although Travers hinted that the Uncle was not

214

happy with this and that most of his and Peru's little audiences were more to do with McSwarve than Earl. It seemed my little digging had maybe found some traction.

I told Travers about Gabriel's meet with McSwarve and all he did was raise an eyebrow and blow out a huge breath through pursed lips. No denial, no warning to keep the hell away. Nothing.

They now had a small army of witnesses to Earl's crimes. Racing corruption was just the tip of the iceberg, but tying the murder of Wentz up with it, was nothing if not convenient. They were working on something more than circumstantial, but for that they really needed Earl himself.

My meet with the big bad wolf was becoming more and more important by the minute.

Chapter Forty-Two – Revelations

We were holding hands as we walked along the sandy beach, revelling in the feeling of the fine grains on our toes. The sun was nearly burnt out and had left a deep, read scar across the darkening sky. I stopped, pulled her close and kissed her full on the lips.

"I love you, Errol," she said.

She moulded her body into mine, her breasts heaving against the flimsy material of her top, her hips pushing sensually against my groin. I ran my hands down her back and felt her shiver. Her breath was hot on my neck.

"Don't go back tonight, honey," I said.

She sighed, before pushing her tongue deep into my mouth, exploring my own.

"I have to."

She dropped her hands to my flies and yanked at the zip.

"But tomorrow, I will be all yours."

I smiled as she took me in her hand and caressed me gently.

"Tomorrow we will be free of all this."

We dropped to the beach, shed our clothes and made love. We were still naked, our bodies entangled and sexual juices running down both our legs, as the tide reached us and lapped at our feet.

The rain was relentless, bouncing a yard high off the platform. The big, ornate clock, hanging from the roof clicked over to 12pm. I had been waiting for what seemed like hours. Shit, it had been hours.

She was late.

An hour late.

The railway station was deserted. There had been a train a half hour ago, but no-one had got on and no-one had got off. The next one was due any moment. Since then not a single soul had appeared.

Until now.

"You need to go, Eezy," said Hermeez Wentz. He too, was soaked to the bone, his fedora shielding his face from the barrage, but providing a neat waterfall for the rest of him.

I looked at the train, that was now no further than 400 yards from the platform, its big, powerful headlight illuminating the otherwise gloomy Casablanca railway station.

I nodded.

"Marcus Trainer has been arrested. He can't protect you, Errol."

The train was now almost in the station. The huge, steel wheels turned magnificently, cutting through the torrential, never-ending downpour.

"You will get short shrift from the Uncle. He always hated the rumours about you and his golden girl."

I dropped the butt of my last Lucky, watching the dying embers in the puddled floor.

"And make no mistake, buddy, they will come. This town needs a clean-up, and until that happens, you and I need to be far away."

The cacophonous horn of the incoming train cut through the noise of the rain and the breaks kicked in, as it drew to a halt.

I looked at my buddy. "She will come," I said.

Hermeez sighed deeply and grabbed me my the cheeks, squeezing hard. His fingers felt rough, in spite of the rain and my fledgling beard caught up in the grip, pinching and hurting.

"She will come."

The doors opened and the guard stepped out, whistle in mouth and flag in hand. He looked at his watch, realising he was going to have to wait until the scheduled departure. It was only two minutes away, but in that time he would be drenched, and he knew it. He looked at Hermeez and got a return glare that dared him to blow his whistle early.

The last few weeks had been tough. It had all gone bad. Rotten to the core.

The Shadow Man Detective Agency was becoming personas non grata in Casablanca. Once we had worked for the mob, for the cops, for the feds, indeed for anyone who had paid. But it seemed we had now lost our immunity. Like a diplomat that suddenly found their country had suffered a revolution and all the old authority figures were now staring blankly from the top of a sharpened pole, we were finished.

Drugs busts were not uncommon, but it was usually us that were giving the juice. My old boss and mentor, Terry Shadow, had fallen foul of the Casablanca PD. He was now banged up awaiting a bail hearing. Hermeez and I were the only ones that could get him out, but it meant that we would have to drop the Chief of Detectives in the pot. And the number one drug runner. Neither of which would appreciate it.

217

We had to leave. Terry would understand. Indeed he would undoubtedly be safer doing a short stretch than he would be on the outside. We would regroup later and go back to New York.

That was the plan. But I couldn't go alone. Sarah was coming with me.

I could hear a car in the distance. It was unmistakable and my eyes lit up. Hermeez broke out in a huge grin.

"She will come," I said again.

Hermeez was now patting me on the back and smiling widely.

"Have you got the ticket?" he asked.

"She will come."

The car drew to a halt in the station lot and the driver's door opened. I craned my neck to see. A large umbrella was opened in the gloved hand of my sweetheart and she stepped out of the car, killing the headlights as she did.

Hermeez was now hugging me and was not looking in the direction of the car.

I was.

The other door opened and out came another figure. But this one was not holding an umbrella. He was holding a gun. And it was pointing right at me.

I dived into Hermeez and we tumbled onto the platform, as the gun spat out a volley of shots. I felt pain in my shoulder and my right arm went numb. Rolling onto the platform I could feel the rainwater puddle splash up into my face, but as I looked down the puddle didn't appear to be rainwater at all. It was red. Dark red.

The sound of the firing gun rang out again and more pain, this time in my legs. Instinctively I reached for my own weapon, but my arms weren't working. Hermeez was quicker. He pulled his own rod and fired back a volley of shots, shattering the windscreen of the car.

I kicked his legs from under him, sending him tumbling back to the platform.

"Stop it. Sarah…" is all I croaked, before he grabbed me by the scruff of my neck and slung me through the open door of the train.

The train was only moving slowly, but I could still make her out. She was looking, and her eyes appeared to have tears coming from them, but it was probably just the rain.

I mouthed, "Sarah" but she looked on impassively. She too was holding a gun.

Although the train stopped unexpectedly after only an hour, we made it to New York without being attacked again. And I made it without bleeding to death, although it was a close run thing. Several days and a hundred telephone calls later, I was resigned to never seeing Sarah again. She sent flowers to the hospital, or at least flowers in her name were sent to the hospital. But they ended up in the trash

And for the next few years, so did I.

"You look better. Drink this."

It was Peru. He was looking more tired than ever; his big eyes had sacks under that Santa would be envious of and his neck was all mottled and blotchy.

I took the steaming cup of coffee and burnt my lips as I hungrily took a drink.

"Travers filled you in?" he asked.

I nodded.

"McSwarve's car has been found in the Rockaways. Both doors open, radio playing, no-one to be seen. Nobody for miles around has seen or heard a fuckin' thing."

"Earl?" I asked.

He sighed and took a great mouthful of his own coffee, not flinching as the burning liquid hit his throat.

"Most likely. If he has killed McSwarve, we are all finished. Might as well empty my mattress and get as far away from Casablanca as you tried to do ten years ago."

I raised an eyebrow.

"You think I didn't know?"

Jackson Travers entered the room, carrying his own mug, with a greyhound on it. He whispered something in Peru's ear and sat back on a chair. Peru looked me hard in the eyes. He looked sad.

"Captain Matthews of the NYPD, has just been arrested," he said.

I took another drink. I had snakes running riot in my belly and I felt like I could vomit at any moment, but I said nothing.

"There is an arrest warrant out for a George Field, investigative journalist. You know him?"

I shrugged.

"Of course you do. Officer Wimpon has filled me in."

Still, I said nothing. I looked at Jackson Travers, who looked back a half smile on his weasel features. Peru sighed so heavily it came out almost as a cry of pain.

"You fuckin' idiot, Black. You fuckin' stupid fuckin' idiot! Did you think Uncle Ishmail would not find out? Did you think you could just pretend to be a federal agent and come here to avenge your friend's death? On Ishmail Ouzanti's turf? After what happened before?"

His face so was red I thought he might actually explode. I had seen beetroots that were less rouge. But still I said nothing.

He took out a gun. It looked familiar because it was my gun. Only he didn't point it at me, he opened the breech, filled it with slugs and handed it over.

"Tomorrow you will meet Jevon Earl, as planned. You will apprehend the dirty son of a bitch and bring him back to me. If you do that," he finished the coffee and slammed the cup on the desk, "if you do that, and this whole sorry saga is ended then I might just let you live and go back to wherever the hell you came from!"

Chapter Forty-Three – Biography

Hermeez Wentz and Senator Ishmail Ouzanti have become close friends. They often dine together, go fishing and take private drinks. Neither will divulge the nature of their friendship, or indeed how it began.

I poured a large cognac and lit up a Lucky. George Field's writing hadn't got any better, but the subject matter was dynamite. I read on...

There is unconfirmed rumour of a rift between IO and JM. For years now JM has been the golden boy, groomed to take over IO as King of Casablanca. But now, it seems relations have chilled markedly. Why?
1. The deal between IO and JE. JE's promise to keep drugs and gangsterism out of Casablanca, in return for freedom over his own slice of territory. Crime to be limited to JE's own turf and kept to an absolute minimum. Just enough to keep JE in power. Meanwhile the CRC inject money and affluence to the rest of the town.

The next bit was written in red. It looked like the musings of my friend...

Maybe HW was the go-between IO and JE. They could never be seen to meet, but they needed to communicate. HW could be the way?

2. JM felt that he was being squeezed out. Was JE taking his rightful place as heir to the throne? He approached IO to help him in his bid to be Governor. IO rejected his overtures, saying it was too soon. SNUB I

3. As the head of the Racing Commission, JM was worried about gambling anomalies and possible racing corruption. Everything points to Earl. IO refused to act and JM felt undermined. SNUB II

4. Disgruntled JM lobbies other members of CRC to put pressure on IO. He has proposals to extend developments into JE's territory. IO refuses to support this. SNUB III

All this looks like the makings of a WAR. The coming man vs the old master. The protégé vs the master. Is HW caught in the middle? Why won't HW talk more to me? We are buddies after all.

HW is now dead. What now?

What now, indeed. The telephone broke my thoughts and I found myself listening to a rather distressed sounding Timmy Matthews. He told me to pack my bags and get the hell out of Casablanca. He was ringing from Sing Sing, and was in solitary confinement at his own request.

I hung up the phone and closed my eyes.

Chapter Forty-Four – Sailing

The sun was up early and the air was fresh, with a cool summer breeze. Birds were singing with gusto, as they chased one another through the trees, weaving between the branches with the aptitude of a fighter pilot dodging debris.

I parked up the car by the bridge that adjoined Samui Bay to Honeycomb Island. Spindly trees, freshly planted, lined the drive up to the wooden bridge, which was too narrow to negotiate by car.

I crossed the sturdy bridge, my footsteps getting louder as the silence around me grew. When I reached the other end, it was as still as the beach at midnight.

Earl's hut lay ahead of me in the centre of the tiny islet, with an array of colorful flowers and shrubs all around. Apart from the footpath that led to a small jetty, where a boat was moored, there was nothing else.

Peters was right, this was a perfect venue to discuss business. There was nothing going to disturb you here.

I looked around, you could see the whole island from where I was standing. The only place out of view was the inside of the cabin, and Peru had given me a clean bill of health only thirty minutes ago. If there was an army in there, they'd been holed up for over twenty four hours, and hired doubles to drive their vehicles around the town for the day.

There was a balcony from the side of the cabin, which presumably ran around the back. There, would be the finest views over the bay, so there I guessed would be the seating area, and so Earl.

The small boat, rocking gently on the water, was the only sound as I silently crossed the grass towards the millionaire's hut.

"Mister Earl? Errol Black. Are you around the back?"

An owl stirred from across the water, the sound travelling across the still abyss. Then it was quiet again.

"It's Errol Black. I'm gonna walk around the back," I said, keeping my voice firm.

Nothing.

I found my gun in my hand and wondered if it was a wise move. Prowler on private land, carrying a piece for jewelry. Shit, you could shoot me down every day of the week. I couldn't bring myself to put it away, however, so I tucked it into my jacket pocket, as if it would make a difference.

"Earl!" I yelled, as I reached the cabin.

A small fish caused a ripple in the water and it made me jump. I smiled wryly and put my face to the door, peering inside.

The window in the door was cracked, but it didn't impinge on the view. From what I could see, there was nothing out of the ordinary inside. It looked like a smart, two-room cabin, with fully fitted kitchenette and lounge, with a landscaped patio at the back, which led to the balcony.

Still, there was no sign of life.

I tried the front door, which was locked, so I headed around the side, along the wooden balcony. My footsteps were like a drumbeat in my head, even though they barely made a sound. Faster and faster the drumbeat rolled. I stopped on the corner, checked my gun again, took a deep breath and rounded it.

"Jevon, are you around here?"

I was getting a bad feeling.

A solid table, with four chairs around it, was in the middle of the patio. On the table were two glasses of what looked like brandy. I sniffed it. It was brandy. A candle was half burnt down. I put my fingers to it; it was cold.

The boat grated against the jetty. My thoughts were now on the boat. Could Earl be in there, hoping to trick me to enter the cabin? Just in case there were any doubts regarding the breaking and entering. Then he could shoot me down with no fear from the law. I watched it bob up and down on the gentle tide and dismissed such thoughts. Jevon Earl had no need for tricks. If he wanted me dead he would have moved before now. Killers killed, they didn't fuck about playing cat and mouse. And Jevon Earl was no ordinary killer!

Earl wanted to see me; to talk to me; maybe to appeal to me. He did not want to kill me.

Yet.

I slid open the door to the cabin and walked into a massacre.

There were three bodies in all. Riddled with bullets, and slumped in a heap against the kitchen table, which was obscured from the view outside. The linoleum was awash with blood and there was a dark, bloody stain spreading across the light, pine table.

I recognized one of the bodies as that of Dave Peters. His head was slumped forward onto his chest at a grotesque angle. His mouth was open, and there was a surprised look on his face; his eyes were wide and staring. Two bullet holes, an inch apart, pierced his forehead, and his chest and stomach were a bloody mess.

The other two were unknown to me. Both were black, heavily built and very dead. They still held onto their handguns, which lay across their white shirts. The shirts were now a dark shade of crimson.

I checked all of their pockets for identification. They had nothing to offer but a deathly stare, boring deep into my head. I turned away and into another pair of eyes, staring right at me.

Only these eyes were not dead!

Jevon Earl was a tall, thin man. A few inches over six foot, with a tough, wiry look to him. His skin was light brown, a few shades darker than an Indian, but lighter than most African immigrants. His head was almost completely bald with a few tufts of curly, black hair above the ears and around the back. Wide, piercing eyes looked out from a tired face, which smiled at me; a smile that contained no warmth, no happiness, just a physical act of thin, purplish lips curling upwards at both ends.

I took off my hat and offered him a hand. Without releasing the gun, Earl shook it and gestured to a chair facing him.

"Why don't you sit down, Black? You wanna drink?"

His voice was Deep South. Cleaned up around the edges, with a hint of East Harlem, but clearly he hailed from down South.

I nodded. "Yeah. Why not?"

Earl produced a bottle of Jack Daniels and poured a couple of slugs. We sat there in silence, drinking bourbon, listening to the gentle waters outside.

"I got myself a problem, Black. I got myself a problem and there aint no easy way out of it."

I nodded, and lit up a Lucky, offering one to Earl. He declined.

"I figured as much," I said.

"Yeah, I'm sure you did. You're a smart cookie, Black, and that's no lie. Some would say brave too, coming here all alone into the big, bad wolf's lair when he asks you for a chat."

He chuckled. "Must have seemed a little strange, you just here on routine inquiries. You are alone, aren't you Black?"

I shrugged and looked behind me. "Don't see nobody else around."

Earl nodded and re-filled the glasses. "I don't see 'em, maybe. But I can smell 'em. For the moment, however, I am going to forgive you that little indiscretion. Most people in your shoes would have done exactly the same. I do think, though Black, that you may well regret it."

He sipped his drink and grimaced. "How is Mister Peru? We seem to have lost touch recently.

Is he well?"

"He's busy."

I was afraid I was losing control of the conversation. I was a little taken aback by Jevon Earl's appearance, his apparent ease of the situation. Something here was wrong. Very wrong.

"I bet he's been telling you all about me. Am I right? Everything that goes wrong here in Casablanca is at my door. Shit, I suppose that's the deal. I'm not as bad as they say I am though, don't believe everything you hear."

I looked around the dead men and drank my bourbon.

"I'll make my own judgments."

Earl kept on smiling. Not for a second had his facial expression changed.

"Good for you, shamus. Tell me also, how is the lovely Mrs. McSwarve? Is she busy too, I wonder?"

"I'm sure I wouldn't know."

"That's your story and you're sticking to it, ha?" Earl shook his head with laughter. "Anyway, from what I hear, you're not the only one, Mister Black. Mrs. McSwarve is a hard lady to please."

I threw the drink down and slammed the empty glass hard on the table. Furious with my lack of composure, I poured another. Jevon Earl just watched, keenly alert. The horrible smile back on his sickening lips.

"Are you gonna tell me what you want, before you fuckin' bleed to death?" I rasped, looking right into his smug, arrogant eyes. Still they looked. Mocking. Unflappable.

"Okay. My problem."

"Your problem."

He chuckled. "Our problem."

I reached over and grabbed him by the scruff of the neck. He swatted me off like a fly and spat blood on the floor.

"You want to cool it, brother. Keep that temper of yours under control. Who knows, maybe I got this all wrong. Maybe you are not the solution to the problem, that I figured you were."

I sighed, "Shoot."

He looked briefly at the Luger in his right hand and grimaced slightly. The wound on his shoulder was clotting, the blood drying black.

He told me about the drug bust a month ago. It had been up the coast, not really within the Casablanca jurisdiction, but apparently that had not stopped the Casablanca PD getting involved.

His team had been waiting for a consignment of drugs. It was coming in on a boat, an old trawler that had made its way, via a number of stops from Mexico. It was carrying a tonne of crack cocaine and a whole cache of weapons.

Earl had not been there himself to meet the ship. He had been busy down the docks, getting smaller, less lucrative, yet very important imports through the container ports; smuggling other illegal materials in on sealed units, with his inside man, Pat Berry to help.

No, he had left a crack team to meet the Mexicans and unload the ship. But after a couple of days he had heard nothing. He sent his top man Tony Kalac to investigate and he came back with bad news. The crew had all been killed; shot from close range in the heads.

Executed.

The ship had disappeared, and on further investigating they figured it had been blown up off-shore. Locals recalled seeing a fireball about a mile out to sea at the same time there was a roll of thunder unlike anything they had heard in years.

"You brought me here to tell me about your turf wars?" I asked. "Come to New York, kid. This thing happens every day of the week."

Earl continued to smile.

"And is it Thomas Dewey that is doing the killing? Stealing the shit? Running the bitches?"

Thomas Dewey was the famous New York special prosecutor. The man charged to take on corruption, to challenge the mafia and to crusade against the vice-drenched filth. He famously took on my old acquaintance, Arthur Flegenheimer, otherwise known as Dutch Schultz.

I listened carefully as Earl told me about the corrupt and increasingly powerful police force, led by the irrepressible Arthur Peru, Casablanca's Thomas Dewey. Although I should have been scraping my jaw off the floor, I actually listened to Jevon Earl with a lot less scepticism than the story he was telling merited. I almost found myself believing him.

"Who killed Hermeez Wentz?" I found myself asking.

Earl let out a hee hee laugh and then looked serious. "That, I don't know," he said.

"C'mon Earl..."

"Clyde Gabriel was killed by Peru's boys, Stone and Vincent. My old buddy, Tony Kalac, was killed by Peru's lunatic sidekick, John Wimpon. The two whores were killed by out of town shooters, hired by Ahmed, the best 'face man' in the Union."

He looked at me unblinking. I was waiting for the name of Jarvis McSwarve to come up, but it never did. I couldn't believe

228

the thoughts that were going through my head; here I was listening to the most heinous corruption and criminality imaginable and still I was hoping for a little personal satisfaction.

McSwarve's name never came up.

"My crew were slayed by a mixture of the two; out of towners with Peru's bandits alongside them to make sure they did the job properly. Have you heard about the spate of killings yesterday?"

I nodded.

"Peru again."

He waved his arms around the room, gesturing to the dead bodies around us.

"Peru."

The silence that followed was broken by the sudden down pouring of rain. There was a crack of thunder and the sky was illuminated by sheet lightning. The beautiful morning I had set off in, only half an hour ago, was now turning black.

"Peru thinks you are behind the Kalac killing, the Wentz killing, the…"

"Of course he doesn't, you dipshit!" yelled Earl, the smile leaving his face for the first time. "It is a classic set up. It fits perfectly, though, doesn't it? Yes, we were involved in racing corruption. Hell, I am the original big, bad wolf. I aint gonna go denying any of that, Black. Tony and Wentz were batting for me, not against me."

His eyes darted to the door and then back to me.

"Peru was trying to fuel a war between me and McSwarve."

He said it!

"Or rather, between Senator Ouzanti and McSwarve, with me as Ouaznti's boy. I aint anybody's boy, you got to understand, but I quite like my little empire here."

He grunted.

"At least, I did."

The lightning illuminated the sky again and Earl looked at his watch. "You've been here thirty minutes already. Peru's boys will be out to finish the job very soon." He chuckled and looked at the window. "You see, he even controls the weather."

"McSwarve has gone AWOL," I said.

There was a dull sound in the distance. You could barely hear it over the sound of the rain, but both our ears pricked. It sounded like the engine of a car, or a boat.

"McSwarve is probably dead somewhere with one of my bullets in his head," came the reply.

The dull humming stopped and footsteps could now be heard on the bridge. It was difficult to tell, but I would wager there were three men. Earl staggered to his feet and pulled out another couple of guns. He threw one to me and tucked the other in his bloody pants.

"We will probably need them both," he said.

He was right.

Chapter Forty-Five – Shootout

"Errol Black, are you in there?"

I said nothing. Earl held a gun to his lips and gestured for me to duck down low. I did as he suggested and he did the same. We were both lying flat on our bellies, trying to avoid the congealing puddles of blood on the lino.

"Black, if you are there you need to come out now. We are coming in and we will be using force."

The sound of our breathing rang out loud in the small confines of the cabin. Earl was still smiling to himself and when are our eyes met he winked at me. I tried to picture the land outside the cabin, visualising where the voice was coming from and where the assailants would be standing.

"Jarvis McSwarve has been shot in the head."

Earl flashed his white teeth at me and nodded his head.

"The man you are in there with was the scumbag that shot him! We are gonna take him dead or alive!"

Earl began talking...

Little pig, little pig, let me come in.
No, not by the hair on my chinny chin chin.

"We know you are not one of Hoover's boys. You need to come out now, with your hands up."

Then I'll huff, and I'll puff, and I'll blow your house in.

Earl flicked off the safety catch on both his weapons, nodded for me to do the same and waited.

"Black, I am going to count to ten. If you do not come outside with your hands held up on the count of ten, then we will enter."

Little pig, little pig, let me come in.
No, not by the hair on my chinny chin chin.
Then I'll huff, and I'll puff, and I'll blow your house in.

231

From the moment the first shot was fired, I quickly lost track of who was firing at what and whom. There were two men, or at least two volleys of bullets, coming from the front of the cabin. The windows shattered and broken glass showered all over our prone bodies. It was a good move to be down low, as the first assault was all at chest height. As the bullets fizzed over our heads, I slowed my breathing down and tried to visualise the attackers approach.

Earl ignored the carnage and crawled through to the other room, a bedroom, keeping his guns silent. I followed and we took opposite positions, me leaning against a mirrored, double wardrobe, Earl resting just below the back window. He continued to smile, although I noticed the wound on his shoulder was once again pissing blood

Momentarily the shooting stopped and heavy footsteps approached the cabin.

Oh what big eyes you have
All the better to see you with my dear

"Will you, shut the fuck up and concentrate," I whispered in as menacing a voice as I could muster.

An artillery shell exploded and my head hit the carpet. Only it wasn't a shell at all, it was merely thunder and the machine gun fire was Earl's laughter.

The lightning returned, illuminating the room and there they were, creeping inside: two men, dressed in black, faces covered with balaclavas. They both had big guns in their mitts and were breathing heavily.

They had checked the kitchenette within seconds and now turned towards our hidey hole. Earl didn't hold back, raising both weapons in one slick movement he fired simultaneously, knocking both men clean off their feet.

I'll huff and I'll puff and I'll blow your fucking guts out!

Only their guts were not blown out. And there was no tell tale claret across the impact point. The split second it took me to realise they were wearing vests, gave them enough time to recover and they came back firing, spitting rounds all over the bedroom. The thunder of their guns, the fiery muzzle flashes, killed the pillows, duvet and mattress.

And Jevon Earl.

He took one in the neck, and even the big bad wolf was not gonna survive such a blow. It looked like his carotid artery had been nicked, and he sprayed blood all over the room, as if someone had turned on the hose. The few seconds before he bled out were crucial; now on his feet he staggered towards the killers and made a good blood splash painting on the magnolia walls.

"Take that, you bastards!" he screamed in a deathly voice.

Even in death he was an immense figure. He took one of the death bringers out, catching him clean in the head with probably his last shot, before pirouetting and collapsing in a heap right in front of my own cold guns.

They didn't remain cold for long.

I fired both barrels at the remaining attacker. He was too quick, diving across the bed, chewing great big holes in the plaster above my head. I leapt up to return fire, trying to catch him before he slipped over the bed and into safety.

The sudden darkness allowed me to crawl over the bloody debris back towards the other room. The kitchenette breakfast area would give me enough cover till I could get to the French windows, where I would try and get the fuck out of this situation.

But once again the lightning struck at an inopportune time and the room was lit, with me crawling like a dog. I rolled and fired both guns again and again, until the sickening sound of empty chambers echoed throughout the room. I tucked my empty weapon down my pants and threw Earl's as hard as I could. A head popped up and caught one right in the face, causing him to scream and drop his own gun on the floor. I kicked out at it and sent it spinning across the floor.

He was on top of me in a shot, smashing a heavy lamp into the base of my back. I pulled him close and grabbed his balls in my right hand, squeezing and yanking hard, laughing uncontrollably as he squealed in agony. I let go for a split second and put both my arms around him in a bear hug, before charging into the glass doors.

We both flew through the disintegrating glass into the heavy rain, my fall cushioned by the whimpering lump I was holding, who was now cut to shit. I scrambled off him, slipped on the muddy grass verge before regaining my footing and scurried into the trees.

I figured he was unconscious, or dead, but was soon disappointed as he screamed out loud, "You fucker!" and disappeared back inside the cabin.

I knew exactly what he was looking for and needed to move fast. My pants were shredded from the impact of smashing the French doors and blood, mud and rain mixed artistically on my soaking clothes.

A shot rang out in the darkness. I pinned my body to the biggest tree in the grounds, the only damn tree that was not bent double kissing the ground in the howling wind.

I heard him snap another clip into the breech and his feet crunching through the broken glass and fallen leaves on the ground. As he splashed into a puddle not two yards from where I was hiding, I stepped out and hit him hard on the head with my empty weapon. I had hit him so hard I could hear the crack, but still he didn't fall. Instead he pushed the gun into my belly and pulled the trigger.

It jammed and this really did make him scream. He kneed me in the balls and kicked me hard in the mouth. Blood ran freely from my split lips.

I stumbled away and dropped to my knees. I could hear him reloading the gun, but could do nothing about it.

When I looked up, he had ripped his balaclava from his face and was staring right at me with his red, angry eyes. His face was cut in twenty places and soiled with blood and mud. He had shards of glass sticking out of his neck, face and shoulders and a huge, blue welt on his forehead where I had whacked him with my gun.

John Wimpon didn't say anything.

He wasn't smiling. He raised the gun again and rested the barrel on my forehead.

"I told you, you would regret it, Black!" he shouted over the rain. "Are you regretting it now?"

I was planning my last act, a feint to my left and a dive to the right when the gunshot stopped me.

I put my hand to my head, expecting to feel a bloody great hole and my brains spilling out, but it was intact.

That was more than could be said for John Wimpon. He had a hole through his chest that you could almost drive a saloon car through. He dropped like a stone, throwing water from the puddled ground every which way.

Then the lightning struck again and showed me the weasel like features of the third man.

"Black. You looked like you were having a little trouble."

Chapter Forty-Six – Back at the Ranch

She received me like a doting wife, smothering me in kisses and tenderly attending to my wounds. Tears streamed down her face and she kept saying, "Oh baby." as she stemmed the blood, cleaned the cuts and bandaged the breaks.

Jackson Travers laid me out on the bed and I could hear them talking in the kitchen, as she made coffee. He was anxious that Peru's henchmen would track him down and would soon arrive to finish the job.

He told her that he was leaving town right away and that we should seriously consider doing the same. She cried when he told her about Jarvis, who had been shot, but was hanging on in the Casablanca hospital. He offered her a lift down there and she accepted, but said she needed to check that I was okay first. He said that he understood and would be back in thirty minutes. He would take her to the hospital and then they would return to pick me up and get the hell out of Casablanca.

As soon as he left she shed her clothes and joined me in the bed. Her eyes were red and watery, but I don't think she had ever looked so beautiful. My body felt beat, but one smile from Sarah, one caress from those soft lips and the life flooded back to me.

She leaned forward and kissed me full on the lips. Her hands were running up and down my back, while her mouth opened and her tongue thrust past my teeth. I grimaced in pain as we moved side-by-side, without loosening our grip on each other, but she whispered sweet nothings gently in my ear and bestowed butterfly kisses all over my body.

Every time I moved, pain shot through me, but the reward was too much to deny. I pushed myself against her, knowing she must be able to feel me, wanting her to. She pressed closer, making my heart thump. Every atom in my body wanted to invade hers. I desperately wanted to seed her, to fuck her brains out. But in the back of my mind I thought of Jarvis.

I thought of Hermeez.

I thought of lying bleeding ten years ago; of being kicked and stamped on as she looked on; of being left to die as she went on to romance and marry the dangerous bar owner, Jarvis McSwarve.

I thought of my time in prison.

I thought of my isolation, my time with Hermeez in Europe. I briefly thought of Teresa and how she must think the same of me that I did of Sarah.

I thought of Sarah.

Her husband was dying in hospital, and I was also close to dying right here in her marital bed. But the feeling was overwhelming. Ever since that day she left me bleeding on the railway platform; leaving me with a thousand questions, and no answers, leaving me a confused and emotionally frazzled wreck. Ever since that day, I needed to fuck her, to exert power over her, to make her want me again.

But really I just needed a reason; a bloody good reason. And yet I knew I would not be asking for it tonight.

I pulled her top over her magnificent breasts and unclipped the bra. They were larger than she claimed, so firm, so white, the large pink nipples hardening immediately to my touch. I began to suck, to nibble and lick, until she could hardly bear the stimulation any further.

I remembered her telling me about the day she realised she could orgasm simply by having her nipples eaten by the man of her dreams and how this sexy thought always made her pussy soaking wet.

I wanted to see her everywhere to explore her whole body, and soon she was naked. I took in the view, taking little pictures in my head, kissing her all over.

She lowered herself down towards my bulging mound at the front of my pants. She smiled knowingly and opened the zip, pushing them down to my ankles, before releasing them altogether. I kicked them away as my erection pushed powerfully against her face. Her dangling breasts brushed against my knees as she got to work, licking along its underside and slowly around its fat head, giving me a mind spinning thrill before elevating me to even greater heights by sucking it directly into her open mouth.

She pulled it deeper into her throat, her rhythmic, encircling mouth driving me crazy. A moment later, she murmured "come on" and positioned me on top of her, my heart pounding faster.

Her legs spread beneath me; I teased her with my fingers. I could sense her desperation as I lingered round the honey-pot, titillating her, teasing her. With one powerful thrust I was deep inside her, revelling in the wonderful, natural feeling. We thrust rapidly, neither worrying now what the other was feeling, letting passion take over.

During this time there was no Hermeez.
There was no Jarvis.
There was no Arthur Peru.
There was no world.

237

I held her breasts, I sucked her breasts. I grabbed her ass and rammed myself into her harder and harder, smiling at the beautiful sound of her whimpering beneath me. Soon, she was screaming out loud, orgasming strongly.

"I'm coming, I`m coming!" she cried.

I felt the onset of my own climax, deep thrills running along the length of my penis, building rapidly to a heated bolt that sent spurt after spurt of ejaculate firing into Sarah Hill.

After that I must have fallen asleep…

Alone at the ranch, I slept soundly in spite of the impending storm blowing the trees and the powerful gusts of wind wailing eerily across the vineyard. The last storm had blown out but the forecast for this evening was even worse.

It was the afternoon before I arose, my head still aching, my body frazzled and exhausted. I fixed myself some breakfast of poached eggs and bacon, and drank strong, black coffee, watching the swell of the choppy waters from the big, open kitchen. The storm was closer now and rain was in the air.

I waited for the telephone to ring, but it remained silent. I checked the dialing tone, only to discover the line was dead, presumably from the electric storm only a couple of miles away.

The cloud filled sky, ever darkening and brooding throughout the afternoon, exploded suddenly, as I rounded up the dogs and attached their leads to take them in the house. Sheets of rain savagely pummeled the waters, and thunder roared, before jagged, silver lightening cracked the heavy sky. I raced towards the house, shivering with cold and soaked to the skin.

Once inside, I fixed some dinner for the dogs, got out of my dripping clothes and took a long, hot shower. Warm and dry, I pulled on some fresh clothes and got back into bed, my body aching and head throbbing. I pulled up the heavy covers, still shivering as the cold was replaced by a burning fever.

There, I lay for what seemed like hours, but could only have been minutes, drifting in and out of sleep, with the top blanket pulled up tight around my neck. Looking out through the long, glass doors. Out there the palm trees were bent double, not exactly kissing the waves, more like an ostrich burying its head in the sand.

Terrified birds screeched and searched for cover or shelter from the machine-gun fire of the rain. And the wind howled against the windows, rattling the doors and squealing its ghostly beat through the vineyard.

When I did sleep, it was fitfully and rather than give comfort and a feeling of warmth, it made me toss and turn and writhe around in a terrible, cold sweat.

I woke when the headlights dazzled through the French windows in front of me. I could just about make out the low hum of the engine, but could not make out the vehicle. Sarah had been gone for hours now and was sure to need help carrying the bags in this god-awful storm.

I swung my legs out of bed and searched for my shoes with my feet. The shooting pain in my head almost made me cry out in pain, but instead I grimaced and got to my feet. I didn't reach the door before the key entered the lock, turned and it began to swing open.

With Sarah's gown swinging loosely around my shoulders I attempted a smile and held out my hand to take the bags.

Only there was no bag.

And there was no Sarah.

"You look like death warmed up, Rolly. Sit down, man. Sit down."

I looked into the smiling face of Winston Bishop and my heart sank.

"Where's your things, Errol?" he asked.

I felt dizzy and sick and staggered to the chair. I struggled to ask, "Why are you here, Winston?"

He ignored the question and pulled out a cigar; it was thick and long and Cuban. He bit off the end and spat it out on the floor, before lighting it with a gold zippo. It was engraved HW.

"You should never have come back here, Rolly. Best to let bygones be bygones."

My head was throbbing and felt like it might explode. Winston was all blurred making his grin look even more

239

malevolent. I had a horrible tingling down my spine, where it had been smashed by the lamp. I briefly closed my eyes and tried to refocus, but however many times I looked away, I could not escape the glare of Hermeez Wentz's killer.

"Where's Sarah?" I croaked. "What have you done with her?"

Winston puffed on his cigar and sighed a deep sigh.

"Arthur Peru wants you dead, Rolly. He thinks that you are the only person who can stop him taking over this damn town."

His blurred shape moved slowly towards me. I thought he was going to hit me, but he stopped close and put a cigarette between my blood encrusted lips. He lit it with the zippo and smiled.

"What did you do, Winston?"

He puffed on his cigar.

"We are all Arthur's boys now, Rolly. He can be very persuasive you know."

"Was it Tammy?" I asked. "Is that why you did it? Was Peru going to kill again? Was it too much for you to bear, to lose another love?"

I looked right at him, although he slipped in and out of focus.

"Kill, or death would be brought to your house again? You're getting old now, it is almost understandable. There is only so much death we can take!"

Winston sucked heavily on the cigar, making the end glow hauntingly in the dusk. His face momentarily disappeared in the thick smoke he exhaled.

"You should be dead now, by rights. You're getting sloppy, Errol. I told you so, did I not?"

I stared hard at the man in front of me. The man I had cherished as a dear friend. The man who was now shattering that illusion, blow by blow.

"Carberry saved your bacon more than once. That puzzled Arthur, so it did. He thought Carberry was gonna take you out, save him a job. I tried, Rolly. God did I try, but he refused to call off the dogs."

"What did you do, Winston?"

240

He looked at me. "I pleaded with Arthur to simply send you on your way. Like in the old days, bundle you up in the trunk and drive you fifty miles. He said that would never work. I knew he was right. You always were a headstrong young man."

He scratched his chin and his arm appeared to move in slow motion. His words were distorted and hard to follow. It all felt dreamlike.

"He was certain that he had you at Earl's cabin. How on earth could any man escape a massacre and a violent assault like that? Only you could walk away from that one, Rolly. My heart leapt when I heard you had escaped alive. You would surely be a hundred miles away by now."

I whimpered, "Winston."

He slammed his fist into his huge paw.

"Why did you not go, Errol? Why did you not get the hell out of here?"

"Winston," I whispered, "tell me where she is, and that is what I will do. Right now."

He shook his head.

"It's too late, Rolly. He arranged for me to borrow McSwarve's red Dodge. Hermeez was always pleased to see me. We talked about old times, agreed on the next fishing trip. Like always, we talked about you, Errol."

I reached to my cigarette and crushed it in my palm, wincing as the burning hot paper singed my hand.

"Hermeez loved you more than anyone or anything in the world. If you had come back at any time in the last ten years he would have welcomed you with open arms."

I wiped the tears with the sleeve of Sarah's gown and rubbed my eyes. Winston followed my every move with the small, silver pistol in his right hand. He was becoming clearer now; I could see the sadness in his eyes, feel the foreboding in his voice.

"He was dying, Rolly. Had six months at best. He knew that Peru was onto him, had him marked as a danger that would need to be eliminated."

"What…"

"Cancer. He was riddled with it. He hid it well, but some days he didn't make it out of bed. It was only my bread rolls that kept him going."

He puffed on the cigar again, blowing the smoke high into the air.

"And of course the girls. I think he decided that if he slept with a different girl each night, it might make him live longer. I'm sure that's something all dying men would like to experiment with, eh? And a few healthy ones too."

He let out a hearty chuckle and his whole body shook. He caught me eyes wander and his expression once again became serious.

"He should never have come here in the first place. Casablanca died the day that Arthur Peru walked through the gates. Rotten it is. Rotten to the fuckin' core."

It was the first time I had heard Winston Bishop swear in thirty years. He stood up and pointed the pistol right at me. His finger curled around the tiny trigger; a pained expression on his face.

"I was helping Hermeez out. It was for his own good, but you Rolly…"

His fat finger pulled ever so slightly.

"Where's Sarah, Winston? Tell me where she is and I'm out of here."

"It's too late, Rolly. It's too late."

His eyes narrowed. He took the cigar in his left hand and leaned over to stub it into the ashtray. It was all the invitation I needed.

I kicked the pistol out of his hand and slammed my old buddy into the wall, smashing his head again and again into the stonework. He gasped slumped to the floor. Reaching out and picking up the pistol, I now aimed it at my friend.

"I couldn't do it, Errol. I couldn't do it!" he screamed.

The door was open and they were back before I could react.

"No, you're not a killer, are you Winston?" came the weasel voice.

I turned and looked into the eyes of Jackson Travers. He winked at me and tipped his hat.

Walking right past me, he went to Winston Bishop, helped him back to his feet and brushed down his coat as if this would stop him bleeding and bruising. With one deceptively strong arm wrapped around the old man's middle, he lifted him so that they could dance quickly towards the doorway.

They stopped half way so that Winston could drop the lighter in my palm and hug me tightly. When he let me go he leaned in and kissed me warmly on the cheek.

"Whitney would have been proud," is all he said, and that was all he needed to say to start up my damn tears again!

"Come on, old soldier. Time to go," said Jackson, his Irish lilt becoming more pronounced.

I watched as they staggered to the awaiting car and Jackson deposited Winston in the passenger seat. He left the engine running and headed back to the ranch.

I dropped back to the chaise long and lowered the pistol. Her eyes were wide with fear and her face was pleading. She looked like an angel; a beautiful, terrified angel. Her mouth was taped up with duct tape, and for that alone I almost gave Jackson Travers a good hiding. Instead, I too hugged him tightly before saying, "So long" and watched him drive off into the torrential rain.

Still Sarah looked at me, stabbing me through the heart with each eye. Each beautiful, dangerous, fuckin' eye!

I tested my legs and was surprised that I didn't fall. Slowly I ambled towards her and gently untied her hands. She just looked at me, killing me softly, killing me brutally. Tenderly, I eased the tape from her mouth and replaced it with my own, kissing her lips, hoping that in one kiss we could erase a lifetime of betrayal and death.

We stopped kissing and I looked down at the pistol in my hand. I could feel her flinch as I did so and the snakes were back in my belly.

I dropped the pistol and kicked it away. Opening my arms we fell into an embrace and held each other tightly, shielding each other from the world.

Chapter Forty-Seven – Marcia Grey

Marcia Grey had left Hermeez a year before I found him dead in the Casablanca morgue. Although we had not spoken for five years; not since the day he walked out of Joe's back room, he was always with me. He had figured that although we could never be buddies ever again, he would still avenge my biggest betrayal. I guess he thought it was Sarah that had made me what I was. And so it followed that it was Sarah that had killed our relationship.

Sarah made me fuck Marcia Grey.
Sarah made me betray my best friend.
Sarah killed Hermeez and Errol.

I tried hard to agree with him, but I would be yellower than a bowl of custard if I accepted this flawed theory. The facts were that I was damaged. I suspected most males on the planet were similarly damaged, although to be fair, some of them did resist the urge to fuck the wives of their best friends. Not all men had Marcia as the wives of their best friend, however!

Sarah made me fuck Marcia.
Sarah killed Hermeez and Errol.

He had decided he would return to Casablanca alone. He would destroy Jarvis McSwarve through a series of fixed races, drug plants and smears. He would enjoy himself, by seducing and probably sleeping with Sarah Hill. In doing so he would return the betrayal that I had inflicted on him. Although, I am sure he reckoned on me never finding out. I don't know whether this made it better or worse. I guess, after he had had his fun, he would probably kill her and put things right. Then we would be even.

Sarah made me fuck Marcia.
Sarah made Hermeez kill Sarah.
Sarah brought Hermeez and I back together.

Then we would be able to be reunited and Black and Wentz would be back in business. Every good story needed a comeback. We would be the comeback to end them all!

Only that's not how it turned out. There were too many players in this town, and Hermeez was becoming old. Old and sloppy. He didn't account for the power of Ishmail Ouzanti, of Arthur Peru, of Jevon Earl. He didn't account for the resilience and the guile of Sarah Hill.

Arthur Peru got in the way. Peru saw his chance to take over the town. Peru cultivated the war between Ouzanti and McSwarve, with Jevon Earl and Hermeez Wentz as his major players. Peru was ruthless and tied up all loose ends. My old buddy was not only deluded, but he got sloppy. In the old days he would never have let a county sheriff get the better of him.

But of course it wasn't Peru that killed him.

Sarah made me fuck Marcia.

Sarah made Hermeez kill Sarah.

Hermeez made Sarah kill Hermeez!

Epilogue – The Big, Bad Wolf

Jackson Travers left Casablanca the same day that I did. Different boats, same destination: as far away from that rotten town as damn possible. I never did catch up with him again, but later heard that he had taken up dog breeding. That was always his passion, and as long as he avoided the Al Capones and Arthur Perus of the world he would be okay.

I would always be thankful that he saved my life instead of ending it. Peru had blinked before sending him in with John Wimpon and Noah Thomas to Jevon Earl's cabin. They had expected that Earl and I would have all but killed each other and that they would simply be finishing the job. They had not reckoned on the astuteness of the big bad wolf.

Even so, if Travers had not made the decision that he did, I would have gone the same way as Hermeez, and for that I will be forever thankful. And for returning Sarah to my care instead of killing her for her betrayal, I also would be eternally in his debt.

Jarvis McSwarve recovered from his head wound, and did run for Governor. He didn't win though. I don't suppose the state was ready for a quadriplegic lawmaker. He was looked after by his brothers, Hunter and Irwin and lived till a ripe old age.

Senator Ishmail Ouzanti acted quickly on the news of his own suffering at the hands of Peru's duplicity. The CRC stepped up a gear and continued to build shiny new developments as westerly as the Western Isle and the Broadlands and instead of incarcerating or even disposing of Arthur Peru, he made him City Mayor, where he took on the role of Jevon Earl. For the interim, Peru was neutered, his whole team disappeared overnight and I heard his crimes remained on a meaty file that Ouzanti kept copies of in ten different locations. But in true spirit of Mayor Cermak, Peru continued to hold high and esteemed office, in spite of having irrevocable ties to gangsterism, extortion and murder.

Vernon Carberry was returned to New York and spent the next twenty years of his life in prison. He was denied access to his lifeline of cinnamon sticks and lived out his latter years no more than a dribbling imbecile. Every year I sent him a bouquet of flowers and raised a glass to the sadistic child killer who had saved my life and befriended my best pal.

And Sarah.

That's for the next chapter, but let's just say that it's not the end. We clung on tight together as the apocalyptic weather battered down and cleansed our dirty souls. We were both as guilty as each other and this time she did not leave me bleeding to death...

Timmy Matthews didn't stay in jail for long. He told me later that Sing Sing was like a walk in Central Park, on a beautiful Summer's day compared with our time in Guadalcanal. I think maybe he was in denial about the horrors he endured, and wanted to make me feel better.

I was enjoying a lazy morning when I took the call. Bacon and eggs, swilled down with two cups of strong coffee. Dizzy Gillespie was singing the blues on the radio.

"Eezy, are you sitting down?" he asked.

"Yes," I lied.

"Good. I just took the call from your favourite town. The feds are all over it. Arthur Peru is in custody and will kill himself tonight."

I nearly dropped my cup of coffee.

"They only found the remains of a body in his garage. Apparently there was a tip off from Tipararee."

Travers.

"It only turned out to be the remains of Aisha Earl, niece of the great man. They think she was killed by Peru's thugs during the war. She was sixteen. Apparently she had run away from home and last seen heading for Casablanca's gold coast, where she had got herself a boyfriend who spent most of his time on the beach. He was a surfer."

I thanked Timmy and smiled.

"Take care, old buddy. See you in Frisco in the Fall."

I'll huff and I'll puff and I'll blow your house down!

247

BIOGRAPHY

Simon Swift is a writer of hardboiled mystery fiction. His debut novel, BLACK SHADOWS, is a bestseller on amazon kindle and a former Authonomy Gold Star Winner. He has been compared to genre masters, Raymond Chandler and Dashiell Hammett.

THE CASABLANCA CASE is his second novel in the Errol Black Trilogy.

He has been writing for as long as he can remember...

A voracious reader from an early age, he fell in love with the adventures of hardboiled detectives Sam Spade and Mike Hammer. His own hero, Errol Black now fills the same pages as these fictional detectives.

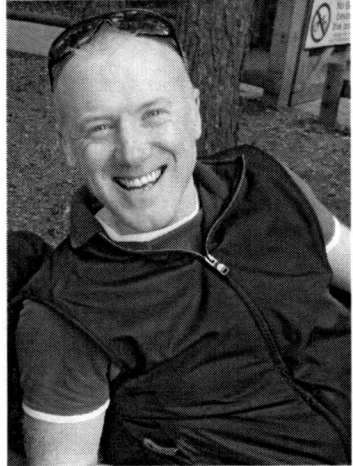

As well as writing, Simon passes the time trying to improve the lives of young children as an Assistant Headteacher at a primary school, playing football with his two young children and being a dedicated husband to his lovely wife. He has previously imported Oriental rugs, delivered pizzas, farmed pumpkins in rural Queensland and served in the Royal Artillery.

As well as his family, his amazing job and writing, Simon loves cricket and very rare, rib-eye steak.

Lightning Source UK Ltd.
Milton Keynes UK
UKOW052135180712

196238UK00002B/25/P